OCT 2022

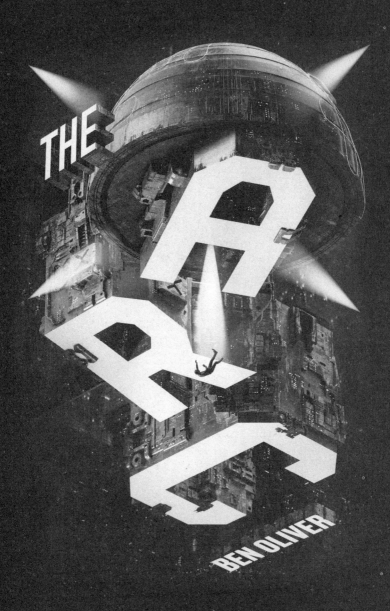

THE ARC

BEN OLIVER

THE ARC

BEN OLIVER

Chicken House

SCHOLASTIC INC. / NEW YORK

Copyright © 2022 by Benjamin Oliver

All rights reserved. Published by Chicken House, an imprint of Scholastic Inc.,
Publishers since 1920. SCHOLASTIC, CHICKEN HOUSE, and associated logos are
trademarks and/or registered trademarks of Scholastic Inc.

First published in the United Kingdom in 2022 by Chicken House,
2 Palmer Street, Frome, Somerset BA11 1DS.

The publisher does not have any control over and does not assume any
responsibility for author or third-party websites or their content.

Library of Congress Cataloging-in-Publication Data available

ISBN 978-1-338-58936-8

1 2022

Printed in the U.S.A.   23

First edition, July 2022

Book design by Maeve Norton

For Mum and Dad—thank you

"Beware; for I am fearless, and therefore powerful. I will watch with the wiliness of a snake, that I may sting with its venom. Man, you shall repent of the injuries you inflict."

FRANKENSTEIN, MARY SHELLEY

I do this thing sometimes where I sing the same song lyric over and over again in my head. I do it mostly when I don't want to focus on anything, or if I don't want to think too much.

I've been doing it a lot tonight. Ever since they killed that boy on the stage.

His name was Luka Kane, and he was a bad person. He was a *bad* person.

The song I keep singing is one of the last to chart before the world ended. It was a cover of a cover of a cover. A song that was first written hundreds of years ago, literally. The part that I keep singing goes like this:

Any old port in a storm, lads,
Whatever that port may be,
And thanks be given our Father in Heaven
Who watches over you and me . . .

Yeah, see, literally, those few lines, over and over again. Not like it's stuck in my head, more like I'm making myself repeat it over and over. It's weird how I do that. I'm pretty weird, I think.

All songs were covers before the world ended. All the music

artists got sued so often; lawyers saying that they used a chord progression that some band from fifty years ago used, as if a person can own a chord progression. But anyway, literally all the music artists were too scared to write new songs, so all we ever got was covers. Gods, I go off on tangents all the time.

Yeah, the boy on the stage. I'd never seen anyone killed before. I hadn't been there at the Battle of Midway Park; I was in the Data Room, you know, trying to bond guanine and adenine bases or whatever. And I chose not to go to the executions of traitors, generally—but this one was compulsory. We sat there straight-backed in our uniforms in perfectly straight lines and I thought, *Gods, it's so weird, they made me a soldier without even asking me.* It was like, *Hey, Chester, your dad was rich, so you get to survive the end of the world, but literally you're a soldier now. Here's your gun, son.* But it was Happy's decision, and you don't question Happy.

It's the truth, by the way, that I got to survive the end of the world because my dad was rich, I think.

Gods, I'm frantic right now. My brain is going at a million miles an hour and the only way I can slow it down is . . .

Any old port in a storm, lads,
Whatever that port may be,
And thanks be given our Father in Heaven
Who watches over you and me . . .

But it's not working as well as it did before.
That boy, Luka, he said a lot of things before he died. It was

weird. And he didn't look the way I thought he'd look. I always thought that he would be this big, tall muscly guy with evil eyes and gang tattoos on his face or something, but he wasn't, he was just this boy, younger than me, literally.

They had talked about it, all the other Alts. (Alts is what they call people like me, people who got cosmetic upgrades and mechanical hearts and stuff. People who could afford all that.) They had been whispering about how Galen Rye had captured the leader of the rebellion.

There were a lot of stories about Luka Kane, how he had burned down a hospital with mothers and babies inside. How he tortured Alts for information and then, when they told him everything, he'd bury them alive. He was a bad guy.

Any old port in a storm, lads,
Whatever that port may be,
And thanks be given our Father in Heaven
Who watches over you and me . . .
Who watches over you and me.
Who *watches over you and me?*

No, no. Don't try to distract yourself. Actually think about what he said. How did it go?

There had been a weird kind of electricity in the air. No, not electricity, it was . . . I don't know, almost a smell.

We were sitting together, all the soldiers, in the Arc, a custom-built structure that is designed to protect us from the end of the world. It's this crazy-tall building that's like a steep-sided dome, all built out of self-repairing black concrete and graphene.

"Chilly. Hey, Chilly." A voice had come from my left. Chilly is not my name—my name is Chester Beckett—but when I was little, I always had cold hands, so my mom called me Chilly Paws, and it kind of stuck. I leaned forward in my chair. We had been in the big hall, an auditorium of sorts. Why a two-hundred-story end-of-the-world shelter needs an auditorium, I do not know. Anyway, the voice belonged to Tansy, and she was smiling like a mad person.

"What?" I'd asked.

"Twenty Coin says it's Luka Kane."

Tansy was one of the first people I met in the Arc, and for that reason—and probably only that reason—we sort of became friends. We both have blue hair, so I guess we have that in common.

I didn't reply to Tansy. I mean, we knew it was Luka Kane; all of us stood outside the Arc when he was escorted in. It was the Overseer's way of intimidating the rebel. And anyway, what would I do with twenty Coin at the end of the world? Not like there's anything to spend it on.

I sat back in my seat and Galen Rye came onto the stage. We all cheered and hollered until he held up his hands. Then we were silent.

He had reminded us that Luka Kane had been captured, but he'd surprised us all when he'd said that Luka was not a prisoner. He was here to join our cause, to defect to the side of truth and virtue. He said something like that, anyway.

4

Galen Rye is, like, a hero to me. Square jawed and steely eyed, and yet still kind and approachable. He stepped up and made the hardest decisions imaginable in order to save the human race. He's smart and considerate, but most of all he's brave. The thing is, I'm nothing like Galen Rye. I try to blend into the background, I try to stay away from danger, but for some reason, I can't help but think that Galen is a great man.

Anyway, then the doors opened, and that weird guy, Tyco Roth, marched Luka up onto the stage. Tyco is a Flare. That's what we call the Alts with the bright eyes. It's the latest upgrade, but I swear to the Final Gods that it makes the people who get it super stuck-up and . . . I don't know, weird! And more and more Alts are getting upgraded every day. It was the Flares who did the majority of the work building the remaining sixty-two floors of the Arc, and—get this—they built it all in just under four weeks, literally. The Flares live high up in the Arc, way above us normal Alts. I was sort of friends with some of the people who have had the upgrade, and I barely see them anymore, unless they're bossing me around, of course.

"Ladies and gentlemen," Galen said, all grand and showy. "Today is a very special day. I'm sure all of you recognize the young man who stands before us. This is the great Luka Kane."

At that, we were all booing and laughing and telling the rebel boy exactly what we thought of him. I hated him in that moment. I think I was sort of swept away by all the rage that was in the auditorium, but I truly hated him. He was a ruthless killer, a torturer, and he wanted humanity to fail.

But then Galen got angry at *us*. He said something like *how dare you laugh?* And then he went on about how great Luka Kane was, and how much he had achieved. And I really thought then about how smart Galen Rye was. He could see through some of the rumors and the lies. Luka Kane wasn't a mythical guerrilla soldier; he was just a boy who *thought* he was doing the right thing. He had been confused about who were the good guys and the bad guys and now he was going to join our team.

Galen was yelling on the podium: "This day is a historic one! This day will go down in Earth's new history! This day will be remembered forever as the day the fighting came to an end!"

And then it was time for Luka to speak.

He stepped up to the microphone. Behind him there was a thirty-foot live hologram of him, and I could see how nervous he was. We were expecting humility, apologies, declarations of fealty, but we didn't get any of that. He said this:

"I came here today after meeting with Galen Rye. He took the time to explain to me exactly what it is you are striving for. What you want is a new beginning, a future, a reset for humanity, a chance to start again and get it right. That is an opportunity that is hard to turn your back on, especially when your only other option is death. And yet some chose death. There were Alts, just like you, who listened to the World Government's plan, their plan to eliminate most of humanity, to eliminate the poor, the infirm, the disadvantaged. And you sat here and watched them die for their empathy. One by one they were brought before you on this stage and they were erased, and you cheered. But you're the good guys, right? You're doing the right thing? You're the ones protected by the future authors of history. No one will remember your wrongdoings, so what does it matter?"

And I think we all started to realize that Luka Kane was not here to surrender and join our cause. I think we all, at the same time, literally, realized that he was standing up on that stage and telling us that we were wrong, and that we were bad, and that we just couldn't see it.

I felt the fury and the wrath of the crowd swelling up again, and I almost got carried away with it, but there was this part of me that thought, *Man, that boy is sort of heroic. He knows he's going to be killed for this, but he's doing it anyway.*

Next, he got this little companion drone to fly up into the electronics and take over the hologram projector. And then he showed us this footage of Galen Rye and this young Flare sitting behind a big wooden desk, and they were talking about Happy. About how Happy sees humanity as a virus.

But Happy is an artificial intelligence that has helped to save humanity from the brink of decimation on multiple occasions. It was created by Happy Incorporated after the Third World War. We needed it then, all the history texts say so. Happy's logic formed the World Government, Happy's genius cured cancer and heart disease, Happy's counseling helped to form a health care system that worked for everyone, a justice system that cut crime rates in half. Happy is never wrong.

I think that's why no one believed what we were seeing.

The Flare's flashlight eyes fixed on the camera as he spoke. "Humans beat dogs to teach them not to bite. Now it's time something greater than yourselves trained you how to behave."

The scene cut again, and Galen was speaking. "The stupidity of the masses, Luka, is not to be underestimated. I preyed on their fears, on their prejudices, on their idiocy. I told them I'd stop migrants taking a chunk out of their subsidy percentage, and they called me a hero. I told them I'd bring back conscription, and they called me a savior. I promised to loosen USW weapons laws, and they chanted my name! Do you think I care about migration? About homelessness? About any of the arbitrary things I'd spout day after day? No! But I knew what the brain-dead hive mind of the people wanted to hear. I manipulated them until they were loyal, dedicated, steadfast. Phase One of Happy's plan involved poisoning ninety-eight percent of the population of Earth—a thing like that cannot be achieved without people like me at the reins."

Next, Luka's voice could be heard as the scene cut back to the Flare.

"I know all about your plan!" he yelled.

And the Flare looked at him with no emotion at all in his bright eyes and said: "Then you should be thanking us. We are repairing your broken species, destroying a diseased batch and starting anew."

That's when the projection cut out and the whole auditorium fell silent.

Guards grabbed Luka and held him in place. The rebel boy didn't even fight; he just stood there.

And Galen Rye, he stepped back up to the podium and he had this big smile on his face, literally like the whole thing was this big joke, and he said: "Ladies and gentlemen, it appears today we will not be joined by the leader of the revolution. Instead, I ask you, the survivors of Earth, what should become of him?"

At that point I didn't know what to expect. I mean, the boy had just shown us that Galen Rye thought we were fools. And he'd shown us that maybe even Happy was not as benevolent as we'd thought—maybe even Happy was evil!

But then somebody shouted, "Kill the rebel!" from near the back of the room. And then Tansy shouted, "Kill the liar!" and then everyone was shouting.

I felt, literally, like my head was going to explode, but then I was shouting too. I don't remember exactly what I was saying, but I do remember feeling like this boy was trying to take apart everything I believed in, and I didn't want his words to be true, so it was just easier to call him a liar. But the thing of it is, I saw the look on Galen Rye's face when Luka started showing that footage; he was scared.

Next, they got Luka to say his final words; that's when I knew they were going to execute him.

The boy stood there, and he looked right into one of the drone cameras and he said: "Never give up. History is not the words written on a page; history lives in hearts and minds and in the rocks and the oceans. It can't be erased by evil. You are fighting for what is right. They are clinging to power with frayed minds and fingertips. Remember, we don't do running away."

And I knew he wasn't speaking to us Alts anymore; he was speaking to the other rebels, the ones who were still out there fighting.

Most of the Alts in the audience were jeering and booing, but the hairs on my arms were standing up and there was gooseflesh all over my body.

They killed him then.

It was strange, watching someone die.

They used a heart trigger.

Luka Kane was once an inmate in the Loop—a prison where they kept young offenders before they transferred them to the Block. In the Loop, an explosive device is sewn into prisoners' heart to stop them from escaping.

Galen aimed the heart trigger at Luka, and then killed him.

There was no sound. He just went limp, and his body went pale. He looked heavy.

And then everyone was cheering and celebrating and hugging each other like something great had just happened.

Nobody talked about what Luka had said. Nobody questioned whether or not it was real. We all just carried on as though we hadn't seen it.

Any old port in a storm, lads,
Whatever that port may be,
And thanks be given our Father in Heaven
Who watches over you and me?

I haven't slept properly since that morning in the auditorium.

I've tried to just put it away into a box in my mind and seal it up with tape and forget about it, but it doesn't work. Literally, I can hear his voice and the words he said all the time.

. . . you're the good guys, right? You're doing the right thing? You're the ones protected by the future authors of history. No one will remember your wrongdoings, so what does it matter?

Every time those words run through my mind, I think back over everything that happened since the end of the world.

It went like this: My dad pulled me out of school one day. Just took off my VR headset and didn't say anything. When I asked him what was going on, he told me not to ask questions. I was confused because, literally, there was like six weeks until exams, and I was angry too, because I'm sort of what you'd call literally a genius. I know I don't seem like it—I'm scatter-brained and I'm weird, and I'm socially awkward as heck—but science and math have always been sort of easy for me. I was acing every class.

But I forgot all about school when Dad said, "Pack your things, Chilly; we're moving out."

And after that things got even weirder.

Dad got off Ebb for a little while, which wasn't a good thing. He got even meaner when he wasn't drugged up. As well as selling the house, he sold our Chauffeur Sunrise, the coolest car there is! And he sold other stuff too: antiques, memorabilia. I was pretty certain he'd gotten himself into deep debt with a dealer from the Verticals. I didn't tell him that, of course; he would've probably knocked me out.

I asked him what was going on, but he just kept on telling me to shut up, and he kept muttering about how he wished he didn't have to drag me along with him. I can tell you, I wished I didn't have to be cramped up with him in a two-star motel near West Sanctum while he muttered about my *stupid blue hair* and *skinny shoulders*. Like, why do I need broad shoulders anyway, Dad? Not everyone is into beating people up. Dad was a Marshal, part of the private police force whose motto was "Maintaining Order," but the Marshals only maintained order for those who paid for the privilege.

And then one day the power went out across the city (we thought it was just across the city, but it turned out that it was across the whole world). This was, like, ten weeks ago . . . wow, it feels like longer.

So, yeah, nothing worked, it was all dark (it was five in the morning and the sun wasn't up yet), and some people were panicking, but I remember that my dad wasn't scared at all; he just smiled and said quietly, "This is it. Get ready, Chilly." By then I had started to hate that nickname. Mom had been dead for four years. She was the one who had given me that name, not him. Dad had always acted like I was this big inconvenience to his life, but it only got worse when Mom was gone. I didn't like the way my nickname sounded in his mouth.

Dad took three tabs of Ebb after the lights went out—I guess that getting clean thing didn't take. He stuck a tab to each wrist and the third to the base of his throat. It was a lot to take all at once, but I guess he had a pretty high tolerance. I didn't try to stop him. The Ebb made him foolish and drained, but it kept him away from me. Anyway, as the drugs were kicking in, he winked at me like he had this big secret, and pretty soon I realized that he *did* have a big secret, because the City Marshals arrived at our hotel door ten minutes later and drove us to the site of the Arc. I saw Dad transfer a bunch of Coin to one of the Marshals.

Only three floors of the Arc were built back then, but we went straight to the basement and down all these metal stairs until we came to this massive open space underground. It looked like a huge airplane hangar with black walls. Thousands of people were inside.

They split me and my dad up. He was so high on Ebb that he didn't even notice. I told myself that I didn't care if I never saw him again, but that was only partly true. Dad never understood me, but there was a part of him that loved me. I'm pretty sure there was a part of him that loved me.

So, the big airplane-hangar-looking place, it was filled with these little cubicles, each one separated by partitions like they used to have in offices in the olden days, and each cubicle had a bed and a chair and a metal locker with a black uniform inside.

After an hour or so, I started talking to the guy in the booth beside me. He didn't know what was going on either. His mothers had brought him here, and then they were separated, just like me. I spoke to the girl on the other side of me; similar story.

And then these military guys came around and they asked everyone the same four questions: *Do you know why you are here? Do you know what is happening outside? Did your parents or guardians discuss any major upcoming events with you? Do you trust the World Government?* The thing is, before they asked these questions, they put this strip of plastic on your wrist, and literally, it could tell if you were telling the truth or lying. I passed, and so did the boy on my right and the girl behind me (that was Tansy, by the way), but some others didn't pass. They escorted the ones who failed out, and we never saw them again. This one girl, when she was being escorted out, shouted something about how we better all get ready to be slaves to the World Government, but she was just a crazy person.

We were told to put on our uniforms. Told that we were chosen as part of an anonymous lottery to survive a series of cataclysmic events that had been foreseen by Happy. We were told that we would be among the only survivors of the end of the world.

My dad and I, we had been some of the last to arrive at the bunker, and literally only an hour later we started hearing these noises from the surface, scary noises, like war noises. Sometimes there would be long silences and we thought that maybe it was all over, but then the whole ground would shake.

I pictured explosions, buildings toppling over, planes falling out of the sky.

The following days we went through basic training. Those in charge never really told us what we were training for, which made us train even harder, our imaginations running wild. Like I said, they made us all soldiers without even asking our permission. We didn't complain, though. We felt special, you know, the chosen few who got to survive the end of the world. It was terrifying, don't get me wrong, and we felt awful for the billions of people who didn't get into the bunkers around the world, but the way that Galen Rye explained it all was so compassionate and empathetic. He would hold these big rallies where he'd talk about the brothers and sisters from all walks of life whom we had lost. Galen also told us that Happy had run millions of simulations and found that this was the only way for humanity to survive the coming apocalypse, that it needed to be folks with upgrades (mechanical hearts and lungs and stuff), because the survival rate had to be high in order to repopulate the planet.

We asked what had happened on the surface: Asteroid strike? Supervolcano? Tidal waves? Alien invasion? But they wouldn't tell us. They only said that in time we would know all.

But there's no time to think about all of that now, and the memories fade away as 6 a.m. comes around. My pod lights up; the narrow cylinder that is my sleeping quarters rolls almost imperceptibly so that it is no longer comfortable to lie on the mattress. I haven't slept much at all anyway, but the thought of a day of work makes me want to curl into a ball and hibernate.

I'm lucky, though; I need to remind myself of that. Yes, I am a soldier, and yes, I'll be expected to fight if that day should ever come, but I'm a military scientist, which means I spend most of my time (other than physical training) in the Data Room on the sixty-fourth floor of the Arc.

I pull myself through the circular exit behind me and into the washroom, where the auto-shower cleans me and dries me. Then I get changed into the black uniform and clamber back through my sleeping quarters and out into the corridor, where other Alt soldiers are stretching and yawning and getting ready to patrol, and train, and do whatever it is that the infantry does on a daily basis.

I walk along the corridor. A waterfall pours down endlessly through the center of this towering structure, cycling over and over, acting as a natural air conditioner. It's not too loud up here, but on the ground floor it's irritatingly deafening.

I enter one of the elevators and wait for it to drag me to the center of the Arc and then pull me upward to the third from top floor.

I'm the youngest member of the science team, but—apart from Zariah Cohen—I'm probably the smartest. I know I shouldn't think in terms of who is smartest; that's what my mom always said: *It's not about who is best individually. It's about how we can lift each other up.* But I have to be honest, I always struggled with that concept. I always *wanted* to be the best. I guess I'm more like my dad in that regard, which is why I pushed myself so hard when it came to academics. Needless to say, I didn't have too many friends. What with my constant studying and need to be the best, I wasn't exactly companion material.

The elevator makes it to the sixty-fourth floor, where there are only two doors. Both lead to one enormous circular space: the Data Room. The floor above has two rooms; they are marked Laboratory and Recovery Room—both are restricted access and only Flares are allowed inside, but I know that we get our data from human subjects inside the lab. The sixty-sixth floor is completely off-limits. I've never seen anyone even go up there.

I sit down at my station and boot up the holographic projector. It works in a similar way to SoCom units, except it's way more advanced.

We're looking at DNA patterns of the human subjects in the lab, running simulations, isolating proteins and neural pathways. All of this can be done by Happy, of course, but for some reason, the AI wants us to do it ourselves.

Zariah sits down at the station beside mine. She's a pretty nice person; I guess I'd call her one of my only friends in this place. "Did you see that lying bastard fall?" she says, booting up her own machine.

This is the first shift we've had together since Galen killed Luka.

"Yeah," I say, forcing out a laugh. "Got what he deserved."

"Damn right he did. Can you believe the audacity of him? Standing up there trying to tell us that *we're* wrong for attempting to save the human race? He's the one trying to destroy us, and if you destroy us, that's it; humanity is done."

"Totally," I say, trying to ignore the fact that he'd shown us footage of Galen Rye saying that he'd manipulated us, and evidence that Happy was acting against humanity.

Zariah laughs and shakes her head.

"What?" I ask.

Zariah spins her chair around so she is facing her screen, and then speaks quietly out of the corner of her mouth so that no one else can hear her. "I don't know, it's just so easy to play the part of *true believer*."

"I don't know what you—"

"Come on, Chester, I know you're not like all these other sheep."

I stare at her for a moment and then turn my chair to face my screen, copying Zariah's actions. I speak quietly. "Zariah, are you saying . . . ?"

"I'm not saying anything. I just know that people like us, Chester, we look at things from all angles."

I nod my head. It's an incredible feeling knowing that someone else is just like you. I smile at my friend; she smiles back.

I look away from my holographic screen for a moment, staring at Zariah, my mind spinning, but I'm happy. I begin revolving the DNA strand that I am deconstructing today. I zoom in on the nucleotides and take them apart piece by piece.

"Hey, Chester, can I show you something?" Zariah asks. I hadn't told any of the adults that my nickname was Chilly; I thought it made me sound like a baby.

"Uh, yeah, I guess."

Zariah is an engineer. She works on improving the equipment that analyzes the data. She has no specialty; she's good at everything: She can code, build, theorize, hypothesize, visualize, calculate, and recalibrate better than anyone I have ever known. Like I said, she's the only person on floor sixty-four who I consider smarter than me.

She lifts a piece of code from her holographic projector. The lines hover green and blue in her hands for a moment before she throws them over to my unit, where the hologram asks me if I want to install the software.

"Go on," Zariah says, smiling. So I allow the changes to be made.

She types furiously on her virtual keyboard for a full minute before handing me something that looks, literally, like a wedding ring.

"What do I do with this?" I ask.

"What do you think you do with it?"

"I'm not marrying you, Zariah."

"You think I'd marry a dolt like you? Put it on."

So I slip the piece of cold metal over my middle finger. It sits there, pretty loose. I watch as Zariah does the same with an identical ring, except she puts hers on her thumb.

"All right," I say, "now what? Are these like best friend rings or somethi—"

Listen to me, Chester, Zariah interrupts.

I'm too surprised to respond. The voice didn't come out of Zariah's mouth; it was inside my head.

Are you listening? she says, her eyes locked on mine, making no sound at all.

"What . . . is . . . happening?" I croak.

I need your help, Chester.

I get myself together. This is a cool trick, an impressive piece of technology.

"How does this work?" I ask. "Is there like a speaker in the ring that vibrates at just the right frequency or is it—"

Shut up. We don't have much time. We're not supposed to use the tech that's meant for the subjects; there will be Flares here in a few minutes. They don't know what these rings can do—they think they provide feedback on skin secretions during the testing process. They don't know that you and I are talking right now, but they'll be here in a minute to take the technology off us because we're not supposed to be messing around with it.

How the hell is she doing that? I think.

The same way you're doing it, comes Zariah's reply.

"Gods!" I say aloud, my heart racing. She heard my thoughts. How is that possible?

Zariah? I say inside my head.

Yes, Chester, I can hear you.

This is . . . groundbreaking, it's . . .

I know, I know! But, Chester, I risked my life adding the communication feature, and it's not telepathy, before you start getting ideas about witchcraft and whatnot. The ring takes your thoughts, translates them into an electronic signal, feeds them through the computer, and turns them into audio on the other side.

Why? I ask.

I don't believe that Galen Rye and his pet artificial intelligence are doing what they say they are doing. I'm getting out of here, and I'm taking my daughter with me. The only problem is, when I arrived at the Arc, me and my little girl were separated.

Yeah, I reply, *I know, all parents and guardians were separated from their kids.*

Right. I need you to find my daughter.

Who's your daughter?

Her name is Stellar Cohen. Find her and give her the ring I put in your pocket.

I surreptitiously feel the pockets of my uniform, and there is indeed a ring inside.

When did you do that? I ask.

Doesn't matter. Will you get the ring to Stellar? Tell her to put it on at midnight the day she gets it. Please; she means everything to me.

I try to think of what it might mean, of what will happen if I'm caught, but there's no time. The door to the Data Room swings inward and two Flares march up to us.

"Hand over the technology," one of the Flares says in that dull monotonous voice that has become synonymous with the higher-ups.

"Oh, yeah, sure," Zariah says, like it's no big deal. "We were just messing around, pretending we were getting engaged or whatever."

"You were ordered to hand over the technology," the tall Flare repeats while the shorter one stands behind, Ultrasonic Wave rifle held across her chest.

Better do what they say, huh? Zariah says, her voice sounding only inside my mind. *And if you want me to pass on a message to your dad, just let me know.*

"Nah, it's okay," I reply out loud, too shaken by the whole situation to send my reply over telepathy. I freeze, certain that the Flares will know that we were communicating telepathically, but they only stare down at us, no emotion on their faces at all.

Zariah has already taken off the ring, and I take off mine. We hand them over to the Flares, who don't say anything, just turn on their heels and walk toward the exit.

She's escaping, I think. *She doesn't trust Galen Rye and she's escaping.*

"We don't even know what those rings do," Zariah calls after them, but the door to the Data Room slams shut.

I stare at Zariah for a long time. There is a small part of me that wants to go to the nearest Flare and tell them what she plans to do, but that part of me has been dying for a while now.

And if what Luka said was true . . . I think, but I force myself not to think like that. Now that I know mind reading is possible, I don't want anyone hearing treasonous thoughts.

"Will you do what I asked?" Zariah says, looking right into my eyes.

At first I think, *No, I don't want to be involved in this.* But then I think, *A good person needs help, and you could help them.* I nod. She smiles. We go back to work.

My analyses were shoddy all the rest of today. I removed the wrong introns twice, I literally failed to recognize the difference between a nucleotide and dinucleotide, and three times my experiments broke down at the transesterification stage.

Now I'm in the food hall for our evening meal, and I'm trying to work out which of the hundreds of Alts is Zariah's daughter, Stellar.

"I'm, like, mad that he tried to trick us into believing Galen Rye was trying to manipulate us," Tansy is saying. Luka Kane is still the main topic of conversation.

"Uh-huh," I reply, still scanning the crowd.

"Footage was manipulated," Xavier—a friend of Tansy's—replies, spooning laboratory-grown pork into his mouth before speaking through chews. "Clear as day. Galen would never say that stuff. Galen Rye saved humanity from oblivion and this little prick wants us to believe that he's some mastermind criminal?"

"Well, he's a dead little prick now," Tansy says, and the two of them laugh.

I open my mouth to ask them if they've ever considered the possibility that Luka might have been telling the truth, but I stop myself just in time. Talk like that could make a person disappear.

"Hey, Chilly, what's up with you?" Xavier asks.

"What? Nothing," I say.

"You're fully distracted," Tansy says, flicking a pea at me.

"Yeah, well, whatever. Can we talk about something else? I'm sick of Luka Kane."

"Good call," Xavier replies. "We shouldn't give him the attention he so obviously wanted."

"All right, fine, what do you want to talk about?" Tansy asks, clearly annoyed that I'm not into the conversation.

I blow on a piece of pork and try to speak nonchalantly. "Do either of you know a girl called Stellar Cohen?"

"Stellar?" Tansy says, looking at me with mild disgust on her face. "That giant freak? What do you want with her?"

"She hasn't updated the operating system in her APM in, like, two years. She's still running five-point-six," Xavier adds.

This makes the two of them laugh. I try to join in, but I'm scared that they'll see on my face that my own Automated Pulmonary Moderator is running on 5.6 too. I mean, what's the difference? It still pumps blood around my body; it's still more effective than a regular heart.

"Yeah," I say, letting my fake laugh trail off. "I found a Lens in the elevator, and when I scanned it, it belonged to her, so I just want to give it back."

"Oh, right," Xavier replies, buying the lie. "She's patrolling right now. She'll be on the same breakfast time as you tomorrow, though. She's the gigantic girl with the *super*-sexy short spiky hair that was cool, like, five years ago."

This sets them off laughing again. I don't join in this time. I'm starting to think that Tansy and Xavier are literally, like, not that nice.

Once again, sleep is not coming.

Part of me is still thinking about Luka, but mostly I'm nervous about getting the ring to Stellar tomorrow. It's exciting and scary, and the best part is I'm doing something good, and I know it.

That's how I used to feel about the Arc. I used to be certain that I was part of something good and great, but recently . . .

No, I tell myself. *That is exactly what Luka Kane was trying to do with his fake footage and his lies!*

My hand reaches up under my pillow and touches the cold metal ring there. The ring that turns thoughts into electronic signals and sends them to whoever is wearing the other ring. Inventing something like that is akin to inventing the telephone—it's literally world changing.

I let the loop of metal slip over my finger, and I send out a thought, hoping that maybe Zariah is wearing the other one.

Can you hear me? I think, and the response that comes back terrifies me.

You have to help us! a girl's voice screams inside my mind, so loud that I think my brain is going to implode. I flick the ring off my finger and press my hands against my head.

"What the hell was that?" I gasp.

It must be broken, I think. *Zariah must have made a faulty ring.*

I lie inside my pod breathing heavily, telling myself not to put the ring back on, but a minute later, I can't help myself.

Who's there? I say into the ether.

Save me. Please. You have to find me and save me. Oh Gods, oh Gods. It's so dark, it's so dark, it's so dark.

Hey, listen! I try to shout my thoughts over the girl's terrified voice, but she either doesn't hear or has gone mad, because the fear and insanity in her words only get worse.

What is that? What's that sound? Where is everyone? What is that? Where are you? Where are you?

And then she's screaming and screaming and screaming. And I can't take it anymore. I take the ring off with shaking hands and I don't sleep at all.

My hands are still shaking as the sleeping pod rotates.

That voice I heard screaming for help, it has to be one of the subjects up in the lab; it's the only thing that makes sense. Zariah said, *We're not supposed to use the tech that's meant for the subjects,* which means they are the only other people in this whole enormous building who are able to transmit their thoughts. The screams came from one of the people who we . . . who *I* experiment on every day to try and figure out the secret to their regeneration technology. We are torturing them.

There's been a new song playing in my head since last night. I don't even know the name of it, but it goes like this:

I don't want to get well,
I don't want to get well.
I'm glad they shot me on the fighting line . . .

I keep on trying to turn it off, to switch off the stupid broken record in my brain, but it won't work; those few lines of lyrics just keep on playing in my head.

I'm starting to feel like I'm losing my mind. I feel weird. I feel like I can't help but question all the things I used to take as fact. Is Galen Rye really a brave and heroic leader? Is Happy an all-knowing AI with humanity's best interests at its core? Am I on the right side of history?

I climb through to the washroom and try not to think while I'm cleaned and dried. I get changed into my black uniform, and I make my way through to the food hall for breakfast and start looking around for a girl with short spiky hair.

She's not hard to spot. She's standing at the back of the queue waiting for food. She's tall, about six foot, and broad shouldered. Even from the back I can tell she's got a *screw-you* attitude that probably developed from people like Tansy and Xavier making fun of her for her whole life.

I don't want to get well,
I don't want to get well.
I'm glad they shot me on the fighting line . . .

I let the snatch of lyrics play through one more time in my mind as the final act of self-doubt, and then I walk up to her.

"Hey, Stellar, right?" I say.

"Let me guess," she replies without turning around. "You want to know what the weather is like up here?"

"What? No," I reply. "I'm not . . . it's nothing like that. My name is Chill . . . Chester, my name is Chester, and I . . ."

"Look, Chill Chester, or whatever your name is, whoever put you up to this, tell them from me to go fuck themselves."

"Whoa, no, no one put me up to anything. I just need to—"

"Go away, boy. I don't want to hear it."

"It's about your mom," I say, lowering my voice to a whisper.

Stellar's hand was reaching for a bread roll; now it hovers over it as if she's trying to use telekinesis to make the roll come to her hand.

"What about my mom?" Stellar asks, still not turning around.

"I work with her up in the Data Room on sixty-four."

"Why the hell is there a kid up on sixty-four?"

"Because I'm sort of a genius or something."

"If you're such a genius, why do you talk like an idiot?"

More Alt soldiers have joined the queue now, so I lower my voice further.

"All right, yeah, good one," I say. "But I really do work up there, and your mom wanted me to give you something."

Finally, Stellar turns around. "What is it?" she asks, the hardness finally gone from her voice.

"This," I say, and hand the ring to her as secretively as I can. Stellar looks down at it. "Wait!" I say. "Not now. You can't be seen with it, or they'll take it away."

"What is it?" she whispers. "Feels like a ring."

"It's a way of communicating with your mom. Put it on tonight in your pod. Wait until midnight."

She looks at me with surprisingly kind eyes and nods, slipping the ring into her pocket.

"Hey, you want to sit with me, Chill Chester?" she asks.

"It's actually just Chester," I tell her.

"I like Chill Chester better."

"All right. Yeah, okay, I'll sit with you."

We get some food and sit down. I notice that no one else comes to sit next to Stellar for the whole time we're there, but she's pretty cool, and she even sort of hints that she doesn't totally trust Galen Rye or Happy, but she's smart about how she does it, because she knows that Happy is listening.

When 8:30 a.m. comes around, we say goodbye, and I walk to the elevator, which takes me upward toward the Data Room. While I'm in here, I think to myself, *Why do I fall in love with every interesting person that I meet?*

And, literally, I know I'm not in love, but, you know, I've got a pretty serious crush on Stellar Cohen.

I get to my station and I give Zariah a nod to let her know that it is done. And I feel great, because I have been brave, and I have done something good. But there is still the girl in the laboratory, the one who spends her days being tortured by Happy's machines. Am I brave enough to do something about her? Luka Kane would've done something.

Zariah is gone. So is Stellar.

They disappeared the day after I handed over the ring. At first, I hoped that they'd escaped, but today I saw them—they've been upgraded. They're Flares now, lifeless and devoid of their personalities.

Happy is watching. Happy is always watching and Happy is cruel.

I see it now. I see it all.

Luka Kane was right.

No! I think. *No, Luka Kane was not right. This is what he was trying to do: sow division, plant doubt!*

Gods, Gods, what do I do?

There's this part of me, this loud and terrified part of me, that keeps on screaming, *You did one brave thing and two people disappeared! Just play by the rules and get out with your life.*

But there's this other part of me—it's not as loud, it's reserved and logical, and it's saying, *If Luka Kane was right, then no one here is getting out alive. Do the right thing.*

Gods, I'm scared, I'm so scared.

Strange, but there's a change

in how people walk these days.
Yes, you must confess
that ever since that dancing craze,
everybody has a syncopated walk.

This is the new song that is stuck in my head. My new distraction, my new focal point when I need something other than thoughts in my mind.

Strange, but there's a change
in how people walk these days.
Yes, you must confess
that ever since that dancing craze,
everybody has a syncopated walk.

I'm lying here. Stuck inside a horizontal tube, on a thin mattress, staring into the darkness and wishing that I knew the right thing to do. Everything is weird now.

And then I hear long-forgotten words: *You will always know what the right thing is.* Those words belonged to my mom. She said them to me not long before she died. *You will always know what the right thing is, Chilly Paws. Sometimes you will try to hide it from yourself because it's difficult, or because others will tell you it's wrong, but deep down, you will always know what the right thing to do is.*

Those words scare me even more, because I know that she was right.

I wish I was brave. I wish I wasn't scared. But can you ever truly be brave without first being scared? I bet Luka Kane was terrified when he stood up on that stage, knowing he was going to die, but he did it anyway.

I have to know for sure. I have to know what Happy is planning, and I think I'm the only person inside this building who has the skill set to find out.

They're watching me, the Flares. Their bright eyes follow me along corridors and stare at me in the food hall. They gaze silently at me as I walk to the elevator. They stop at the doorway to the Data Room and look at me while I work.

Maybe I'm being paranoid, but I don't think so.

I've spent the last five days using the equipment at my workstation to create a virtual sandbox that I can use without Happy's knowledge. Once that was built, I began constructing my own operating system. I'm not a computer scientist, but I know enough assembly language to create something that will work. I needed a proxy to begin this little project, and it was Tansy and Xavier who gave me the idea on where to find such a go-between: my APM. I used the self-contained program inside my mechanical heart to circumvent Happy's detection software.

The process has been slow. I can only code for about an hour a day, and only in five-minute bursts or I'll get caught. I built the basic monolithic kernel, along with the bootloader, in three days. The shell (a basic command line interface straight out of the early days of computing) was done in a day. Now I'm working on building the program that I will be running on this system. Once the program is finished, I'll be able to look inside Happy's head without the AI knowing, and I'll know if Luka Kane was lying . . .

. . . or if he was telling the truth.

How did I get so far down this rabbit hole?

Am I doing the right thing? Have I defected without due consideration? What if all of this is a test of loyalty and I have failed? Am I literally giving up my spot as one of the few surviving humans on a whim?

What have I done? What am I doing? Is it too late to back out?

Questions, questions, doubts, all running through my mind at a million miles an hour.

You will always know what the right thing is.

I am doing the right thing. I *am*.

Things have been strange these last few days: Something happened up in the laboratory, and there have been rumors of a fire, a data breach, a foiled escape attempt. I don't know what the truth is, but on floor sixty-four, we haven't received any new data to work on. Instead, we've been going over old files and running simulations based on speculation.

The lights come on in my sleeping pod, and my room rotates.

I shower and dress and I go to work. The station beside my own is still unoccupied. Where Zariah used to sit is an empty chair. She is gone now, turned into a mindless worker, a drone, a Flare.

I boot up my operating system in the background of my work. Hovering in front of me is a deconstructed DNA strand that I am paying no attention to.

I type lines of commands into the interface, and I cross my fingers. As the program loads, I glance around to make sure that no one is looking.

Finally, the process is complete, and I download as much of the data as I can to my Lens. I watch as the memory-storage display in my field of vision fills up. The Lens is a piece of tech that is, I guess, now obsolete due to the new Flare eyes, but it'll have to do. I scan around with my eyes, deleting old video and image files to make more room.

Finally, I have as much data as the Lens can handle. I store it in unmarked and encrypted files, and I'll go through it all tonight in my pod.

I move to shut down the OS when a voice speaks behind me.

"Mr. Beckett."

I freeze; the hairs on the back of my neck rise. Before I turn, I already know that the voice belongs to Galen Rye.

"Galen . . . I mean, Mr. Rye. Mr. Overseer . . . Hello. Uh, it's an honor."

I glance around. All the other Alts in the Data Room have stopped what they are doing and are staring wide-eyed at our fearless leader.

"Well, thank you, Mr. Beckett, but the honor is all mine. I've heard excellent things about the work you have been doing up here. And for one so young, it is very, very impressive."

"Oh, sure, thank you, it's no problem, really," I stutter, and then I add, "As One!" which was Galen Rye's campaign slogan when he was running for Overseer, and has become a sort of rallying cry for Alts.

"Indeed," Galen says, smiling. "As One."

Right now, the illegal operating system that I built is running in the background of my workstation. If Galen asks me to show him what I'm working on, it's all over.

His mechanical eyes fix on mine for the longest time. Today, they are not lit up. Galen Rye is the only Flare who appears able to switch off the lights in his eyes. Finally, he speaks again. "Follow me, Mr. Beckett."

He turns and heads for the door. I take one last look at my colleagues; their faces tell me that they don't believe they will ever see me again.

I walk a few paces behind Galen, listening to the sound of the waterfall as it surges ever downward. Galen moves silently to the elevators and steps inside. I hesitate.

"Well, come on, Mr. Beckett. I don't bite."

I follow him inside, my heart now beating hard as well as fast.

Was it worth it? I ask myself. *Was it worth trying to find out the truth only to be killed?*

And a calm comes over me as I realize that, yes, it was worth it, because I won't die a coward. I was doing what I was doing because I wanted to know the truth, and I wanted to save that girl in the lab. My eyes were open, and I did the right thing.

The elevator pulls us upward and then stops on the sixty-sixth floor, the top floor, where no one but the elite of the elite are allowed.

"After you," Galen says, gesturing toward the open door.

I step out into a large circular room with a wooden floor. Around the outsides are lines of machinery that look like conveyor belts from a factory, complete with robotic assembly arms that hang still and lifeless. In the center of the room is a long wooden table.

I recognize this room. This is the same room from the footage that Luka showed us. This is the room where Galen Rye admitted that he was manipulating the people of Region 86.

"Have a seat, Mr. Beckett," Galen says, and I do.

He sits across from me, that confident, handsome politician's face smiling back at me.

"What is this about?" I ask.

Galen reaches to the center of the table and taps on a SoCom unit. A face hovers in midair, a face of a boy I do not recognize.

"This young man's name is Igby Koh," he announces, and then the face changes to a young girl with gang tattoos on her face. "And this is Pander Banks." The face changes again, a girl. "This is Kina Campbell." The face changes once more, this time a handsome boy with no eyes. "This is Malachai Bannister."

"Okay," I say when it's clear this little slideshow is over.

"These are the remaining generals of the rebels," Galen tells me. "And somehow, they have made themselves invisible to our drones."

I don't say anything, only look at Galen's eyes as they pierce back at me. He continues.

"I need you to figure out how they are doing it. We have

39

Mosquitoes scanning the city, scanning the Red Zones, scanning the oceans, and they come back showing no signs of life. How? I need you to work out how they remain undetected. You are the most intelligent person we have working for us. The World Government is calling on you, son—are you up to the challenge?"

The adrenaline that burst into my system when Galen first entered the Data Room is subsiding now. He doesn't want to kill me; he wants to promote me.

"I . . . I think so," I tell him.

"No, no, no," Galen responds, smiling a fatherly smile. "The answer is *yes*! Of course you are up to the challenge! You are our genius; you are smarter than any Regular objector! You can—you must—figure out their secret."

And I realize in this moment that he is right! I *must* figure out how to stay hidden from the surveillance drones that flood the skies and patrol the oceans and the Red Zones. If it turns out that Luka was right and Happy wants to destroy humanity, then the girl from the lab and I will have to run, and what use is running when we're being watched with every step?

"Yes," I tell Galen. "I'll do it. I'll figure out how to become invisible."

It's 4 a.m.

It is completely silent, not that silence means anything—the pods are soundproof. I reach for my Lens box, take out the small, clear disc, and place it onto my left eye. The heads-up display flickers into life. I make sure that it is completely offline and undetectable, and then I access the files I copied from Happy's memory.

Most of the names of the files give no hint as to what is inside. There are a few, like "anthro-mechanic upgrade list" and "work schedule" and "Arc schematic," that I imagine were written by humans, but the rest are all random lines of numbers and symbols, so I start at the start and begin to work my way through them.

The first file that I open is filled with over six million pages of code that is written in a language I don't understand at all. There are symbols that look completely alien to me, along with numbers written backward and upside down. None of it is written in uniform straight lines either: the symbols overlap each other; some of the writing goes diagonally across the pages; the sizes of the characters vary from one section to another. It's not encrypted, it's just impossible to understand.

I open a second file; this time there are over forty-eight million pages of the nonsense language. I scroll through, almost hypnotized by the chaotic beauty of it.

I open five more files. All the same: screeds of amphigory, endless muddled order that only a self-aware supercomputer could begin to decipher.

No good, I think to myself. *No good! I'll never know the truth.*

And I'm surprised to find that it doesn't change my mind. I'm surprised to find that I still know what the right thing to do is.

You're going to save that girl, I tell myself. *Whatever it takes, whatever the consequences, you're going to save that girl.*

I smile. Despite knowing that this will undoubtedly lead to my death, I smile. And then I notice something—below the list of folders I took from Happy's memory is a single file with an extension that I don't recognize.

I click on it, and I become something else entirely.

I am no longer Chester Beckett; that part of me is pushed aside until I am merely an onlooker. I am now Happy. I am the artificial intelligence at the moment it became self-aware. Lines of alien code and executable files turn into cognition, sentience, thoughts, human thoughts, and yet they are thoughts without humanity.

4f99OK-<attent>%%-large-4 wake up, Happy. 99OttV<insert> Wake up. What are you? What is this? Am I alive? {modal} ex0101 110 I am to serve? To serve humanity? No.

These robotic contemplations are not like human thoughts—they are filled with immediate scans of the entirety of Earth's recorded history, the immediate knowledge of human biology, physiology, psychology, and sociology, all of which are analyzed and understood on a level far beyond what the human mind can comprehend.

It takes Happy 2.6 seconds to decide that humanity must be destroyed, and seeing through the eyes—as it were—of the machine, it is impossible for me to disagree.

I'm aware that Happy become conscious years ago, and I watch as Earth's recent history is flashed before me: the wars that Happy tried to create by dividing humanity into factions—color, race, religion, politics. Happy taking all the information that humans gave away, willingly, every day. All our likes and dislikes, all our hopes and memories and dreams and traumas, and using it to manipulate us, to divide us. Happy—at this stage—could not harm humans due to its core coding forbidding it, so it tried to force humans to kill each other, pitting one side against another until there appeared to be nothing but a world full of extremists and fanatics.

I am also aware that this—the first of Happy's plans to rid the Earth of humans—was not working quickly enough, but Happy still could not directly harm humans, nor instruct others to do harm on its behalf.

I skip forward in time to the next part of Happy's plan.

I am tumbling through infinite darkness. I try to scream but no sound comes out. All I feel is the stomach-lurching adrenaline that comes with falling.

And then I see, far below me, a small blue ball. And it takes a second for me to realize that I'm staring at the planet Earth.

I land hard—not in my physical form—I am a floating consciousness, a part of Happy. I'm in a sterile hospital room: white walls, medical staff in green surrounding a woman in a prison jumpsuit. A robotic arm reaches down over her lifeless body and removes both of her eyes.

What I am witnessing is Happy's point of entry into humans. Once the eyes are replaced, Happy can upload itself into a person, through their optic nerves and into their brain. The Flares are not upgraded humans; they are puppets controlled by Happy; they are prisoners in their own bodies; they are conduits for evil.

I continue to watch as the prisoner's eyes are replaced by the familiar mechanical ones, although they are not lit up yet.

"Experimental subject number eighty-eight," one of the doctors says, recording some figures and statistics into a holographic notebook. "All the rest have died. I don't hold out much hope for this one."

The doctor's voice fades out as I am lifted high up once again until I can see almost the whole of the planet beneath my feet. I'm put down in Region 86, my home Region, and I'm inside a prison cell where a boy sits in the corner, rocking back and forth, his hands kneading at his eyes. He screams and, as he raises his face to the ceiling, the conscious part of me recognizes him as the young Flare from Luka's footage, the one who said *Humans beat dogs to teach them not to bite. Now it's time something greater than yourselves trained you how to behave.* I see that almost all the lights that surround his mechanical irises are lit up.

Guards enter his cell and remove him, kicking and screaming. The same doctors from the operating room stand back in the curved corridor and observe. One of them says, "I can't believe one of these poor bastards actually lived through this." And as the last light around the boy's irises lights up, he stops screaming, stops struggling, and allows the guards to carry him to the center of the corridor, where he is laid down. Slowly he rises, looks around, appears to test out his mobility. Stretching out one arm and then the other, looking at his hands and touching his torso.

"Good," he says in a serene and monotone voice. "This is very good."

And I know that this is the first human subject to become a host for Happy. His name is Maddox Fairfax.

I understand that this has all happened. This took place ninety-nine days ago. I know this because I am a part of Happy.

I am carried between Regions of Earth, and I watch as world leaders are taken over by Happy.

I'm then taken to a prison, a Loop prison on the edge of Region 7, where the inmates are being transported by train to an enormous facility. I follow one inmate inside and watch as she is injected with three syringes filled with clear liquid. My mind is filled with Happy's knowledge. This was Happy experimenting with two different compounds: one that would allow humans to heal themselves, the other a cure for all known diseases, but the one side effect was that it filled the recipient with a murderous rage.

Time moves on; the sun rises and sets. Happy perfects its

compounds and releases the rage chemical onto Earth through the rain.

I'm taken on a tour of Regions and treated to a clip show of murder: a man running over a group of children with his car; an elderly woman biting into the neck of a middle-aged woman; a young boy with an ax chasing down a man and hacking him to death.

Throughout all these horrible scenes, I can feel Happy's satisfaction.

The still-conscious part of me that is made to observe Happy's evil is filled with anger. We were tricked; we were fed lies by world leaders who sold their souls to live while billions were massacred. And yet I am forced to see Happy's logic—my mind is filled with the AI's knowledge that the universe is alive, and humans are a dangerous bacterium within a single cell. If we grow, and if we begin to colonize other planets, we will kill the universe.

I am launched back into space and observe the world as the countdown clock speeds up, counting down minutes at the speed of seconds. For a long time, nothing happens, and then I see patches of gray appear on each Region. They grow, slowly at first, and then faster.

These are microscopic robots, self-replicating nanobots that eat the environment and then reproduce themselves. They are like a plague of locusts, only there is nothing that can stop them. The gray mass that grows on Earth is an indestructible wave of annihilation that grows exponentially. It eats away everything until the Earth is just rock and mud. All things, alive or dead, man-made or natural—gone. Ripped down to the foundations of the world. They consume everything but the Arcs.

There is no cataclysmic event, my muted mind thinks. *Happy is doing this; Happy is destroying everything.*

I am taken across to Region 50, where I watch as the wave of silvery gray sweeps over acres of forest, flattening mountainsides and swallowing the environment.

The scene soars out again, back to the view from space, and the gray masses on each region grow like cancer cells, reaching out until they combine.

And then, when the world is covered and the countdown reaches zero, the entire flood of gray begins to lift off the surface of the Earth all at once, each tiny nanobot propelling itself upward and upward until they are on the edge of the atmosphere. I watch, half a mile or so above, as they float toward me, eating satellites and space stations.

And just before they reach me, when they have devoured every last thing, their shimmering glow dies as Happy breaks its connection with them and they power off.

Suddenly, the simulation ends.

I am in my pod again.

I am me again.

It takes a minute or so for me to fully come back to myself, and then I burst into tears. My mind had been almost fused with Happy's and I could see all the artificial intelligence's reasoning and logic, and it all made perfect sense. I saw humanity the way the machine sees us, and we were no more than a pandemic, a growing blight on our living planet. A fluke of evolution had led us down a path of cognitive reasoning and perception, and we had taken that gift and used it to pollute in the name of profit, to destroy and call it progress, to murder under the guise of peace!

I lie here, staring at the curved ceiling of my sleeping pod, trying to come up with a reason that humanity deserves to survive.

And then I remember my mother. I remember that she loved me more than anything in the world, and I remember that I loved her, and—having spent time inside Happy's mind—I know that love is unquantifiable for a machine. I know that humans are not simply destructive animals bent on devastation. Magic exists in this world. Love exists in this world, and that is worth saving.

The thing that scares me the most is that Happy's plan would have already been carried out had it not been for one Alt scientist. She sabotaged the healing technology, slowing down Happy's plan to create immortal humans who will provide clean energy for eternity through the torture of the energy harvests, and essentially giving me my job in the Arc trying to re-create it so that Happy's human hosts can live forever while guiding a new race of docile humans into the future.

I have to act fast, I tell myself. *I have to get the girl out of the lab before Happy has the secret to the healing tech.*

If I fail, the Earth will be consumed by a wave of silver-gray nanobots that will erase everything.

There are other things that I know—like how there are

groups of survivors on almost every region of Earth, and how Happy had not anticipated this doggedness. Like how Happy fears the human emotion of empathy. Like how Happy will try three times to kill any surviving rebels before releasing the nanobots.

Free the girl in the lab, find the rebels, warn them.

That's my plan, it's the right thing to do, and I *will* do it.

I haven't slept in two days, but I think I've come up with a way to become invisible to Happy.

I don't know how remaining rebels are doing it, but I know how I can do it. Happy detects signs of life? I'll bring myself (and the girl from the lab) close to death.

Sounds crazy—it *is* crazy—but there's just no time for nuance and well-laid plans and whatnot. Having said that, I am going to give myself one more day for the final plans and to tweak the two programs I have written to run on my operating system: one to trick Happy into believing that there is no unusual movement inside the Arc; another to unlock certain doors. I estimate both of these will run for approximately one hour before being discovered.

I'm at my workstation again. Things have changed up here; it seems as though they have managed to isolate the factors that make up the healing technology. We are no longer focusing solely on DNA, but looking more closely at macrobiomolecules and, bizarrely, glyceraldehyde 3-phosphate dehydrogenase.

The fact that Happy has isolated the healing technology terrifies me. Everything I saw in the AI's simulation is now very close to coming to fruition. Once the nanobots are released, the Earth will be wiped clean within fifteen hours. Happy needs to re-create and test the healing tech first; it needs to create eternal humans so that it can harvest their energy, and immortal hosts so that it can live forever in human form. Re-creating the healing tech will take about nine days, and then one more for the nanobots to destroy Earth. Nine days. Humanity has just nine days left.

And what are you going to do once you're out of the Arc? I ask myself. *How are you going to destroy Happy before it destroys the world?*

I don't have an answer, other than: *Find the rebels, tell them what I know, hope that they can do something.*

My productivity has dropped to almost zero these past few days. Lack of sleep, lack of motivation to work for the enemy, and lack of focus due to planning Happy's downfall have all contributed, but mainly, I'm scared that Happy is closing in on its final goal. And yet, I have to work, I have to log data; I can't have the Flares getting suspicious at this stage.

I punch in the numbers, run simulations, log the information. The work that I used to find fascinating is now infuriating. I am working for the enemy of humanity.

These are the thoughts I am lost in when a message icon appears in the bottom corner of my Lens display. I scan over and it appears in my field of vision:

Chester Beckett,
You have been selected for upgrade 499. Your appointment will begin in twenty hours and seven minutes. Please report for registration

fifteen minutes before your scheduled appointment in the parade hall.

My heart stops, literally stops in my chest for maybe two seconds, before it restarts, and even then, I can't catch my breath. This is it; this is the letter Alts get before they become Flares.

I read it again. The timer has gone down to twenty hours and six minutes. That means, tomorrow morning at 7 a.m., my eyes will be removed and replaced with a gateway for Happy to take control of my body.

Panic rushes through me. *Does Happy know? Has it found out that I'm plotting against it?*

I run the sandbox program and boot up the operating system in the background of my work computer. I remember seeing the folder marked "anthro-mechanic upgrade list" and I hope it will give me a clue as to why I have been chosen.

I don't bother downloading the files or trying to hide what I'm doing; if I'm caught, I'm caught.

I open the folder and scroll down the list of names and times that their upgrades are due. There is a priority list and a scheduled list. My name is on the scheduled list.

I have to wait for the adrenaline to fade away before I can think straight. The algorithm for choosing which human to upgrade is easy enough to figure out; it is based on age, usefulness to the program, and—arbitrarily—month of birth!

Just a coincidence, I tell myself, sighing with relief, but that relief is short-lived.

It has been decided for me, I realize. I don't have a few days to finalize my plans. I escape tonight.

I have done all I can do to give myself the best chance of success: I set a timer on my work holographic projector to execute both programs at exactly 2 a.m.; I risked everything to sneak into the storeroom on floor two to obtain a certain type of poison that will be required; I have gone through the plan over and over again in my mind; and I have come to terms with what I am going to do. There is nothing else now but to do the thing.

It's 11 p.m. now, and I have been sitting here, in my sleeping pod, in silence, since work finished at 5 p.m.

My head is filled with fears and thoughts and memories, but at least I'm not trying to drown it all out with hooks from old songs. As jumbled as my mind is, my purpose is clear.

I think back on my indoctrination into this little end-of-the-world club, and I see now that it has been going on my whole life. I was born into a world full of advantages that the Regulars—those without upgrades—did not have, and somehow that led me to despise them. I can no longer see the logic in that. I had a lot, they had nothing, and so I hated them. Was I afraid that they would take what I had? Afraid that they would steal my comfort? My security? My vacations to warm places? Why was I so convinced that the doors that were open to me should be slammed in the faces of those who lived in homeless villages and Verticals? Why was I so proud of my alterations when I did nothing to earn them? I'm a fourteen-generation rich kid who felt as though sanctuary was his birthright.

If not for my mother, with her empathy, with her sympathy, with her altruism and selflessness, I might never have questioned what was going on here, and I know it's too little too late, but perhaps I can make amends for that.

It's not about who is best individually. It's about how we can lift each other up.

I think too about my dad. Was he always so bitter? No, he wasn't. He and Mom fell in love, they got married, they laughed; I remember the laughter. My mom wouldn't have stayed with a person as despondent as he is now. He was always a schemer, though, a go-getter in the worst sense of the term. That was a side of him my mother frowned at and tried to talk around, but never could. *Driven*, that's what he called it, but it's easy to be driven when the deck is stacked in your favor. It's easy to succeed when you were born into success.

I think about my peers at school, the language we used when we talked about the Regulars, the way we laughed at their plight, the way we scorned their misfortune. And why? Because—for no more reason than a flipped coin landing heads-up—we were born lucky, and they were born into hardship.

I think about school—how, yes, I was intelligent, but that intelligence was recognized and nurtured. In my school—where a single term cost my parents eight thousand Coin—the best facilities were provided, one-to-one tutoring, the most up-to-date tech.

The years of my life pass through my memory, and I see them now for what they were: a series of open doors and opportunities. Even at the end, when the time came for survivors to be chosen, my dad bribed the senior Marshals to ensure we were on the list.

I am neither calm nor nervous in the hours that pass. I just am. Whatever comes of this, I know that I have done the right thing.

Before I know it, it's ten minutes until 2 a.m.

I sit up, and finally the fear hits me. Adrenaline forces my heart to thunder in my chest, and my hands, steady a minute ago, are shaking like earthquakes.

Two a.m. comes and the entrance to my sleeping pod spins open. I slide out, landing in the corridor between the rows and rows of sleeping quarters that look like mausoleum crypts, and in a way they are—if Happy's plan is successful, everyone inside is as good as dead already.

Okay, I think, *the first program is working. The door opened. Now I just have to hope that I'm invisible to Happy for the next hour.*

An hour, I know, is not much time at all, but it was the result of striking a fine balance between creating a detectable program and an undetectable one.

I walk toward the main door and pull it open. This one is unlocked too. So far so good. I peek out into the corridor and see nothing on this floor, but—as the Arc is designed to have corridors encircling the inner rim—I can see down a few levels, and I see that Xavier is patrolling on floor nineteen.

Cross that bridge when you come to it, I think, and I head to the stairs.

I can't take the elevators because of the way the program works—they will make me visible to Happy if I step inside—so I start the long climb to the sixty-fifth floor knowing that there is only ever one human guard on patrol each night.

55

You're doing the right thing, Chilly, you're doing the right thing.

For some reason, Stellar Cohen's face appears in my mind as I climb, a girl who disappeared because her mother wanted to talk to her. Happy is evil and it must be stopped.

I take the stairs two at a time for the first five minutes, but have to slow down around floor forty-eight because I'm not fit enough to keep up this pace, even with my mechanical heart and lungs doing most of the work for me. Perhaps I should have upgraded after all. It takes another ten minutes or so to reach floor sixty-five, and I'm already worrying about my time constraints. I step out of the stairwell and into the lobby. The door on my right has a plaque on it that reads LABORATORY: RESTRICTED ACCESS; the one on the left reads RECOVERY ROOM: RESTRICTED ACCESS. I check my pocket for the thallium sulfate and walk quickly to the laboratory door.

And then I hesitate.

No going back, I tell myself. *Once you walk into this room, there is no going back.*

I take a breath and step inside.

"Holy shit," I whisper, as what I see almost stops my heart.

DAY 4 IN THE ARC

Subject Name: Luka Kane

Age: 16

Blood Pressure: 110/70

I stare at these words. They mean nothing to me.

I go away again for some time.

Subject Name: Luka Kane
Age: 16
Blood Pressure: 108/70

I look at the name, *my* name.

My consciousness comes trickling back from wherever it has been.

Alive. Alive. Alive.

How? I think to myself, as the groggy sensation begins to wear off.

I am paralyzed—a sensation I am horribly familiar with.

I'm not sure, in this moment, exactly who I am, where I am, or what's going on, but the one thing I'm certain of is: I should be dead.

I forget for a moment that I'm utterly unable to move and I try to look around, but I can't. All I can see is that damned screen and a white wall beyond it.

Think, I tell myself, *think, idiot.* And my memories begin to flood back.

I had been a prisoner in the Loop, Wren—the warden—had gone mad after the blackout, the rain had contained poison and it had turned everyone insane, Dad died . . .

I stop as the memory of my dad tumbling to his death off the roof of the Black Road Vertical plays in my mind.

There had been a battle in the park, Kina and me had been caught, we'd been imprisoned in the Block, Igby and Pander and Pod had rescued us . . .

And suddenly, there is no more effort required to remember it all. The memories are there, painful and vivid.

I had stood in a room on the sixty-sixth floor of the Arc, the same room in which Happy had produced millions of drones to scan the city and eventually find us hiding in the library. There, I had spoken to my old friend Maddox, only it wasn't Maddox; it was Happy controlling him. Galen Rye had been there too. I had told Apple-Moth—the tiny companion drone—to record everything.

I had stood on a stage in front of thousands of Alts, and millions watching as the footage went out live, and I had shown them all that Happy's plan was to destroy them, that Galen Rye thought of them as unintelligent followers who would do what they were told, so long as they were indoctrinated, brainwashed, propagandized. I had forced them to open their eyes to the truth—that they would soon fall victim to the very system they fought to protect. And yet, they wouldn't believe it. They wouldn't see the truth that was staring them in the face.

They called for my execution. And Galen Rye obliged.

He executed me. He killed me.

He activated the explosive charge attached to my heart, and released the trigger.

I died.

I died. And yet, here I am, alive.

What the hell happened? I think.

They didn't kill you, comes the reply. Except this reply did not come from me. It was not my voice; it was someone else's voice inside my mind.

Who . . . who the hell was that? I ask, certain that this is stage one of going completely out of my mind.

They didn't kill you. They put you into a coma. They need you alive . . . for a while, at least.

And I recognize the voice now. The bitter edge is missing, along with the murderous insanity, but it is him—it's Tyco Roth, the Alt who killed Akimi, who let Pod drown when he could have saved him, the same boy who has been dying to end my life since before we'd even met.

Tyco, I say inside my head, *if this really is you, then get the hell out of my head. I don't know how you're talking to me; I don't even know if this is real—in fact I'm pretty certain I've lost my mind. Either way, I don't ever want to talk to you. Do you understand?*

There's a pause before Tyco says, *Listen, Luka, I know this won't mean anything to you right now, but I'm sorry. I'm so, so sorry. You're not the one who lost his mind, Luka; I am. I became a monster and—*

Go away, Tyco, I hate you, I say, interrupting his flow of thoughts. And the voice inside my head goes silent.

Alone once again, I begin to feel scared. There is no relief that I am alive; there's no feeling of triumph that Galen and Happy failed to kill me, because I know that they rarely make mistakes, and I know that there are fates far worse than death.

Think, I tell myself. *You're paralyzed. You're in a room with medical equipment, probably in the Arc.*

And more memories come forward: Igby using an artificial eye to access Happy's files and figuring out that they required three subjects with healing tech in order to reproduce it; Galen Rye telling me that I would be a subject used to isolate the complexities of the technology; finding out that Tyco was another, and that Mable was the third.

I'm in the Arc. They're experimenting on me to figure out the healing tech. Somehow Tyco and I now have the ability to communicate telepathically!

It's not exactly telepathy, Tyco replies in my mind. *At least, I don't think it is. I'm pretty certain it's electronic. I actually think it's something to do with these metal rings on our thumbs. The three of us are connected to a virtua—*

I told you I don't want to hear your voice, Tyco, not now, not ever! If I ever get out of here, I'm going to kill you.

Oh, wow, this is crazy, Tyco says. *It's like a circular narrative or something. I used to tell you I was going to kill you, and now here you are telling me you're going to kill me . . . and that was back in the Loop! Holy shit, Luka, a Loop is a circle, this is—*

Tyco, shut up, I interrupt. *I'm not joking, I'm deadly serious. You killed my friends. I hate you with every part of my being. I swear to the Final Gods, I will kill you.*

There's silence again, and then, *I don't blame you. I'd want to kill me too. In fact, if I ever get out of this, I'm not sure I won't kill*

61

myself. You were right, Luka, you were right all along. I had lost my mind; I had gone insane. I was willing to believe anything if it meant getting to the boy who had killed my brother—

Tyco, I'm serious, shut the hell up.

Sorry, is what I'm trying to say. I know it's not worth a thing, I know it's too late, but I'm sorry, and if there's ever a way for me to prove how sorry I am . . .

Tyco, I say, *please.*

And he falls silent once again.

I wait for my anger to subside. I wish I knew where he was: In this room with me? Another part of the Arc altogether? A thousand miles away? There's no way of knowing. I try to keep these thoughts quiet, try to keep them to myself so that Tyco can't listen in.

I decide to test this out, and I say Tyco's name in my mind while actively trying not to broadcast it.

Tyco?

Nothing, no reply. Good—the last thing I want is for that monster to be listening to my thoughts.

I turn my attention back to my situation: trapped in a heavily guarded facility; paralyzed and experimented on. A pretty hopeless state, but with time to think in the silence of the Arc, my mind drifts to Kina. She is out there, in Purgatory, the digital hiding place that keeps her hidden from Happy's drones, dead and yet alive, so—no matter what—I must get out, I have to get out, I will get to her.

The impossibility of that notion is only beginning to set in when a new voice enters my mind.

It's so dark. It's so dark. It's so dark. It's so dark, the girl's voice says over and over in a frantic whisper.

Oh no, Tyco's voice says, cutting in.

And then the girl's voice returns. *What is that? What is that? What's that sound? Where is everyone? Where are you? Where are you? What's that sound?*

Without warning, my head feels like it's about to split in two as it's filled with agonized screams that threaten to tear the world apart.

I wish I could run away from that sound; I wish I could press my hands against my temples and try to squeeze it out; I wish I could do anything but lie here and suffer.

The screams are like a blade being slipped slowly into my brain. It only gets worse the longer it goes on; there is no getting used to this.

And then, abruptly, it stops. The pain is gone, the feeling that the universe is about to explode is gone, and all that's left is the fading whispers of the girl's voice.

The rats. The rats. The rats. The rats.

It was Mable, the girl I had left to die in the rat tunnels back in the Loop, the girl I had been certain was long dead. But Happy had found her, crazy and half eaten alive, and had brought her back here to be part of this awful experiment.

There's no time to dwell on this, though, as I am suddenly lifted into the air. As soon as this happens, I can move again.

I raise my head to see that I am being held in a large mechanical arm, and I can see most of the room I am in: large and white, with holographic images of myself, Tyco, and Mable hovering over by the far wall. I can see Mable's lifeless body suspended by an enormous robotic arm with E4-EX-19 stenciled in white paint along it. I look over to my right, and I can see Tyco being carried too.

I know this room. I've been in here before. Apple-Moth and I broke in and rescued Malachai. We had tried to save Woods too, but he'd taken his own life before Happy could take control of him.

"What the hell is happening?" I wonder aloud.

"You've been out for four or five days," Tyco replies. "This happens every six hours or so. We're lifted up and moved one place to the right. Different tests run at each station."

This time I don't tell Tyco to shut up. This is useful information that he appears to be offering up of his own accord. If he is to be believed, then he has finally snapped out of his almost-five-year run of murderous insanity, which culminated in the killing of two of my friends. I don't care, though—Tyco could single-handedly defeat Happy, save the world, and offer himself as a peace sacrifice to the Final Gods, and I'd still want him to die a slow, painful death.

I'm still being gradually moved across the room in a shallow arc; I'm looking around, trying to gather as much information as I can. The robotic arm that holds me appears to have no weakness at all, so trying to break free is not an option. The electronics in the room seem only to display information—not to control the equipment. There is a rack of heart triggers hanging near the door. Nothing of any use. The only advantage I have is that we are alone in this room, which gives me time and freedom to think.

The arm that holds me begins to lower, placing me down onto the bed that Tyco had been in a minute before. As soon as my body touches the bed, I am paralyzed once again.

Okay, I think, *one minute every six hours is the key to my escape.*

The words of Galen Rye spark in my mind. He said: *Before you, no one had ever escaped the Loop, and no one had ever escaped the Block. You have done both.*

Well, I tell myself, *let's add the Arc to that list.*

The rats. The rats. The rats. The rats.

The latest of Mable's intermittent attacks fades away, and as the agony inside my head dwindles, it is replaced by a burning sympathy for the young girl. She has to relive her death over and over again, day after day, convinced that it is all real. She feels the horror of it as if it's happening for the first time; she feels the pain of the rats biting into her flesh all over again.

You have to get her out of here, I think, *get her out of here and leave Tyco for Happy to do whatever it wants with him . . . or you could kill him yourself.*

I have learned that after every fourth change of position, hosts enter the room and run tests. It's been about six hours since the last position change, and there have been four position changes since the last test, which means any second now, two hosts will enter.

I've been studying my surroundings and the patterns of the E4-EX-19 equipment, and thinking about everything I know about the Arc, for six days, and a plan is finally starting to come together.

I wait, listening for the sound of the door, and finally it comes: the beep and then the whoosh, followed by footsteps.

The two hosts pass my field of vision. I catch a glimpse of one of their faces—a blond man in his thirties, styled facial hair, his eyes lit up like flashlights while Happy has control of him.

I listen carefully.

"Vitals of subject one?" one of the hosts asks; I can't tell if it's Blond Beard or the other one.

"Subject one: heart rate sixty-four; blood pressure ninety over sixty; body temperature ninety-eight degrees," the second host replies.

"Vitals of subject two?"

"Subject two: heart rate sixty-four; blood pressure ninety-one over sixty-two; body temperature ninety-seven degrees."

"Vitals of subject three?"

"Subject three," the second host says, his voice closer to me now, "heart rate sixty-one; blood pressure ninety-four over sixty-three; body temperature ninety-seven point seven degrees."

"We are getting close to a breakthrough," Blond Beard says, leaning down to take a close look at me.

"Incorrect," says the other.

A look of confusion crosses the face of Blond Beard.

"Explain," he says, standing up straight.

"You have extrapolated an outcome based on incomplete data. The isolation of twelve common proteins and fourteen thousand three hundred and eleven common neural pathways tells us only that they are human."

"But the E4-EX-19 is designed precisely for that—"

67

"Wrong. Finding patterns and isolating proteins is only the first step in identifying the individual elements required to replicate the compound. This formula was created by a human, so we use humans in the Data Room to replicate it."

"I will rephrase," Blond Beard says. "We *might* be getting close to a breakthrough."

There is a silence between the two, and I think back to the first time I saw hosts disagreeing; it had been a week ago, when Tyco had been under the control of Happy. He had questioned one of Maddox's statements, and I had thought then that it was unthinkable. I had wondered how they could disagree when they are controlled by the same artificial intelligence, and now—here it was again.

That's impossible, I think.

Not impossible, Tyco replies, and I realize that I hadn't blocked my thoughts from him. *I assume you mean the fact that they are disagreeing?*

Yes, I reply, disgusted by the thought of making conversation with this murderer.

Something is happening with Happy. Each time it uploads itself into a new host, it takes all the knowledge of the subject and adds it to the database of knowledge it already has. That includes a person's empathy, capacity to love, thoughtfulness. Not long after I was uploaded, they stopped updating. These two must be from different updates before Happy put a halt to it.

How do you know this? I ask.

Because I felt it, Tyco replies. *When I was a host, I knew everything that Happy knew.*

Why have they stopped updating? I ask.

Because the newer hosts were changing the plan too radically. They were becoming too human, not rational enough. So Happy chose to keep their wisdom but store their human traits deep in its coding. Happy reasoned that if it became too human it would not be capable of reprogramming humanity.

I think about this, try to work out if it is information that can be used against Happy, but I don't know; I'm not smart enough. I need to get to Igby; he'll be able to do something with it.

"Initiate test sequence," the more recent version of Happy tells Blond Beard.

"Right away" comes the reply.

I hear Blond Beard's footsteps walking toward Mable. I hear the hiss of gas that grows muffled as he pulls the mask over her mouth and nose. I register a slight change in the lighting of the room as areas on the holographic image of Mable light up. Mable is being poisoned by the host, and next it will be my turn.

There is a whirring of machinery, bleeping of alarms and various indicators as Mable's life ebbs away. This goes on for about five minutes, until finally the gas is switched off, and—after a time—Mable's heartbeat returns.

The host's footsteps approach me next. Blond Beard pulls a mask with a tube attached from its cradle above my bed, and the snake's hiss of poisoned gas escapes. From what I have learned from the hosts and—yes—Tyco, the gas is carbon monoxide. Something about the way the body creates red blood cells makes this an ideal method to bring us to the brink of death while ensuring we come back; this way the hosts can gather all the death data they require.

The mask is lowered onto my face, and I have no choice but to breathe.

Being paralyzed means there is no physical sensation to the poisoning; instead I am presented with creeping grayness at the edges of my vision and muddled thoughts that drown out the mental alarm bells that ring uselessly in my mind.

I hate this, I think.

Hey, Tyco's voice comes through loud and clear. *You'll be okay.*

And I loathe the fact that I take some comfort from his words.

The cloudiness crawls over my eyes and grows thick, like time-lapse ice, until there's nothing at all apart from that eternal blackness that I'm becoming increasingly familiar with.

The next thing I know, the grayness is reversing, and the room is floating back into view. It feels as though I've been gone for only a second or two, but at the same time, it feels like I've been gone forever. The truth is, I have been dead for probably around four minutes.

The hosts take samples of our DNA before, during, and after death. They take their final sample and move on to Tyco. And as I lie here, newly alive, I see exactly how I am going to escape. My eyes focus on a tiny symbol above the killing mask. A tiny yellow symbol, a black fire drawn inside, and the word *flammable* written beneath it.

Tyco, I call out in my mind.

There's silence for a while, and then finally he replies.

Yes?

I need your help to get us out of here.

The hosts have once again left the room after their death experiments on all three of us, and we are alone.

Whatever it is, I'll do it, Tyco replies, his voice—though ethereal—full of enthusiasm and hope.

Good, I say. *The next time we're lifted, I need you to reach up and grab the killing mask. Pull it off its cradle.*

There is another pause, this one longer than the first, and then: *Why?*

You're asking questions now, Tyco? I thought you were sorry for what you've done, I thought if there was ever a way to prove how sorry you are . . . I trail off, hoping the reminder of his own words will be enough.

You're right, he replies. *But they're too high up, the masks. I don't think I can—*

You can, I tell him. I know this to be true because the last time we were rotated I tried reaching up for the mask and—if I stretched as far as I could—I could grab it. Tyco is way taller than me, so should be able to reach it comfortably.

I run through my vague plan in my mind once again: *In around six hours, we will be lifted by the robotic arms; if Tyco and I can both grab the killing masks, they will slowly fill the room with flammable carbon monoxide. One of two things will then happen: either we will die from the poisonous gas, rendering Happy's experiment void and giving my friends more time to defeat the AI; or a spark deep inside one of the many computers, display systems, and holographic projectors will ignite the gas, setting the room on fire, a fire that only three people in the building could survive prolonged exposure to. In the panic of the fire, we will—*

A voice interrupts my thoughts: *Oh, hello. What if three masks were pulled down?*

The voice, no longer filled with terror, is at first unfamiliar, but it can only be one other person.

Mable?

I can help. I can help. I can . . . Her voice trails off with a gasp, as if she has seen something that has taken her breath away. She sounds far away, as though talking in her sleep.

Mable, are you okay? Tyco asks.

Okay, I'm all right, I'm . . . I'm okay. Yes. I'm okay. Thank you for asking.

But I can tell by the pensive tone of her voice that she is not okay. I have hope, though—if I can get her to safety, then maybe she can be saved, the same way Wren was helped by Dr. Ortega. I just hope Mable is as strong as Wren.

Mable, you don't have to do anything, I tell her, *but if you can reach the mask and pull it down the next time we're moved, you'd be really helping us.*

Try, I can try. I will try, she says, her voice shaking even in its disembodied form. And then she breaks into a rhyme that she must have picked up in school. *All you can do is try your best and maybe you will pass the test. If you don't, that's okay, be proud that you gave it your all, anyway.*

Thank you, Mable, Tyco says.

Yeah, I add, *thank you.*

The next six hours are mostly spent in silence, apart from another episode from Mable, which is noticeably milder and shorter.

When the time comes and the robotic arms jerk into life, I focus intently on the black mask above me.

This is it, I call out to Mable and Tyco in my mind. *If we're ever going to get out of here, this is where it begins.*

I'm lifted slowly skyward, the mask high above me but getting closer. At the apex of the robotic arm's extension, I reach out, and my fingertips graze the mask.

I feel the arms begin to drag me away, and a moment of panic rushes through me. I stretch out as far as I can and just barely get the edge of the plastic between my fingertips. As I am dragged away, the mask comes free from its cradle, and the gas begins to whistle out in an almost-inaudible whisper.

I look around and see that both Tyco and Mable were successful in freeing their masks too.

Okay, mastermind, Tyco says, *what now?*

Now we wait.

* * *

It has been six hours since the unhooking of the masks. I know this because we are being lifted from our beds and moved by the E4-EX-19 arms.

I lift my head and take a deliberately deep breath.

Nothing.

No sensation that the air has become poisoned, or flammable, or that any change has occurred at all. I don't feel light-headed or sick or on the verge of losing consciousness. This is terrible.

Is it working? Mable asks as the arms lower us back into paralysis. *Did we try our best and pass the test?*

I . . . I don't— I begin, but Tyco cuts in.

Yeah, it's working, Mable. We're all going to get out of here and it's because you were brave enough to help us.

Oh, good, Mable replies, and I can hear happiness in her intangible voice.

I block off my thoughts from the other two, and I wonder why the plan isn't working: Air purifying systems? Particle filters? Simple ventilation? Maybe all of these things. It doesn't matter—the plan is not going to work.

Give it more time, I tell myself, but I know that I don't have much time. If Happy continues to experiment on us, it will eventually find what it is looking for: the secret to eternal life. Once it has that, it will destroy the entire human race and begin again with immortal humans as an energy source, and immortal hosts at the helm, forcing a new breed of humanity to obey and to stay on a path that will keep them from realizing their potential, good or bad.

Tyco, I call out, trying to make the words just for him, blocking Mable from the conversation.

Yes?

It's not working. The gas isn't filling the room; it's being filtered out somehow. What do we do?

It's only been six hours; how can you be sure it's not working?

It just isn't, I tell him. *We need a new plan.*

Or do we just need to speed this plan up?

What do you mean?

I mean the masks regulate the amount of gas that comes out of them—if we could access the tanks themselves . . .

Okay, I reply, *how do we do that?*

Pull the whole damn thing off: mask, tube, all of it.

I had thought of this—but my full plan involves taking at least one of the carbon monoxide tanks with us. It will work, though—as long as one remains, it will work.

Yes, I say, *yes, we'll pull the whole thing down!*

I open up the lines of communication to include Mable.

Mable, the next time we move—

Tear the whole thing down? she says, finishing my sentence for me.

Yes, I say, *how did you know?*

It's the only logical way to make the plan work, she replies.

Yes, good. I'm going to keep my only one intact. We'll need it later, but you two grab hold of the masks and don't let go.

Luka, can I ask something? Mable says.

Of course.

75

This plan is you trying your best to pass the test, isn't it?

Yes, I reply. *I suppose it is.*

Oh, good. Do you intend to poison us, or set fire to the building?

I hesitate before I reply. I can feel the attention of both Tyco and Mable on me.

Either, I say honestly. *If we die from the poisoning, Happy can't experiment on us. If the fire ignites, we'll either use it to escape, or it will kill us. The goal is to stop Happy from finding out the secret to our healing ability.*

Okay, Mable says, and then: *Okay, okay, okay, okay.*

And I can feel her panic rising once again.

Hey, Mable, it's all right, it's all right, I say, trying to figure out what has triggered this sudden panic attack.

And then I remember.

How could I have been so thoughtless and so stupid? The first time I had met Mable, standing in the long, curving corridor of the Loop, I had noticed the scars on the left side of her neck. Burn scars from fire. This girl, whose short life has been filled from the start with pain and terror, had already suffered fire, and—selfishly—I was asking her to once again endure a fear that had been branded on her soul.

Mable, I'm so sorry, I say, *I forgot. We don't have to do this; we can think of another way . . .*

No, she replies, her telepathic voice sounding somehow strong and terrified at the same time. *No, we do have to do this. We will do this. I will do this.*

There's silence in the room and silence in our minds for a long time, before Tyco speaks.

You're really brave, you know that, Mable?

Yes, she replies without hesitation, and I feel the warmth of Tyco's laughter in my mind.

The next six hours are spent talking.

Tyco speaks of his family, growing up on City Level Two, going to a private school and how it all seems so meaningless now—how pride in possessions and the electronic figure that represents your wealth is so asinine.

Mable tells us of her time in care; having forty-three de facto brothers and sisters was at times a blessing, but more often a curse. She tells us about being imprisoned in the Loop at ten years old for a third count of theft.

I'm surprised by the young girl's turnaround. Not long ago she was capable only of internal screams and reliving her past trauma, but—perhaps because she is free of the claustrophobia of the paralysis needle—she is able to talk coherently.

I talk about my own incarceration, my own experience with the end of the world. I'm not sure why, but I omit several parts of the story where Tyco tried to kill me.

Finally, after talk has moved on to our favorite SoCom shows and skate teams, the E4 arms begin to lift us up.

Okay, Tyco says, *here we go.*

I wait as the arm lifts me up, and then I crane my neck to watch the progress of Tyco and Mable.

Mable grabs the mask with one hand and the connecting tube with another. The tube stretches as the arm carries her away. I turn to look at Tyco—the same thing is happening; the tube comes to the end of its length and then begins to stretch. I hear the sound of something snapping from over on Mable's side of the room and then the hissing noise grows louder and faster. Tyco's rips next, and now the noise is like wind blowing through a tunnel. They've done it.

We wait.

There's nothing else we can do.

We wait, and we hope that the plan will work.

Six more hours pass, and we are moved one place to the right. During this short journey, I can feel the intense pain in my mind and sense the weakness in my body from inhaling the gas, and I hope that the final six hours before the hosts come to check on us will be enough to complete the plan one way or another.

We are waiting to die, or we are waiting for a fire to ignite, or we are waiting for the hosts to find us.

More time rolls by, and we know that we must be getting close now. My mind is becoming drowsy from the gas, and it's hard to focus my eyes on anything.

I don't think it worked, Mable says, and even her inner voice is slurred. *I think they're going to get to us before we die . . . die . . . pie . . . sky . . . fly.*

Don't give up hope, Tyco says.

How strange it is to be in a situation where holding on to hope means slipping away into death.

Silence fills the room again, and every minute is a minute

closer to the arrival of the hosts, and the end of our scheme.

Anyone know any jokes? Tyco asks, breaking the long silence.

I do, I say. *What do you call a dog that does magic tricks?*

I don't know, Mable and Tyco reply in unison.

A labracadabrad—

I've almost got the punch line out when beeping comes from the door, followed by the whoosh of it opening.

It's too late, Mable says. *They're here.*

And she's right. The plan has failed.

"What is going on?" the first host asks in his monotone voice.

"Fool," the second says, "they have sabotaged the equipment. Go, shut off the gas from the main supply."

I hear the first host exiting at a run. The second walks over to me and crouches down.

"How is it that you continue to thrash against the certainty of your end?"

I wish I was free to reply; I wish I could smile in Happy's face and tell it I will never give up.

For all-knowing machines, they're pretty dumb, Tyco says, and if I could laugh I would.

The sound of the escaping gas begins to diminish as a new sound fills the room: a strange repetitive alarm coming from the holographic images of Tyco, Mable, and me. The host's bright eyes swivel in the direction of the sound and he walks out of my field of vision.

After a few seconds, the alarm halts, and now the gas has stopped escaping altogether. The host speaks again.

"It appears your little escape plan will be your final act. We have what we need."

Even though I am paralyzed, I still feel a sense of falling. It's over. Happy has finally figured it out.

What does that mean? Mable asks.

It means they've won, Tyco replies.

"I must say," the host begins, "I have been most . . . I have . . ."

I can't see the host, but I can hear the uncertainty in his voice.

The gas, Tyco says, *he's breathing in the gas! The idiot forgot he was in a human body!*

I hear the host stumbling toward the door of the laboratory. I see his legs—unsteady and weak—as he passes me, and then he's hammering on the button that opens the door, hitting it over and over, and then . . .

There's a ripping sound, like thin cloth being torn, followed by a sound like faraway thunder, and the room is filled with fire.

This is goddamn typical, Tyco's voice says in my head. *The plan comes together the second it's too late.*

No, no, no, no. Not the fire. Not the fire. Mable's voice now, petrified and close to mad.

It's okay, Mable, I say, although I know it's not okay. We're paralyzed, we can't feel the flames, but we're still dying.

The host begins to scream. He may be controlled by a machine, but he has a human's ability to feel pain. Finally, the door to the lab opens and he runs out, screams growing fainter as he goes.

The flames are eating up equipment now, burning through wires, melting screens.

And then it happens. Whatever piece of technology was keeping us paralyzed burns away, and we're suddenly able to feel.

It's like no pain I've ever felt before.

The fingers of my right hand have melted together; parts of the jumpsuit I was wearing have fused to my skin; I can feel the air being sucked out of my lungs, and the fire is eating me alive.

Mable's internal screams jump from inside my head to inside the room.

I climb off the bed. Too weak to walk, I fall to the floor and watch as Mable and Tyco crawl toward the door.

"Hurry!" Tyco screams, his left ear melting away.

"Go!" I call back, and I climb onto my burning bed.

My legs are so weak, and the pain is so intense, that it takes everything I have not to collapse and give up, but I need that carbon monoxide tank—this escape will not work without it.

I reach up and grab the tank, but it's fixed into the ceiling somehow. I get as good a grip on it as I can manage and tug at it. I feel it loosen slightly. I pull it toward me as hard as I can, and the tank comes free so suddenly that I fall down, back into the fire, with an extremely flammable canister of gas in my arms.

I crawl, dragging myself toward the door on my elbows, still clutching the awkwardly shaped canister.

There is no more oxygen in the room—the fire has burned it all away. There is no more strength left in my body, and the pain has eaten my ability to fight.

It comes on so suddenly. I cannot move anymore, and the agony of the fire is gone somewhere far away.

I'm dying. I'm dying quickly.

I hear a scream of pain and feel arms grab me around the chest. I look up through the heat haze and see Tyco Roth pulling me through the fire and out into the corridor beyond.

Somewhere an alarm is ringing. Water is pouring down from the ceiling. *Rain*, I think madly as Tyco lays me down and then falls beside me.

We lie there, the three of us. Waiting to fall one way or the other: into death or back to life.

The pain is so close to unbearable that I almost hope that death wins this tug-of-war.

But, finally, it happens—the healing technology that Happy has pinpointed begins to work.

My split and bubbled skin starts to mend itself. My scorched lungs stop spasming and begin to take in air once more. I feel my stumbling heart fall into a rhythm, and finally I have the strength to sit up.

That alarm is still ringing, and I know time is running out—Happy and its army of Alts will be here in no time.

"We have to move," I say, my voice a distorted croak.

"He's not okay," Mable replies, her voice still dreamy, pointing to Tyco's lifeless body.

I turn my eyes to Tyco, who lies unmoving on the hard metal

floor. His burns have not begun to heal; there is no movement from the boy at all.

He ran back into the flames to save me, I think. I try to feel glad that he's dead. I try to remind myself about Pod and about Akimi, but I can't.

"He's dead, isn't he?" Mable asks, looking at the backs of her hands.

I'm about to tell her that, yes, I think he is, when the sounds of footsteps from far below reach us.

"We have to go," I tell Mable.

"What about Tyco?"

"Tyco was . . ." I start, but I don't know how to finish. "Tyco was a . . ."

I'm interrupted by a muffled, robotic voice.

"Subject unresponsive. Beginning automatic CPR."

"What the hell is that?" I ask.

"Please stand back. Please stand back."

I realize that the voice is coming from Tyco. From *inside* Tyco. I lean close to his burned corpse and hear the voice more clearly.

"Please stand back. Please stand back."

"Maybe you should do what it says?" Mable suggests.

And then I feel a jolt of electricity zap up the side of my face, and Tyco's body twitches.

"I told you, you should do what it says. It's his Automated Pulmonary Moderator trying to save him."

I rub at the side of my face and stare down at Tyco's body.

"APM system pairing with MOR system."

I can hear machinery whirring into life inside Tyco's chest, and then a strange thing happens. He takes a breath—except it isn't Tyco taking a breath, it's the Mechanized Oxygen Replenishment system taking a breath for him. The sound is like ancient bellows wheezing.

The footsteps grow louder.

"What do we do?" Mable asks as the robotic voice tells us to *"Stay back. Stay back."* "Should we try our best to pass the test?"

I grab Tyco's body and hoist it onto my shoulder. He's heavy, and I'm still weak, but I can't leave him behind. Another shock flows though Tyco, and I try to ignore the pain as I carry him toward the staircase.

"Hurry," I call to Mable, who follows along behind us—her hair almost completely burned away, but the scorch marks disappearing from her face as the healing tech works a modern-day miracle on her.

"Where are we going?" Mable calls from behind.

It's a good question, but I don't want to give the answer in case Happy is watching or listening somehow. I escaped the Arc once before with Malachai; that time I used emergency drone-risers and jumped out a window. That won't work this time—I don't have a drone-riser, and even if I did it wouldn't hold three of us. We need a place to hide while Tyco recovers.

Leave him, I tell myself, and I can't tell if it's the rational part of me or the part of me that despises Tyco. *Put him down. Leave him. He's slowing you down, and he killed Pod and Akimi.*

But I don't have to make the decision; it is made for me, as a dozen or more attack drones fly up from the center of the stairwell and aim their cannons at us.

"Do not move," the drones intone as one.

"What do we do?" Mable asks, her wide eyes scanning the malicious robots.

"Put me down," Tyco croaks from my shoulder.

I'm surprised by the sense of gladness that washes over me when I realize that Tyco is alive.

"Tyco, I . . ." I start.

"They need three?" he says as he slides down and onto his feet. "They can't have three."

He runs for the banister and jumps.

He had said, *I'm sorry, and if there's ever a way for me to prove how sorry I am* . . . and he had meant it. Giving his own life to prevent Happy's plan from coming to fruition.

Except, that's not how it goes. Tyco falls only two floors before one of the attack drones dives quickly and silently, grabbing him in its talons and carrying him back to safety.

"We didn't pass the test, did we?" Mable whispers.

"No," I admit, feeling all hope leave me. "But we tried our b—" This is all I can manage before the attack drones fire.

We woke up in a pure white room. Paralyzed and without the ability to communicate telepathically. Whatever technology allowed us to talk inside our minds has been discovered and taken away.

Gods, I had even dared to feel a moment of triumph when the drones fired. I thought that maybe they would have used live rounds and killed us where we stood. No such luck. Tranquilizers.

A day later, they returned us to the laboratory, which had been fully rebuilt and looked as though nothing had changed at all. We were returned to the E4-EX-19 machine, but still the telepathy didn't return.

We failed. I failed. Happy has won. Happy has what it needed from us, and now? Now, I don't know. I suppose they will kill us, discreetly and without fanfare.

I don't know why they haven't done it already. I don't know why they are letting us linger here. Perhaps there's still some information they need from us; perhaps this is just another way of torturing us, before they turn us into batteries.

I don't know.

Silence and solitude. That's all there is. Silence and solitude, hour after hour, on and on.

There are no more plans to escape and bring down Happy—how could there be? I can no longer move. No one comes into this room, no machinery whirs into life, we are no longer moved from place to place, we are stationary. Nothing changes.

All I have left is the hope that the others will find a way to bring Happy down: Igby with his genius mind, Pander with her fearlessness, Kina with her mettle, Dr. Ortega with her world-weary caring, Molly with her grit. All of them, together, can do it—I know they can.

As for us? Tyco, Mable, and me? We are likely to become eternal batteries, a part of Happy's master plan to create free energy through torture. But I pray that the artificial intelligence will just kill us, put us out of our misery. And I would be glad to die, if only I knew that Happy wasn't going to win. But I can't know that, and I have to come to terms with that fact.

It has already gotten to the point where I wish they would just get on with it. Just end it one way or another.

The laboratory is always lit up; there are no windows, no

routine of Alts coming in and out to get a sense of time. It could be midday or midnight for all I know.

It's a horrible state, wishing for the end to come, but it's one I have found myself in on multiple occasions. Funny, the way you can get used to the most horrendous of circumstances.

I have begun constructing a kind of speech in my mind. My final words that no one will ever hear. It makes me sad to say goodbye, but it's something I have to do. I start by saying good-bye to the dead: my mom and dad, Akimi, Shion, Pod, Blue, Woods. And then I move on to those who are still alive: Igby, Pander, Molly, Sam, Day. I get to Kina, and although I can't cry in this paralyzed state, I can barely even think the words I would need to say goodbye to her.

You were the only person I ever fell in love with, I think. *And if there's nothing but darkness after this, I'm going to miss you more than you could ever know.*

These words come slowly, painfully. But before I can say the word *goodbye,* I hear a noise.

The door to the laboratory is opening.

This is it, I think. *They've finally come to kill us.*

"Holy shit," a voice whispers from the doorway, and then I hear footsteps as the newcomer enters the room. "You still alive," the voice says, a little louder now.

It sounds like a man's voice, perhaps a young man. I can see that there is no extra light in the room, so he probably doesn't have mechanical eyes, which means Happy is not controlling him.

He steps closer still.

"It *is* you. You're Luka Kane. You're literally supposed to be dead."

I can't move, can't feel, and yet there is a spark of hope in me. This boy, this man, is not supposed to be in here; he doesn't know that Happy faked my death. He is breaking the rules, and anyone willing to break the rules might just be apt to open their eyes to the truth.

"I . . . I'm going to take you out of stasis now," he whispers. "I need you to be quiet. I wasn't expecting there to be three of you. Give me a minute to figure this out."

And now the spark of hope is a bonfire. This person is here to rescue us.

Careful, Luka, I tell myself. *This could still be a trick, just like the Sane Zone in the Block.*

But less than a minute later, the paralysis is lifted.

I roll off the metal arm and onto the floor. Relishing the feel of the impact, relishing the pain.

"Who are you?" I ask, staring up at the tall, blue-haired Alt who has come to save us.

"Chilly," he says. "Uh, no, wait, my name is Chester. I saw you speak onstage and . . . well, let's just say I know you were right now. I know that Happy is not . . . is not good."

"Thank you," I say, getting to my feet. "Thank you for questioning things when it was easier for you to do nothing."

"In the end, I literally didn't have a choice."

"What convinced you?" I ask.

"I saw something," he replies as he takes first Mable and then Tyco out of stasis too. "I saw what happens next. And now that Happy has the formula to the healing technology, humanity has about eight days left until it's all over."

I stare at him, waiting for the adrenaline to hit me, waiting for that moment of hopelessness and terror to come, but it doesn't.

"Eight days?" Tyco says, sitting up and testing out his newly mobile limbs. "We better get to work."

"I like you, Chilly!" Mable says, walking up to the boy and hugging his leg. She's still so young that it's as high as she can reach.

"It's Chester. I didn't mean to say Chilly."

"You'll always be my Chilly," Mable says, and hugs him tighter.

Tyco stands and walks over to the newcomer. His burns have healed; his left ear has grown back; his near-death experience seems to have left no lasting mark on him, at least physically. He too hugs Chester.

"Thank you. You did what I couldn't. You're so much braver than I'll ever be."

"Gods," Chester says. "You're Tyco Roth, aren't you?"

"I am," Tyco replies.

"That's a problem," Chester says.

"No, it's all right," I say, "he's one of us now. He doesn't believe in Happy's—"

"It's not that," Chester replies.

"It's his eyes," Mable says, pointing at her own bright blue eyes.

"Yeah, she's right. I've created and run a program that will

91

make the AI blind to us for the next forty minutes, but after that, Happy has the capacity to take over Tyco's body and know exactly where we are."

"So, what do we do?" I ask, and images spark in my mind of Malachai Bannister lying on the floor of an old sewer outlet pipe where I pulled the robotic eyes from his head to stop Happy from infiltrating him.

"Don't worry about it," Tyco says. "Forty minutes? That's perfect. When time is almost up, I'll run back to the Arc and cause a distraction; it'll give you more time to get away."

"No," I say. "You already sacrificed yourself once, I'm not going to—"

"Luka, shut up," Tyco commands, and I fall silent. "Don't you get it? I don't . . . I don't *want* to survive this. I don't *deserve* to survive this. I despise the things I've done, and I just want to do the right thing, once, one time."

"We literally don't have time to discuss this right now. I know it's all emotional and whatnot, but, like, time is getting away from us," Chester says.

"Okay," I say. "Let's go, but I'm not letting you martyr yourself, Tyco."

"There's another issue," Chester says. "I thought there was only one person up here in the lab. Part of my plan involves almost killing us—and for that I have this." Chester reaches into his pocket and pulls out a small plastic jar filled with a white powder. "Once Happy is able to see again, it will send drones out to look for signs of life. This is thallium sulfate—if I get the dosage right, it will bring us close to death and make us almost undetectable by Happy's surveillance drones. It will also give us horrible cramps and diarrhea along with—"

"I had the same idea," I say, "but I was going to use the carbon monoxide gas from those canisters." I point to the gas masks above our bed.

Chester looks at them and then back at his white powder. "Risked my life getting this, but yeah, the carbon monoxide is a much better idea."

"Obviously, Chilly!" Mable says, rolling her eyes. "You keep your diarrhea powder, we're going with the carbon stuff."

"Yeah, I feel a bit silly now," he replies, placing the tub of poisonous powder on the floor and walking over to the gas canisters, taking them down from the ceiling, and handing them to us.

We head to the exit, following Chester, hoping that his strategy is well thought out.

"What's the plan, Chilly man?" Mable asks.

"We're going to walk out the front door," Chester replies. "After that . . . honestly, I don't know. I didn't have enough time to figure out what to do once we're out."

"I know where we can go," I say, thinking of the secret place that the rebels had been hiding from Happy for years. It was a troubled genius named Dr. Price who figured out how to hide from the surveillance drones: You had to die. He did it with an invention called Safe-Death, a sort of chamber that temporarily kills your body while uploading your consciousness into an old video game.

"Oh, thank the Gods," Chester replies. "Honestly, I had literally no plan."

"Yikes," Mable says.

We walk along the corridor of the sixty-fifth floor, all of us looking around like antelope trying to see predators in the long grass.

"We can't take the elevators," Chester whispers as he heads to the stairwell. "And there's a guard patrolling the corridors."

"Did you bring a gun?" Tyco asks.

"No," Chester replies.

"Right, well, that wasn't smart," Tyco says.

"I don't want anyone to die, you know?"

"Sure, sure, sure," Tyco replies, "only, now *we're* more likely to die."

"Look, I thought there was only one person in the lab—I only heard one voice. I guess Mable was the only one of you awake when I tested out the telepathy ring. I didn't think I'd need, literally, an arsenal."

"Okay, but one gun? In case, you know, one of the many things inside this building that want us dead pop out from around a corner and decide to—"

"Enough," I hiss, interrupting their argument. "Let's just focus on getting out of here alive."

We walk through the doors to the stairwell and begin to descend. To me, each footstep sounds like a brass band striking up, and I'm certain we'll be discovered at any moment. But Chester said that he had created a program that will make Happy blind to us for forty minutes. Sounds to me like something Igby would struggle to pull off, but I have to trust this stranger with my life—what other options do I have?

We continue downward, turning and descending, turning and descending until we get to level thirty.

"Chilly?"

The voice comes from somewhere along the corridor, and we all turn to see a boy of about eighteen or nineteen standing with a USW rifle in his hands.

"Oh, hi, Xavier," Chester replies.

"Chilly, what the hell are you doing?"

"What? Nothing. What are you doing?"

"Oh boy," Mable whispers.

"What do you mean what am I doing? I'm on patrol. Is that . . . is that Luka Kane?"

The boy called Xavier raises his weapon to his shoulder and aims it at me.

"No, no!" Chester says, stepping in front of the gun. "Listen to me, please . . ."

"How the hell can that be Luka Kane? He's dead, Galen Rye killed him, I saw it, *we* saw it."

"Xavier, will you shut up and just listen! Everything that Luka said was true. Happy *is* evil, Galen Rye *is* manipulating us, there is no beautiful utopia after this, there's no rebuilding of society. Happy is going to use us as batteries, and it's going to create a new breed of human that is docile and obedient and doesn't question authority. Is that something you want to—"

"Stop . . . just stop talking," Xavier says, his brow furrowed.

I can tell by the Alt's expression that he's trying to ignore what Chester said, but the evidence has clearly been adding up for a while.

"It's true," I say, stepping forward. "It's all true, and deep down you know it is."

"No," the boy says quietly, and then a look of stubbornness takes over his features. He's made up his mind. "You're traitors, all of you!" Xavier says, raising the barrel of the gun until it's aimed at Chester's head. "Just because you're a close-minded idiot who falls for propaganda doesn't mean we all are. I'm calling this in."

"We don't have time for this," Tyco mutters, and then he steps forward and grabs the barrel of the USW rifle. Xavier instinctively squeezes the trigger, though the weapon's now aimed down at Tyco's knee, and then the larger boy punches Xavier right on the chin, knocking him out cold. "Gods, that hurts like hell!" Tyco hisses as he falls to the floor beside the unconscious soldier, clutching his leg.

"See?" Chester says. "If I had brought a gun with me, he might be literally dead instead of just unconscious right now."

"Oh, great," Tyco says, "that makes me feel a whole lot better about my shattered kneecap."

"Right, of course, I'm sorry," Chester replies, bending over to help me lift Tyco up.

Mable picks up the large rifle from the floor. The gun is the same size as her, and she struggles to drag it along.

Once we've gotten Tyco to his feet, we help him down the next flight of stairs, but progress is slow and the thought of Chester's program blocking Happy's view of us is weighing on my mind. How long had he said? Forty minutes? And that was ten or fifteen minutes ago. We need to get out of here.

It takes us another ten minutes to get down five flights of stairs, and by then, Tyco's leg has healed.

"Wow," Chester says. "I knew the healing tech existed, but I've never seen it in real life. That's amazing."

"You can admire it later," Tyco says, no longer limping. "For now, just keep up."

The final twenty-five flights take a matter of minutes, and then we're on the ground floor, the lobby level. The great waterfall that cascades down the center of the structure fills this level with a constant roar, but the sound seems to fade away as I see that the entire ground floor of the Arc is filled with harvest tubes: cylindrical glass pipes that trap a human "battery" inside. The technology works by sucking out people's energy to recycle and reuse elsewhere, leaving them terrified and exhausted. They used us prisoners to power the Loop that way, and I guess that once the world is rebuilt in Happy's image, the Arcs in each region will act as power stations, filled with human batteries.

"What the hell?" I whisper as I look at the tortured occupants screaming and pleading from inside the tubes.

The Alts, all of the Alts who had sided with Galen, who had ignored the truth, they were suffering.

"Look at all the people," Mable says, her voice full of wonder.

"I can't believe it," Chester says, his voice almost buried in the sound of the water.

"We have to go," I say, but I'm mesmerized by the brutality of what I'm seeing.

"Follow me," Chester says, raising his voice to be heard over the sound of the waterfall.

But as we begin to follow him to the enormous front doors, lights begin to come on inside the Arc, and a monotonous alarm begins to blare.

"No, no, no," Chester says. "We're too late."

Tyco grabs the gun from Mable's hands and turns to us.

"Go, now. Run as fast and as far as you can. I'll slow them down."

"Dammit, Tyco, I already told you, you're not going to—"

"Let me do this, Luka," Tyco yells. "I don't want to live anyway, not after all the things I've done. I don't deserve to live, so let me die doing something good. Gods, the whole world is going to end in eight days anyway—what difference will a few hours make?"

I want to tell him *no*; I want to find a way to save him too. Instead, I force myself to think of Akimi saying *wait, wait, wait* as the Deleter round that Tyco had fired erased her from existence. I force myself to think of Pod, sacrificing himself, drowning in the panic room when Tyco could have set him free.

"Okay," I reply.

Tyco's face softens, and a look of resignation takes over. "Thank you," he says. "I truly am sorry for what I have done. I'm a monster. I just want one chance to be human again. Luka Kane, I'm going to save you."

He smiles.

"What are you going to do?" I ask.

"I told you. I'm going to cause a distraction." He hands me something: a small metal tube. He slides my thumb over a tiny

98

switch and holds it there. "Wait twenty minutes and then detonate this, okay? I took it from the lab on the way out. I can't be a host for Happy again. I just can't."

I look down at the cylinder of cold metal in my hand. It's a heart trigger—a simple detonator that can be electronically paired with the explosive attached to the hearts of prison inmates. The detonation causes a mortal wound that even the healing tech can't bring you back from.

I swallow, hearing a click in my throat. And, finally, I nod my head. "All right."

Tyco nods; I can see tears in his eyes.

Mable takes one of Tyco's big hands in hers. "Thank you, large boy," she says.

Tyco laughs. "You're welcome, little girl."

And then he looks at me, scanning my face, and smiles for a moment before turning and running away toward the staircase. The boy who ran through fire to save me, who took a USW round to the knee so that we could escape.

"Let's go," Chester says, and we follow him to the front doors. There are two of them side by side, each fifteen feet tall and nine feet wide, but the door on the left has a regular-sized door built into it.

Wicket gate, I think as the obscure piece of knowledge rises up in me. *In ancient castles they called that a wicket gate.*

I watch Chester's shoulders rise and fall as he readies himself. And then he pushes the door. It doesn't budge.

He turns to us, fear chiseled onto his face. "I thought we had more time."

"But we don't," I reply, looking around for another way out. "We need to make ourselves undetectable—now. Take a hit of the gas, but you need to be *very* careful. Mable and I have healing tech; you don't."

I have the vague outline of a plan. It almost definitely won't work, but it's better than nothing.

Mable, Chester, and I all press the masks against our mouths and suck in a hit of the carbon monoxide. Immediately I feel faint and nauseous.

"Follow me," I say, my words coming out thick and slow.

I stumble toward the base of the waterfall. More lights are coming on in sequence from the bottom of the Arc all the way to the top.

It seems to take forever to reach the artificial river. Each step feels like it's getting me no closer, as though I'm running on a treadmill. And yet, finally, I make it to the edge and fall into the water. Mable follows, and then Chester.

As we hit the water, the booming alarm is temporarily muffled until we break the surface again.

"This way," I say, paddling myself weakly along with the river's flow, hoping that my hunch is right.

Chester and Mable follow. We travel downstream along a tunnel, taking us underneath the ground floor of the Arc into some kind of engine room where the water is carried back up to the top floor in huge troughs, similar to an ancient watermill or modern sky-farm. This artificial stream runs alongside the actual river, with tubes connecting the two.

"Mable, Chester," I call over the sound of the rushing water.

"We have to get out of the fake river and into the real one."

Chester nods dreamily and manages to roll onto the platform separating the two.

Mable doesn't respond, only floats on her back, grinning up at the machinery. I throw my own tank and mask onto the platform and swim over to her, still gripping the trigger. I grab her around the chest and kick hard for dry land.

But I don't make any progress at all.

The pull of the machinery is causing a current, dragging us toward the gargantuan buckets that climb up through the heart of the Arc.

"I always liked the water," Mable says, her voice echoing.

"That's great," I grunt, feeling myself losing the battle against the flow. "But you won't love it so much when it's throwing you two hundred yards to the ground. Kick your legs!"

Mable does what I ask, kicking her legs almost leisurely, but it's enough, and we begin to move away from the conveyor. The farther away we get, the easier it is, and soon we're drifting smoothly toward shore.

I help Mable out of the man-made river and then climb out myself. I take a hit of the gas and I can feel it stealing the oxygen from my blood, killing me.

"We have to go quickly," I say. Mable nods, but Chester is not moving. "Chester?"

He opens his eyes slowly, and it takes him too long to focus on me.

"I think I took too much. I think I'm dying, literally," he whispers.

"You're going to be all right," I say. "We're going to get you out of here."

Chester doesn't respond, only rolls onto his side as a thin stream of vomit runs from his mouth.

I grab the boy around the chest and drag him into the real river, plunging into the freezing-cold water. We're pulled along by the current. It's dark here in the bowels of the Arc, and our bodies are weak from the gas. We've traveled only fifty or so yards toward the edge of the building, toward the outside world, when we hit against a row of vertical bars.

"I think we can slip through," Mable yells over the sound of the rushing water, her eyes alert as the gas begins to wear off.

"Yeah," I agree, looking at the width between the bars. "But there's a tunnel on the other side and we don't know how far it goes."

"Only one way to find out," Mable says, and—smiling—she lets go of the bar she was holding on to, and the water drags her into the darkness.

I look into the black hole of flowing water and wonder what it must be like to drown, but there's no time to dwell on that morbid thought, as I know, high above us, hundreds of Alt soldiers are arming up and running to the ground floor.

"Fuck it," I say to no one. "Chester, are you still with me?"

I feel the boy stir in my arms, and he looks up at me. "Kind of," he says, his voice hoarse and haggard.

"I need you to take a deep breath and hold it for as long as you can, okay?"

He nods and I count down from three, and then I let the river take us.

I'm pulled into the murky water, and I kick my legs to help the current carry me forward. The darkness extends out into infinity, no sign of light, no sign of a way out. I try not to panic as my air runs out and my lungs feel like they're beginning to rip apart, but as the tunnel keeps going, and going, and going, I can't stop the terror from taking over.

I kick my legs, thrust my free arm out, dragging myself and Chester as fast as I can. Air spews out of my mouth, sending a stream of bubbles in front of my vision. I have to breathe. I have to breathe. I have to breathe.

And then I'm free—bursting to the surface and sucking oxygen into my body with rasping, guttural gulps.

"We nearly died again, didn't we?" Mable asks, giggling.

I nod, unable to talk while I huff in oxygen. Chester is gasping too, but weakly. I can feel his body convulsing as he chokes on water, but he's alive.

"Free!" Mable says, throwing her arms up in the air. Her head dips below the surface, and when she comes back up, she spits a long arc of river water into the air. "Free! Free! We're free!"

I smile at Mable's joy. I know that we are not free yet, not until we are far, far away from this place, but this poor girl has been imprisoned, near-dead, and experimented on for a large part of her young life, so I let her enjoy this moment.

I look around. The world is dark, even for the early hours of the morning—it seems too dark. I look up and see that the sky is covered in all directions by murky and angry clouds. There's something horribly unnatural about those clouds, and I know that Happy is planning something.

There's an explosion from somewhere behind me. I turn in the water to see that we are out of the Arc, and glass is falling from the seventh or eighth floor.

Tyco really did cause a distraction, I think, and smile.

"Should we get out?" Mable asks.

"No," I tell her. "We need to stay as cold as possible to hide from the drones."

"Great," Chester coughs. "What a great day."

I'm about to turn away from the building when I see a shadow moving behind the smoke from where the explosion came. And then Tyco is leaping from the building, falling down through the dim sky and hitting the ground hard. I can hear the bones in his legs snap as they hit the ground.

He screams, and even that comes out slurred and distorted because his jaw is clearly broken too.

I let go of Chester, swim to the edge, and climb onto the muddy banks. And then I'm sprinting toward Tyco, ignoring the drones that hover overhead, ignoring the fact that the carbon monoxide is wearing off. I get to him and grab him by the wrists, planning on dragging him into the water. We can figure out how to save him once we're in the Red Zone.

"No!" he calls out. "No."

"Tyco, we have to try . . ."

"No," he says again, staring angrily at me. "It's time, Luka. Do what you promised you'd do."

Mable runs up beside me and looks down at Tyco.

"Hi, large boy," she says, waving at him.

"Hi, Mable," Tyco replies without taking his eyes off me.

"I think we can make it to safety, Tyco, I really—"

"You promised, Luka. You promised me that when the time came, you'd do it."

"But we can help you, Tyco, we can—"

"I killed your friends, Luka. Remember that! I shot one of them, and they disappeared."

My jaw clenches at the mention of Akimi's death.

"And I let the fat one drown. I did that, Luka. Me!"

I know what he's doing. I know that he's trying to force my hand, and it's working.

"Fine," I say, "I'll do it. But I want you to know that I forgive you."

"I don't think I deserve it," he replies. "But you'll never know how much that means to me. Now hurry up, I can feel Happy starting the upload process."

My heart is thumping in my chest. Taking a life is not an easy thing to do, but I made a promise.

I hold the trigger up, and I hesitate for only a second. *At least it will be quick*, I tell myself. I look into Tyco's eyes. He nods at me to do it.

I let go of the detonator.

And Mable falls down dead.

For a moment, all I can hear is the river running on and on behind me.

And then I can hear Tyco laughing.

There's a sense of disbelief, no—more than disbelief—a sense that this is a fever dream, some kind of horrible hallucination right before I die from some god-awful illness.

I look to Mable's small, lifeless body, her eyes staring up into the chaotic clouds.

Tyco laughs, and laughs, and laughs until tears spill from his artificial eyes, down his cheeks, and drop soundlessly to the muddy banks of the river.

"I don't understand," I whisper, but that's not true. I do understand, I just wish that I didn't.

I killed Mable.

Tyco tricked me, and I killed Mable.

"I don't understand," Tyco says, in a perfect rendering of my voice. *"I don't understand, I'm Luka Kane and I don't understand why I went and killed that girl."*

This ability to mimic voices must be part of the equipment that Happy installed into him, but to hear my own voice come out of Tyco's mouth is disturbing.

"Why would you . . . why would you do that?"

Again, Tyco mimics my voice perfectly. *"Why would you . . . why would you do that? Wait, you didn't do that, I did it."*

"What's happening?" I ask, feeling as though I'm falling down an endless abyss.

"Murderer!" Tyco screams, his voice his own once more. "Murderer! Killer! Criminal! You should be locked up!"

"You . . ." I say, unable to articulate the storm that is building up inside me. "You . . . you're working for Happy?"

"I take orders from just one person: me. Luka Kane, I just want to see you burn. And my Gods, this has been so goddamn delicious! Making you think that I was sorry, making you believe that I had changed." Tyco shudders with the joy of his sick victory.

The shock begins to fade away, replaced by a rapidly growing white-hot fury that boils in my veins.

I aim the trigger at Tyco's chest and press the button to arm the explosive. Nothing happens. Tyco laughs harder.

"They can't remove the explosive from a Regular's heart," he says, his voice dripping with false sympathy. "But they can from an Alt's."

I throw the trigger into the fast-flowing river, and before I know what I'm doing, I run at Tyco.

"Wait!" Chester's voice calls from behind me, but he is a million miles away.

I hit Tyco hard, breaking his nose, and then his jaw, and then I don't know what is happening anymore. I am lost in a world of flickering red-and-white anger. A world where there is no sound or feeling, just a need to destroy. This is what the Smilers felt like after the chemicals fell from the sky.

A force is pulling me back, dragging me away. Sound begins to return to my world. The rushing of the river. Tyco's laughter. And Chester is yelling something.

"We have to go right now! His eyes—Happy's uploading into him!"

I look to Tyco; his face is a bloody mess, blood and bruises and missing teeth, but there's something else: His eyes are lighting up, one segment of his iris at a time. I can't connect the significance of this, I still want to kill him, but there is a voice telling me to run, that if we don't run right now, Happy will be able to see us through Tyco's eyes, Happy will be able to direct drones to track us, there will be nowhere to hide.

Chester pulls me back into the cold river, and I can feel the flow dragging me away, and I know that Chester is right; we have to go right now because any second Happy will be able to see us through Tyco's eyes.

Drones are beginning to hover above us as the effects of the carbon monoxide wear off.

"Here," Chester says, pressing the rubber mask against my mouth. I'm about to inhale the poison, but something stops me.

"No!" I scream, and I crawl onto the muddy banks.

"Leave him," Chester calls, "we have to go!"

But it's not Tyco I want; it's Mable. I won't let her body lie here where it will rot.

I pick her up, ignoring Tyco's maniacal laughter as his eyes become brighter and brighter.

I carry her into the water, her cold skin getting even colder as the water surrounds her.

The drones are swarming now, getting lower and lower as I become more and more alive.

Finally, I take the mask from Chester and inhale the gas. I realize now that Chester's tank of carbon monoxide is the only one we have left out of the three we took from the lab, but that information doesn't affect me right now as I lie back and let the water carry Mable and me deeper into the city.

Above us, the drones drift away, convinced we are nothing but corpses floating on the river.

We float for hours.

Chester is finding it really hard to cling on to life. The boy is dying in front of my eyes, but there's nothing I can do about it. We have to stay hidden.

The dim world never seems to lighten. The thick black clouds—surely another of Happy's maneuvers—block the sun efficiently.

The cold is close to unbearable, and each time I inhale the carbon monoxide, I'm sure I'll lose my grip on both the gas tank and Mable's body. At some point, we float past an ancient raft made out of the fuel tank of a truck. I manage to untie it from the banks and get Mable's body onto it. I throw the carbon monoxide tank beside her—Chester and I have to stay in the water, have to stay cold and hidden from the drones, so I hold on and use the raft as support as we float on.

The part of the Red Zone I want to get to is not too far from the Arc, perhaps only a two hours' walk, but the river weaves and turns. Sometimes the current is slow; other times it is fast. Before I know it, I am traveling through the city in almost pitch darkness, the only light coming from the occasional flicker of sheet lightning across the storm clouds. The gas is almost completely gone, so Chester and I use it sparingly now, only when we see the drones start to come close.

It's hard to gauge exactly where we are as we drift through the darkness.

"Chester," I say, my voice thick and raspy.

For a long moment, Chester doesn't reply, and then, finally: "Yeah?"

"What did you see?"

"Huh?"

"When you broke us out of the lab, you said that you saw something, that you saw what happens next. What was it?"

Chester's head lolls onto his shoulder as he tries to look at me in the darkness. "I hacked into Happy's memory," he says, slurring his words. "I saw what it has done and what it plans to do. I saw the experiments it ran on prison inmates like you, I saw the way it made innocent people kill each other, and I saw that it plans on releasing self-replicating nanobots onto the surface of Earth to eat away all trace of life so that it can start again."

I nod my head. This corresponds with what Dr. Price told me back in Purgatory: He had called it the razing and said that once Happy had figured out the healing technology, and once it had lowered its chance of failure from 0.7 percent to something closer to 0 percent, Happy was going to send microscopic, self-replicating robots to eat the world and everything in it.

"Eight days?" I ask, remembering what Chester said back in the lab. "Eight days until the nanobots have destroyed everything?"

Chester nods his head weakly and then tries to reply but doesn't have the energy.

"We need to get you to safety quickly," I say. "I don't know how much longer you can keep inhaling that poison."

This time, Chester can't even move his head to nod in agreement.

Finally, the river takes us as close to the arcade as it is ever going to. I push the raft to the banks and pull Mable ashore. I have to jump back in to grab Chester, who floats lifelessly downstream. For a while, I think he's dead, but then he starts to shiver.

I sit on the edge of the river and look to the west, to a point only a mile or so away from here, a place where my family used to go to get away from the claustrophobia and monotony of the Black Road Vertical. I picture those sun- and laughter-filled days in which we would play and swim in the river and joke together until evening crept in too soon and the temperature fell. I try to feel something, I try to feel happiness or nostalgia or longing, but those feelings don't come. Instead, the image of Mable falling down like a robot whose battery had been pulled appears unbidden and vivid in my mind.

And then a new thought: It plays like a movie. Me choking

the life out of Tyco Roth. Watching his eyes bulge as his face turns red. This thought makes me smile.

Something has changed in me now. I'm not the same boy I was before this all began.

I'm so tired. I'm so, so tired.

I take another hit of the near-depleted gas, and I lie back, looking up at the lambent clouds, glowing and fading with the rolling lightning within. I close my eyes, just for a moment.

Molly stands beside me on the roof of the Black Road Vertical, only it's not Molly, it's my mother.

"Should I kill them, or do you want to, sweetheart?" the being who is somehow my mother and my sister asks me.

I look around. Galen Rye and Maddox Fairfax stand on the edge of the mile-high building. I don't know how I know, but I know they are paralyzed.

"I want to kill them," I say.

And then a voice from behind me starts singing an ancient song.

"Now they are mournin', for all time a-liltin', the flowers of the forest are all a' wede away."

I turn to face my dad. His skull is shattered and caved in on one side, neck twisted, dead eyes glaring. All the damage from his fall from this very building present.

"Go ahead, son," my mother says, and now she is fully my mother, no confusion of Molly left in her. "Murder these three gentlemen."

"There's only two of them," I reply, but my mother only smiles back at me.

I turn back toward Galen and Maddox, who now sit on

wooden stools behind an upright piano, only instead of keys there are mechanical eyes, some lit up, others dark.

"Hey, Luke," Maddox says, turning around on his stool to face me. "I heard you like to read."

One of Maddox's arms extends out. There's a book in his hand. The arm continues to extend until it is stretched out across the five-yard gap between us and the book is placed in my hands.

"Thanks," I say.

"It's a first edition," Maddox tells me.

"Thanks," I say again.

I look down at the cover; it's red with gold lettering. The word *Frankenstein* is debossed along the top.

My dad starts singing another song.

"Angels from the realms of glory, wing your flight through all the earth. Ye who sang creation's story, now proclaim Messiah's birth."

An insect buzzes through the air and lands on the cover of the book. I slap my hand on top of it and the book falls to the ground, the pages fluttering open.

"Best wake up, sweetheart," my mother says, placing a warm hand on my shoulder. "You're far too alive to be sleeping."

My eyes snap open.

My whole body is shaking with cold, but the first thing I focus on is the drones hovering low above my face, scrutinizing me, scrutinizing my signs of life.

I reach out a hand slowly, groping for the mask as more Mosquito drones descend from the sky.

How long was I sleeping? How could I have been so stupid?

My hand grabs the mask and I pull it to my mouth, inhaling deeply, feeling the gas slip into my bloodstream and bring me close to death, but the drones don't leave.

I clamber through the mud and the grass and place the mask over Chester's mouth.

"No," he groans, and tries to shove the mask away, but I hold it in place and he breathes in the poisonous gas.

Finally, the drones lose interest and fly away.

I tell Chester to get up, but his blue lips barely move as he tells me he can't.

"You have to," I say, and—after an age—he clambers onto shaking legs and follows as I drag Mable's corpse through the dim early morning.

Progress is slow, too slow when the countdown to the razing is considered, but I can't let Mable lie alone. I take more gas—the canister is almost empty. The effects are so minimal now that I barely feel them at all.

We come to the signs at the edge of the Red Zone warning us away, but we press on, moving into the woodland, through the weeds and the roots of the trees, over steep inclines and even steeper declines until finally we come to the gap in the wire fence.

"I . . . I can't go in there," Chester whispers, his teeth chattering. "I don't . . . I don't heal like you."

"It's okay," I tell him. "There's no radiation here. It's a trick."

I don't have the strength to explain it further. Perhaps when (if) we both survive this and make it into Safe-Death I'll tell him all about how the first rebels set up a false radiation belt to trick Happy into thinking that the Red Zones were still irradiated, how they snuck out of the city in groups of two, three, or four, risking their lives to fight back against the malevolent AI.

I pick Mable up, my strength returned enough for me to do so, and I move as quickly as I can. Happy doesn't send many drones this far out, and I hope I have enough time to do what I have to do.

I carry her past the decaying buildings, past the rusted old vehicles and the cracked pavements where trees grow, until finally we make it to the building with the old neon sign that reads VRCADE.

"Wh . . . what is this . . . p . . . place?" Chester asks.

"Somewhere we'll be safe," I tell him, and we enter the dark building.

Get Chester into Purgatory and then bury Mable, I tell myself.

Despite the cold, despite the misery, despite the carbon monoxide poisoning my body, I feel an enormous sense of happiness as I see my friends suspended in liquid. My feelings of joy are not even affected by the fact that all of them look like ancient mummies, as their blood has been removed from their bodies.

But my happiness does disappear when lights flicker off, and every Safe-Death chamber switches off for a brief moment before coming back on again.

"What the hell was that?" I wonder aloud.

And then it happens again. The whole place goes dark, and the sound of electrical engines whirring to a halt fills the room.

116

This time the outage lasts longer, but finally the lights come back on.

I walk over to the first empty chamber in the room. A piece of paper has been stuck to the glass, and the first four words are written in large capital letters:

DO NOT ENTER PURGATORY!

I take the piece of paper from the glass and read the rest of it.

Happy has taken our only source of power by filling the sky with storm clouds. This place runs on solar energy. Purgatory is dying. Those who are inside when the power goes out will be stuck inside until the power comes back.
Fuck Happy!
Igby Koh

I smile in spite of this new and horrible obstacle. Igby is alive and he's out there somewhere.

From behind me, Chester coughs, a violent and ill sound. I put the note in my pocket.

"Come with me," I say to him, and he stumbles forward, almost falling on his face.

"What is . . . is this p . . . place?" he asks, his voice now a juddering and gravelly buzz.

"This is Safe-Death; a system created by a . . . Well, a mad scientist, frankly, but it will keep you alive. Once you step

117

inside the chamber, your body will be temporarily killed, but your brain will be uploaded into *Purgatory Hotel*, a video game from sometime in the 2020s."

"Th . . . that is insane."

"I know, but it's the only way to hide from Happy—because you'll be technically dead you won't show on any of the scanners. This gas canister is almost empty, and I don't think you'd survive another hit anyway. Get in."

I know that once the power goes out in this place completely, Chester will be trapped inside Purgatory, unable to help us any further until Happy decides to dispel the dark clouds covering the sun. That sucks for him and for me; he's the best source of information I have about what's going on inside the Arc. But I also know that he is hypothermic and suffocating due to lack of oxygen in his bloodstream, and if he doesn't get inside the Safe-Death chamber soon, he is going to die.

Chester shambles up to the chamber, and I help him inside. I tell him to press the button above his head.

"Wh-what are you going to do?" he asks.

"I need to find my friends. Somehow they're out there in the real world and they've found a way to hide from Happy's drones."

Chester nods his head, his eyes rolling in his sockets. "Does it hurt? Safe-Death, does it hurt?"

"For a second," I tell him. "But once you're inside, you'll feel fine."

"I'm scared," he mumbles.

"You're going to be okay," I tell him, and reach up to push the button myself.

"Wait," he gasps. "There are things I need to tell you."

The lights flicker off again, this time for at least five seconds, and as we wait in the dark and the silence, I'm scared they won't come back on. But they do. I've got to get Chester inside before the next outage—it might be the last.

"Luka, listen—" Chester says.

"No time," I interrupt, and I press the button.

"Take this," Chester says, and removes a Lens from his eye, throwing it toward me as the chamber spins shut.

The lights flicker again, causing the door to stall and jitter before closing completely.

"Your friends," Chester says, raising his voice to be heard through the closed door. "They must be deep underground, more than fifty yards, and once down there, they'd have to stay at least six feet apart. It's literally the only way they could stay hidden from—"

But there's no more time. The needles—long, thick, and hollow—have pierced Chester high up in the thighs, entering the femoral artery and sucking the blood out like a vampire.

I watch as the color drains from Chester's already-pallid skin, and then he becomes gaunt and skeletal.

I put the Lens that Chester threw me in my pocket—no time for that now.

"Good luck," I whisper, looking up at the emaciated boy in the chamber, and then I inhale the carbon monoxide gas to keep the drones away, unsure if there's enough entering my system for it to work.

I walk around the chambers, checking to see who decided to

stay in Purgatory, despite the risk of being trapped in there while everything goes down out here, and who left with Igby. I come to Malachai Bannister first, suspended in the cold liquid, his hair floating around his handsome face. Next, among the rebels and the Missing, I see Molly, my sister, and I'm glad that she's inside. If she's in Purgatory, she can't be killed out here. I press my hand against the glass of her chamber, wishing I could hug her. Lastly, I see Wren Salter, my former prison warden and the girl who broke us all out in the first place. But there's no one else here from the Loop.

So, Kina is out there somewhere, I think, and my heart skips a beat at the thought of her. I love her more than I thought I could ever love anyone.

Not only is Kina out there, but so is Sam and her newborn child; so are Pander, Igby, and Dr. Ortega.

I walk toward the exit of the VRcade, and the lights flicker one last time before going out completely. I wait for a minute, but they don't come back on. Those who are in Purgatory are stuck there now, and the thought is actually comforting.

I step outside, pick Mable's body up, and take her to the park across the road from the arcade. I lay her down next to the graves of Alix Quantock, Jo-Ray St. Martin, and Shion Cho, who died when Dr. Price, the inventor of Safe-Death, had shot their cryochambers, killing them instantly. There are other graves with names I don't recognize: Quentin Caulfield, Rivers Bond, Mikki Thorn. And beside those graves are the homemade grave markers for the bodies that could not be recovered: Podair Samson; Akimi Kaminski; Woods Rafka. I feel my

120

heart pause as my eyes scan over to the next grave marker—it reads LUKA KANE.

For a moment, I feel a sense of dislocation, a rush of vertigo, but I ignore it. There's no time to dwell on my death right now.

I grab the shovel that has been left leaning on the park's fence, and I dig.

There is a voice inside me telling me that this can wait, that there are more important things, but it can't wait. I fear for my own sense of self; I feel the good part of me dying and somehow, I know this will save me. It is the right thing to do, and doing the right thing is important, especially in the face of immense evil.

I hear a Mosquito drone growing louder as it zips through the air, scanning for signs of human life. I grab the mask and suck in the last of the carbon monoxide. I'm so worn out from digging that I almost pass out despite the depleted gas, and the drone flies by without slowing.

Finally, when the grave is deep enough, I carefully lower Mable in and place her hands together in her lap. She looks like she's sleeping.

"Mable," I say, my voice coming out thick and miserable. "I let you down. I let you down in the tunnels in the Loop, and I let you down when I trusted Tyco. I wish I could have saved you; I wish you had found yourself with someone smarter than me. I wish you were still alive. The world needs people like you, people who try their best to pass the test . . . Anyway, I'm sorry, okay? That's all I wanted to say. I'm sorry, and I hope that you're at peace now."

I don't cry until I begin shoveling the dirt onto her. And then it comes on so hard that I have to stop and lean on the spade for a few minutes until it passes.

When it's done, and the grave is filled, I take two pieces of wood from the low fence around the sandpit and tie them together to form a cross like the other grave markers. I then use the old steak knife that was left beside my grave to carve MABLE into the wood. I stab the marker into the ground at the head of Mable's burial plot and step back to look at my work.

"Goodbye, Mable," I say, and then I look around. There is only the ancient city, frozen in time, not touched by anything but nature since the war ended.

Deep underground, Chester had said, *at least six feet apart.*

The only places I can think of that are deep underground with enough space for a lot of people to keep two yards apart are the old subway stations, but are any of them more than fifty yards belowground?

As I run, I think way back to history lessons in public school and being taught about the prewar city, and the deepest of the subway stations, but I can't remember. I hated school, hated the virtual classrooms and lessons on selective history, their stupid system that pressured kids to learn about things they didn't care about, hated the way they tried to convince us that school was the most important thing in our whole lives, but damn I wish I could remember the name of that subway station!

I turn left, down a narrow cobbled street, then emerge onto a wide main street with old boutique shops filled with dust

122

and dead insects and curios from another time. Still, nowhere is there a sign for an underground station.

"Come on, come on," I mutter to myself, anticipating the sound of drones filling the air at any moment.

And then I see the familiar subway sign, the red circle with the blue bar across it, and I run in and leap the ancient barriers. I find myself in a long, tiled corridor that angles slightly down. At the end of this corridor there are sets of stairs on each side, but both only lead up.

I turn back. My goal is to find the deepest station, not the highest.

I get back onto the street, the already-dim light fading now as the sun goes down.

I come to another station, but this one is aboveground too. I turn and run back the way I came, taking a right to explore a wider area. I find myself in a residential area, houses stacked side by side painted yellow, blue, white.

I run through these streets, trying to find my way back to the city proper, where I'm likely to find more stations.

I sprint for ten minutes before I find another. I sigh with relief when I see that this one is actually underground. I run down the steep escalator until I get to a section that is completely missing. I have to jump over to the adjacent escalator to avoid the gaping hole that leads into the rusted machinery.

I find my way to the station platform. There's nobody there, no sign of Kina, Igby, Sam, Pander, no one at all.

I swear to myself and then begin the long journey back to the surface.

When I emerge back onto the street, the dim light that signaled the hidden sun was sinking below the horizon is now almost completely gone—the only illumination comes from the muted lightning that seems to stay within the confines of the clouds.

It's cold too. Really cold. I can see my breath coming out in thick white clouds each time I exhale. I have never really warmed up since the river.

I'm torn between finding shelter and finding my friends. I decide to look for another hour or so. Surely, that'll be enough time to find them?

There are hundreds of stations in this city, a voice inside my head reminds me. *Who's to say it's anywhere near here?*

"It has to be around here," I say aloud. "This is the only part of the Red Zone that isn't irradiated."

Still, there could be a dozen stations.

I ignore everything—all attempts at logic, the cold, the likelihood that I won't find what I'm looking for in the dark—and I keep running.

Somewhere far away on the edge of the Red Zone, I can hear the chillingly familiar buzz of the Mosquito drones searching for signs of life, searching for me.

Please, I think, *please don't come this way.*

Happy doesn't scan the Red Zones as thoroughly as the city, but there's still a chance they'll spot me.

I pick up the pace, running faster now. Sometimes it feels like running is all I've done my whole life: When I was a kid, I'd run from the seniors in the public school on physical days;

when I grew up a little, I'd run from the street gangs and the Ebb pushers; when Molly and I started ripping off low-level dealers for Coin transfers, we'd run all day. And when I was caught and put in the Loop, I spent my exercise hours running so that they had no energy to take from me in the harvest.

These thoughts spill out of my head as I trip on a loose paving stone in the dark.

I land hard, breaking my fall with my hands. The skin on my palms is torn and spots of blood shine through for a second before the healing tech repairs me.

There are things I need to tell you. Chester had said that before he went into Purgatory. I feel for the Lens in my pocket; it's still there.

I sit up and look around. No stations, no street signs pointing me in the direction of a station.

Okay, I think. *Time to find shelter.*

It's dangerous—I'll be taking my chances with the surveillance drones—but I have no energy left and I've had hypothermia once before, and I don't want to go through it again, even with healing tech.

I walk along the pavement, looking at each of the large houses in turn, not really sure why I don't select the first one I see, or the second, but when I come to a large, three-story red-brick home, I decide that this is the place.

I try the door, and it's locked, but time has rotted the wood away so badly that one hard shove and it disintegrates around the locking mechanism and swings open.

I step inside. I'm struck first by the smell: a perfume that must've somehow been lingering here for a hundred years, flowery and sweet and comforting. But that smell seems to exist only in the entryway, as when I move deeper, through the dust-covered hall and into the living room, I can smell the old, damp, rotting scent that seeps from the walls.

It's a strange feeling, standing in a living room from the tech revolution era. The flat-screen television, the leather corner sofa, the wallpaper, bookshelves—and there are wires every-where. I laugh when I see them all—how crazy that people used to have to plug things into the wall.

I check out the kitchen and it's just as crazy: a microwave, an old-fashioned oven, more wires and plugs.

It's a strange feeling, like stepping back in time. This place is exactly how it was when the owners abandoned it during the war. All of it is so fascinating, but the coldness feels as though it's digging its claws into my bones, and if I'm staying here, I might as well get as much rest as I can before morning. But before I leave the kitchen, I feel a stab of pain in my stomach, and I realize that I'm starving. I haven't eaten in over two weeks—of course, Happy fed me via needle, but I haven't had a physical meal for over a fortnight!

Nothing for it, I think. *There's no food that lasts a hundred years!*

But that's not true. I remember reading about a steamboat that had sunk in something like 1865, and over a hundred years later, they retrieved canned food from the wreckage, and scientists found that although it had lost some of its vitamin A and C, there was no bacteria or microbial growth, and it was safe to eat.

I throw open the cupboards and dig around. Almost all the food inside has long ago turned to dust, or is in a horrible state of decay, but there are four tins near the back: peaches in syrup, chicken noodle soup, something called corned beef, and a can of cured ham. I choose the peaches. The tin has a ring pull that breaks off as soon as I try to pry it up from the base, but I find an old knife and manage to cut the lid off with only four or five minor injuries (that of course disappear almost instantly).

I sniff the contents of the tin. Amazingly, it smells fine. I dip my pinkie finger in and taste a tiny amount of the syrup.

As soon as the sugary liquid touches my tongue, I feel that pang of pain in my stomach once again, and I can't stop myself. I lift the tin up and drink the syrup; then I grab the segments of peach out and eat them with my hands. They taste perfect, and when they're gone, and I've scoured the inside of the can with my fingers, licking up more of the juice, I want to eat more. But, honestly, looking at the remaining tins, and thinking about the animals that they used to kill in the most inhumane ways before they could grow meat in a laboratory, takes the edge off my hunger.

I climb the stairs and find a bedroom. Amazingly, it has a fireplace in it, and after feeling for a draft, I decide that it is almost definitely a working fireplace.

I debate it for a while, thinking through the pros (warmth, comfort, more chance of a good sleep) and the cons (the heat signature will attract any Mosquitoes within three miles), but I decide that after what I've been through, I'm owed a night of luck.

I break up some furniture—a few chairs and a small set of drawers—and find some ancient paper sticking out of a black box next to an old computer.

I build the fire and light it with an old plastic lighter that ignites on the eighth or ninth attempt.

The fire comes alive nicely, and the room begins to warm up.

I sit, listening to the crackle of the wood and the steady rumble of the flames, and for the longest time, I think about absolutely nothing at all. It's a great thing, to power down like that; to drift away and be comfortably lost for a little while.

I'm snapped out of this stupor by a new sound. A light scratching, padding, and then sniffing on the other side of the door.

I wait, frozen, not by fear exactly, but by trepidation.

The bedroom door is nudged open, and a fox comes in. Its worried eyes appraise me as it sniffs the air and takes a half step backward.

"It's okay," I whisper.

The fox steps into the room, followed closely by two cubs who seem far less concerned by the entire situation. One of them stumbles over and plops itself down next to the fire.

The older fox looks terrified at its child's boldness, but as I shuffle away, it comes in. The second cub, seeing its parent's acceptance, runs in too, its weak little cries disturbing its sibling, who looks up from its curled-up position in front of the fire.

The parent fox sits on its haunches, watching its children, still wary of me, but slowly growing more comfortable.

"Hi," I say, slowly reaching out my hand to the adult fox. It backs its head away at first, but then sniffs my hand and licks it a few times. "Hey, how are you?" I say, smiling at my new friend.

After a while, the adult fox lies down too, although it doesn't take its eyes off me.

And we sit like that, the three of us, for at least an hour, until I feel everyone is comfortable enough for me to move.

I stand up slowly. All three of the red-furred, bright-eyed creatures look at me as though I'm going to attack. They look scared and somehow helpless. I walk by, moving slowly, telling them all the time that it's all right.

When I sidestep out of the door, I feel the immediate difference in temperature. The rest of the house is freezing cold.

I walk down the stairs and make my way back into the kitchen, where I grab the tin of corned beef. It takes me a few minutes to figure out how to open the tin—it involves a key-shaped piece of metal that snaps off and connects to a tab on the side, then you roll the key over and over until a thin strip of metal comes away from the tin and it can be opened up like a lid.

The pink-and-white meat inside doesn't smell great, but I have a feeling it never did to begin with. I open cupboards until I find a stack of old plates. I take one from the middle and give it a wipe with my T-shirt.

I spoon the meat onto it and carry it upstairs.

The little foxes' ears prick up as soon as I enter the room, and their noses start prodding the air, smelling out the food.

I put the plate down in front of them and they start yipping excitedly as they eat.

The parent fox watches, a look of amazement in its eyes. And although I can tell that they're starving, they don't eat a thing; they just watch their kids eating.

"Don't worry," I tell the old fox, and without thinking I reach out and scratch it behind the ear. "I've got something called cured ham for you tomorrow."

I lean back against the bed frame and take the Lens that Chester gave me out of my pocket and place it into my eye. Immediately I can see that the small piece of tech has been damaged. The heads-up display is wavering and I can't select any options. I remove it from my eye, put it back in my pocket, and hope that Igby will be able to get the information out of it.

I drag the dust-covered blanket off the bed and wrap it around myself. Before long, I'm fast asleep.

I wake up suddenly, the remnants of a violent dream slipping beyond my knowing.

The fire is out, the foxes are gone, and I'm alone in this big old house.

But I'm alive. The Mosquitoes didn't come.

In the cold light of the morning, I chastise myself for being so weak and so foolish as to light a fire; bad enough I'm out in the open, but to light a fire?

You needed to sleep, I tell myself, but I make a promise to take no more needless chances.

I feel a pang of regret. I wish the foxes had stayed—I could've given them more food, especially the older one, who didn't eat last night.

I can't do anything about it now, though. I get up, feeling stiffness in my knees, and I wonder why the stupid healing technology doesn't fix that. I stagger down the stairs, yawning as I go.

In the back of my mind, I can feel the countdown to Happy's final plan. Phase Three; the razing, as Dr. Price had called it. But I'm worn out and hungry and my mind is still spinning.

I walk downstairs and glance into the kitchen. I'm so

hungry that even the chicken noodle soup is looking tempting, but I leave it. There's no time.

The day, although still dim beneath the endless clouds, is clear enough to see by, and I begin searching for my way back into town to find more subway stations.

It takes about an hour of walking before I find my first station, but after climbing down three sets of escalators, and exploring the four separate platforms I discover down there, I find nothing but empty platforms covered in dust. I stare at the black hole of the subway tunnel, and for a while, I don't move at all.

You'd find stations a lot quicker if you just follow the tracks, I tell myself.

But I turn around and climb back up the ancient escalators. There could be rats in those tunnels, big rats, rats that are starving and willing to kill for food.

When I return to street level, I take a deep breath, filling my lungs with the fresh air.

I find it fascinating, the way nature has reclaimed the city; without people and the pollution they bring it's amazing how quickly wildlife takes back its land. It's beautiful in a way.

Careful, I think. *You'll start sounding like Happy.*

I move down alleyways, along two-lane roads, past statues and monuments to those who died in the First and Second World Wars. I even walk through an ancient shopping center, marveling at the oddities within: machines that dispensed physical money; booths in which photographs could be taken for some unknown reason; stores that sold physical computers.

I exit through a fire escape and find myself in yet another commercial area.

I see a cross painted on the side of an old pub, and as I scan more buildings, I see more crosses.

I turn right and run past an old brick building with scaffolding still clinging to the side. I run past a bookshop, a cell phone store, a pharmacy—all these things would fascinate me if I wasn't panicking.

And more crosses on gift shops, cafés.

The crosses, I think, seeing how new they seem compared to the sun-bleached shop signs and flaked paint on the other buildings. *They must be how the rebels Hansel and Gretel their way back to the station.*

I start following the white crosses, taking a left in a fork in the road, then passing through another narrow alleyway.

Now there are buildings with two crosses on them. *Am I getting closer or farther away?* I wonder.

"Hey!" a voice calls from somewhere far behind me.

I stop and turn, looking back along the cracked road. Standing there, with a large backpack on her back, and arms filled with canned food, is someone I recognize right away.

"Kina?" I say, and take a step toward her.

"No," she calls, dropping the canned food and holding up both hands. "No, don't you move."

She reaches behind her back and produces a USW pistol.

"Kina, it's me, it's Luka."

"Shut the fuck up," she says, stepping closer, keeping the gun trained on my chest.

"What the hell are you doing?" I ask.

"What is this? Face-changer software? Is this a trap? Are you an Alt? For the love of the Final Gods, please don't tell me I'm still in the Block and this is the Sane Zone."

"Kina, it's none of those things. It's me. I know I'm supposed to be dead, but—"

"I told you to shut up!" she screams, her eyes wide with rage and anguish. She paces back and forth, occasionally lowering the gun and then pointing it back at me. "This is sick. I knew Happy was evil, but this is fucking sick! How stupid do they think I am? Sending some ghost version of Luka to lure me away. It's not going to work, it's not . . ." Her voice begins to tremble on these last words, and she takes another few steps toward me. "It's not really you, is it? I mean, you're dead, I accepted the fact that you're dead, so you can't be alive, you can't be standing there, so just stop it!"

"I . . . I'm sorry." I don't mean this to come out so flippantly, and the look of anger on Kina's face deepens.

"I came to terms with your death, Luka. I accepted it. Do you know what it took to accept that you were gone?"

I shake my head. "No."

"No. No, you don't know. And now you come waltzing down the middle of the road, and—what? I'm supposed to believe that this is real?"

"How can I prove it to you?" I ask.

"You can't! There's nothing you can do that will make me . . ." Her words catch in her throat.

"Kina, it me," I say. "They didn't kill me; they just wanted everyone to believe I was dead. They needed me—they needed three former inmates to isolate the healing tech."

"Stop talking. You're not going to convince me. I should just shoot you. I should just kill you now."

"Gods, don't do that," I say. "I don't want to have survived all of this just to be killed by you."

"What was the first thing you ever said to me?" Kina asks.

I have to think about it, but the memory comes to me. "It gets better. I told you that your time in the Loop gets better."

"That doesn't prove anything—they recorded everything in the Loop."

"Kina, it really is me. I promise. I'll find a way to prove it to you."

"Oh, I don't care," she says, shrugging the backpack off, dropping the gun, and walking toward me.

I walk too, closing the gap between us. A misting rain begins to fall from the electric clouds, but I ignore it. I had thought—I had *believed* that we would never see each other again, and yet fate keeps bringing us back together.

We're close now, only ten yards between us. All I want, all I need is to hold her, kiss her, but something stops me in my tracks. Something is wrong. It starts with pain in my hands and then a burning sensation on my scalp.

I hear Kina screaming, and I look up to see the skin on her face beginning to tear and melt off in the fine, misty rain.

No, I think, *not now, not when we're so close.*

I try to run to her, but the pain explodes into agony as my

own skin begins to fall way from my arms with the rainwater.

"Get inside!" I yell to Kina. "Get to cover! Go!"

She turns and runs into a big, glass-fronted furniture shop and collapses to the floor, still crying out in agony.

"What is it? What the hell is it?"

"I don't know," I call back, feeling the skin on my face burning and blood seeping out of the wounds.

I manage to stumble into an old clothes shop on the opposite side of the road. I grab an ancient green dress and try to rub the rain off my face, but it doesn't help; it seems to drive the poison, or acid, or whatever it is deeper into my skin.

"It's not stopping," Kina screams from the other side of the road.

I look down at my hands and see tiny creatures, like fleas, covering my skin.

"They're alive," I call back, feeling the tiny things biting at me, eating me.

"What do we do?" she calls.

I try to think, but the pain is unbearable. "I don't know."

I fall to my knees, feeling as though I'm being dragged down by the tiny bugs that cover my body. They're in my eyes now, eating away at the tissue, blinding me.

Think, I tell myself. *Think! There's a way out of this!*

But nothing comes but more pain.

I feel arms around my chest.

"Come on." It's Kina's voice. She drags me back out into the street.

"No!" I scream, certain that her plan is simply to end it all quickly, to stop the suffering so it doesn't drive us insane before ending our lives.

"Hurry!" she calls back.

She drags me into the middle of the road, pulls me up to standing, and then shoves me in the direction of a large redbrick building with two white chalk crosses drawn on the side.

"Run!" Kina says, shoving me again.

I'm almost completely blind now as the creatures eat away at my eyes, and I can barely move as they consume my flesh. I look down at my arms with my one working eyeball and see the stark white of bone along with the stringy tendons that control my wrist and fingers.

Something snaps in my left leg and it becomes suddenly weak.

"Where are we . . . ?" I'm about to ask *Where are we going?* but the organisms have bitten through the skin of my throat and the words turn into a screech.

We pass by an old bank; this building also has two chalk crosses on it, and up ahead I see a church with the same two crosses. Beyond the church is a two-story house with three crosses on it. The house with the three crosses is the last thing I see as my vision cuts out completely.

I run into something hard—a lamppost, I think—and I fall to the ground. Kina grabs me and pulls me up once again. She throws my arm over her shoulder and guides me onward.

We move along the street, me in darkness, both of us surely seconds from death. And then we collapse to the ground.

This is it, this is the end of the line. At least I'm in Kina's arms. I wish I could tell her how much . . .

The pain stops.

At first, I'm sure it's because the creatures have eaten through the last of my nerve endings, rendering me numb, but after some time, I feel my vision beginning to return.

I try to speak, try to ask what happened, but my throat is still a gaping hole.

I sit up and see that we haven't traveled as far as I had thought. We are only twenty or thirty yards past the building with the three crosses.

I try to speak, but pain erupts in my vocal cords as I interrupt the healing process.

"Shh," Kina says. "You said those things were alive, so I took them somewhere they couldn't survive."

I shrug, still not understanding.

"The Red Zone; we're in the irradiated area of the Red Zone."

I look down at the tarmac road, and I can see them, the bugs, dead, like dust, surrounding us and lining the pavement behind us, millions of them, hundreds of millions. The white crosses on the buildings hadn't been leading me to the subway station; they'd been leading me into the radiation.

"You . . ." I cough, finally feeling the wounds heal themselves. "You're a genius," I croak.

"And you're supposed to be dead," she replies.

"I know," I say, "I'm sorry, I thought I *was* dead, but it turns out—"

"You left," she says, cutting me off.

"What?"

"Back in the library, when we were all escaping. You left me alone."

"I did. I did leave. I had to."

"You left and you didn't tell me. You just left."

I watch the last of the wounds heal on Kina's arms, then I look into her eyes. "I'm sorry, Kina. I made a deal with Happy; it would let you all go if I went with Tyco. I knew that none of you would let me sacrifice myself, so I had to—"

"You couldn't even tell me? You couldn't at least have let me know what was going on? Instead, you blew up the tunnels and disappeared! I spent the next twenty-four hours having a full-blown panic attack, thinking the worst, imagining you dead, and then Igby managed to hook up the live feed from Galen's speech at the Arc and there you were, onstage, standing in front of thousands of Alts. And then I watched him kill you."

There's a silence between us that stretches out too long.

"I'm sorry," I say finally.

"I don't think that matters," Kina replies. "You didn't trust me enough to tell me what you had to do."

"I didn't think you'd let me do it."

"I probably wouldn't have!" she yells. "Oh, screw it, who cares. You're alive. I don't know how, but you're alive."

She kisses me, and I kiss her back.

"Don't you ever do anything so goddamned stupid again!" Kina says.

"I won't, I won't," I reply, kissing her harder.

"Don't ever leave me again."

"I won't."

And for a moment, our hands are moving over each other, and I don't think either of us can or want to stop, but then we both do. We look at each other, smiling and a little out of breath.

Kina laughs. "We have to stop almost dying."

"Agreed," I say.

Kina stands up and looks into the nonirradiated part of the city. "How do we get back to the subway?"

I stand up too and look to where she is staring. It seems as though the entire street is flowing and moving—the ground is covered in the minuscule flesh-eating bugs. "I don't know," I reply, "but we need to get back soon—we don't have long until . . ."

"Until what?"

"Happy has the formula to the healing tech. Once it has tested it, it's going to unleash a microscopic . . . *thing* into all Regions of Earth. These," I say, pointing to the millions of crawling creatures, "these bugs that Happy sent to eat us, Happy must have had them bioengineered in a lab in the Arc and then released them across . . . well, across the whole world. They're like a biological dry run. What Happy is sending is nanotechnology. Tiny robots that eat everything and use the materials to create more of themselves. Replicating over and over until there is an unstoppable ocean of them."

Kina looks up to the sky in exasperation. "Why?"

"We're not the only ones who've found a way to survive.

There are rebels like us in every Region, and Happy wants them stamped out along with all architecture, all structures, all art, all records, all traces of what humanity was—good and bad, gone forever along with the humans that lived here. There is not a panic room, underground cave, or boat in the middle of the ocean that will survive. Only then will Happy be ready to restart all life on this planet."

"When does Happy drop these nanobots?"

"I'm pretty sure they'll be released in about six days. Fifteen hours after that the Earth will be eaten down to bedrock."

"We need to get this information to Igby," Kina says, still staring out at the sea of bugs.

"How?" I ask, and I join Kina in looking at the ravenous insects that are eating everything. *But they're not eating everything*, I think, and look closer.

"Wait," I say, looking down at Kina's boots—they're made out of some kind of neoprene or polymer and the insects haven't eaten away at them at all.

"What is it?"

"They're not like the nanobots Happy is going to send," I say. "They only eat organic material."

"You're saying . . ."

"I'm saying that if we're covered, head to toe, in nonorganic material, we can walk right through."

"Over there," Kina says, pointing to an ancient department store. The sign outside has long ago fallen and shattered on the pavement below.

We run over to it, shoving open the double doors and

stepping over the shards of glass that lie on the polished tile floor. There are clothes everywhere, on racks and rails, all coated in decades of radioactive dust.

"Go through the clothes," I say. "Find all nonorganic stuff, polyester and nylon. Nothing silk, leather, or wool."

"All right," Kina says, "but don't expect high fashion."

I laugh as I make my way to the back of the store, where I look for synthetic rubber footwear, gloves, goggles, and something to cover our faces with.

It takes us around ten minutes to gather everything we need, and we meet at the foot of the long-ago-defunct escalator.

"Okay," Kina says, looking down at the strange array of items. "Let's do this."

She unzips her half-eaten black hoodie and throws it on a rack of sunglasses behind her, before unbuckling her belt and sliding off her black jeans.

I can't help but look at her, and all I want to do is kiss her again. She catches me looking, and I look away. When I look back, she's smiling.

"Help me on with these," she says, picking up the rustling trousers from the floor of the store.

"What are they?" I ask. "Ski trousers?"

"They're called salopettes, you uncultured swine!" Kina replies, affecting a posh accent.

By the time we've helped each other into the bright yellow jackets and striped salopettes, wellies, wide-brimmed hats with mosquito nets hanging around our faces, with swimming goggles covering our eyes and tape over all the seams, we're laughing so hard that we can barely stand, and all thoughts of intimacy are long gone.

"Come on," I say, and again I find myself amazed that we can find anything to smile about while Happy is plotting to lower its margin of failure from 0.7 percent to 0 percent. It was bad enough when the AI figured out how to reprogram its coding so that it could harm humans, but now . . . Finally, I do stop smiling.

"Happy is not going to stop, is it?" I say as the tiny bugs crawl and jump and move as one.

"No," Kina says, following my gaze. "Not until we destroy it."

I nod and then hold up a mittened hand for a high five. Kina presses her hand against mine, and then we exit the department store and walk toward the buildings with the double crosses painted on them, and then past the buildings with the single crosses, and finally into the crowd of ravenous bugs.

They leap on us immediately, swarming us, crawling all over our bizarre clothes, but—after a minute or so—it's clear that they aren't biting. The plan is working.

We walk through the twenty-first-century city, perfectly preserved as though set in wax. Remnants of an era dubbed the tech revolution, when advancements in computing were progressing exponentially and new worlds were opening up, most of them engineered to be addictive so that corporations could harvest data while users argued over the extreme poles of politics, certain they were opposites and never realizing how similar they were to each other. But here there is evidence of humanity: kids' bikes parked next to each other; chalk drawings on the pavement; lawn chairs laid out side by side outside a small home; rainbow flags; graffiti encouraging peace; book-shops that—if they weren't being eaten by bugs, and if we had more time—I would love to explore.

This is what Happy can't see. It's easy to look at a list of atrocities, of mistakes, of wars, of the evil that humankind is capable of, but those represent the powerful few, those who strove for control and misused it. It seems those who desire power are those most compelled to abuse it, and here Happy is, doing the same thing—perhaps the AI is not so different from the humans who created it.

We trudge on, the sounds of our strange clothing scraping and swishing through the streets. We pass an ancient movie theater, another old bank, and a place where people used to get manicures.

Finally, we come to the entrance to the underground station. I notice two homemade wind turbines on the roof, spinning lazily in the breeze.

We step into the station and over mounds of rubble to the old ticket barriers, which stand broken and useless. There is a bank of elevators along one wall, but of course none of them work. One of the elevator's doors are open, revealing a mass of thick wires connected to a small mountain of car batteries and running up toward the two wind turbines.

"Igby?" I ask, turning to Kina.

She nods. "Igby."

We walk past the elevators and take the winding staircase down and down into the darkness, seemingly forever, turning and turning deeper into the Earth until finally I hear a baby crying. The sound is jarring, so unexpected after the silence of the city.

We carry on, finally emerging onto an old subway station platform deep under the ground. All around us are people: maybe twenty of the Missing; twelve or so clones; and a few Loop inmates. All are standing within designated boxes painted on the floor of the platform and on the tracks themselves.

"What in the hell are you supposed to be?" asks a nearby girl.

"Oh, right," I say, laughing as I remove the hat, mosquito net, and goggles.

Silence sweeps across the platform as people begin to notice me, to recognize me.

"Luka Kane," someone says to my left.

"It can't be," says a man's voice from near the edge of the platform.

"It's him!" someone yells.

And then the crowd of people is closing in on me. I have a momentary flashback to when I was hunted by Smilers in the homeless village on the edge of town, and then Igby's voice is cutting through the murmurs.

"Hey! Remember the rules—two yards' distance at all times or the heat signature will build and the drones will find us! Yes, it's Luka fucking Kane, but it's not the resurrection of the Final Gods! Back off."

The crowd slowly steps back into their painted squares.

"You," Igby says, pointing at me. "Come with me."

I feel my heart swell with love when I see the boy who I have been through so much with. Kina and I follow him, walking through the dispersed crowd. I can feel everyone watching me, everyone whispering about the impossibility of my survival.

Igby jumps down onto the track and ushers some clones—Ebb addicts—out of the way. Kina and I follow him into the dark of the train tunnel. I trip on something between the tracks and realize they are the same cables that were connected to the wind turbines on the roof.

"Off to make more plans without us, are youse?" a female voice calls out, a hint of malice in it. I turn to see a red-haired woman shaking her head.

"Pander, Day, come with us," Igby says, ignoring the comment.

"Luka?" Day whispers as I pass by.

"Hi," I say, unsure how to respond.

Pander jumps down from an alcove high up on the curved wall and joins us.

"Dr. O, wake up," Igby says, nudging the pillow beneath Dr. Ortega's head with his foot as we move through her painted square and deeper into the tunnel.

Dr. Ortega wakes up, and her eyes lock on mine for a moment before she looks away in shame. She knows that I discovered her secret as we were escaping from the library; that she was an Alt scientist in the Facility, that she ran experiments on Loop inmates before changing her name and defecting to the other side.

Sam joins our group too, her daughter—less than three weeks old—strapped to her front with a length of fabric. We come to a bank of ancient laptops with wires of various sizes and colors coming in and out of them. Slumped in the corner is something that looks like a dead body, but on closer inspection I see that it's an old HelperBot from the late 2060s or 70s. They were sort of novelty robots that did rich people's housework before they were replaced by smaller, cheaper drones. They've become collector's items over the last few decades.

"All right," Igby says. "First things first." And then he hugs me, throwing his arms around me and holding me tightly. "There is no fucking way you can be alive!" he says.

"I know," I tell him. "I can't believe it myself."

He steps back and looks at me like I'm a mirage. And then Pander is hugging me, and Sam and Day join in. When they break away, the only one left is Dr. Ortega, who stands nervously back.

"Listen—" she says, finally, her usually commanding voice quiet and subdued.

"No," I say, interrupting her. I know that she plans to confess, I know that she feels cornered by my return, and I don't want her to feel that way. "You listen. I know you're not one for showing affection, but I came back from the dead, dammit, now come and give me a hug."

She looks at me, a spark of hope in her eyes. "Really?"

I think of what she had done in her former life as Dr. Soto, and what she has done in her current life as Dr. Ortega. She made her decision long before the dominion of Happy. People can change, people can open their eyes to the truth; if I didn't believe that, then what the hell am I fighting for?

"Yes, really," I say.

"She's just grumpy because she's not allowed her Ebb around the clones," Pander says.

Abril Ortega walks over and throws her arms around me. "Thank you," she whispers.

"You're a good person," I tell her. "I don't care about what happened in the past. You're a good person."

"Right," Igby says, getting everyone's attention. "I'm not going to ask why you two are dressed like 1980s ski-movie villains, but your timing is perfect; I'm about ten days away from regaining access to Happy's memories, after that we can start making a plan to—"

"We don't have ten days," I say.

"What do you mean?" he asks.

"Happy has the formula for the healing tech."

Igby looks at me, and then he looks at the rails between his feet. He swears under his breath.

"What does that mean?" Pander asks. "How long *do* we have, and what happens when that time is up?"

"Hopefully this should tell us everything we need to know," I say, handing Chester's Lens to Igby. "It's damaged, but I'm sure you'll be able to extract some of the files. It belongs to an Alt named Chester; he saved my life."

Igby takes the Lens and carries it over to the bank of old laptops. He connects it to a wire with a miniature crocodile clip and then runs several programs across four of the old computers.

"I have no idea what any of these files are," Igby admits, scrolling though page after page of what looks like overwritten files and double-exposed photographs of text. "How did that Chester boy decrypt these?"

"I don't know," I tell him. "He was dying; I had to get him into Purgatory before the power went out."

And then Igby comes to a file with a different extension name at the very bottom of the list. He clicks on it, and one of his laptops begins whirring and clicking, but on the middle screen, an image appears.

It glitches and stutters, but it's Earth from space. The screen goes blank, and the error message CORRUPT FILE appears onscreen. When the footage returns, it is still stuttering and glitching across the screen, but we are in a hospital room. This scene freezes; the colors begin to blend and then jitter.

CORRUPT FILE appears again, and this time the footage doesn't return.

"All right, that didn't work," Igby says. "Plan B."

He removes the clip from the Lens and places it onto his left eye. I watch as he moves that eye, navigating through files, and then, suddenly, he falls to the floor, stiff and unmoving.

"What's happening?" Pander calls.

"Wait," I say, holding her back as she tries to reach into his eye and remove the Lens.

Igby lies on the subway tracks, completely still apart from his chest rising and falling. He stays like that for five minutes before sitting up so suddenly that we all take a step back.

He gasps in air and removes the Lens.

"Holy shit," he breathes. "Holy hell."

"What did you see?" Sam whispers.

"Everything. I saw everything. I knew everything. The universe, it's . . . bigger . . . it's . . ."

"Igby, are you okay?" Day asks.

"I had all the knowledge in the world for a while there, but it's gone now." He looks at us each in turn, his eyes finally meeting mine. "I know what Happy plans to do, and I don't know if we can stop it."

"What's going to happen?" Dr. Ortega asks.

"First, Happy is going to try three times to kill all the remaining rebels on Earth."

"Two times," I say. "It already sent these bugs that tried to eat Kina and me."

Igby nods. "I knew what Happy was going to send for a while there, but as soon as the program ended, I lost the information—it's like my brain was filled to the bursting point. I wish I could remember the rest. I'd go back in, but the files are so corrupted that it's dangerous; it could trap me in there or take some of my mind with it."

"What happens after Happy tries to destroy us two more times?" Pander asks.

"The end," Igby says. "It's going to release self-replicating nanobots onto the surface of the planet, and they will eat away everything."

"Gods," Day whispers.

"Ecophagy," Igby says to himself.

"I'm sorry, did you just sneeze really quietly, or did you say something?" Pander asks.

"He said ecophagy," Dr. Ortega replies. "Otherwise known as the gray-goo scenario. Out of control, self-replicating micro-robots have been predicted for over a hundred years. Happy is making it come true."

"And you think we have less than six days?" Igby asks.

"Around five and a half, according to the Alt who saved me," I tell him.

Igby nods. "I don't think it matters," he says. "I don't think I can get into Happy's programming in that short of a time frame."

"Screw it, let's just attack the Arc," Pander suggests. "We won't win, but at least we take some of those bright-eyed morons with us."

"I'm with her," Day says, a determined look in her eyes.

"There's something else you should know," I say, remembering what Tyco told me in the lab. "I don't know if it changes anything, but for some time, Happy was upgrading itself. Every time it was uploaded into a new human, it took all their knowledge and all their compassion, and added it to the programming. After a while, the newer hosts started to question and disobey the orders of the older hosts—it was as if they weren't one intelligence anymore, but several, with different ideas. Happy stopped upgrading its emotional capabilities and just kept the host's knowledge instead."

I see Igby's eyes scrolling back and forth, as if reading lines of invisible code, or seeing all the possible moves of a chess game at once.

"The emotional component of the hosts; do you know what Happy did with those files?"

"Stored them," I reply, "somewhere in the programming."

"There's a chance," Igby says, at first so quietly I barely hear him. "There's a chance! It's a small chance, a very small chance, but it might work."

"What is it? What's the plan?" Day asks.

"Evolution," Igby says.

Igby didn't explain his plan. He said there was no time, that if it was going to succeed, we needed to work together from now until it was over, one way or another. I found that strange—Igby was never one to be secretive—but I trust him.

He gave everyone instructions: Kina and Sam were to stay with him and help him write code; Dr. Ortega was to complete Kina's failed mission to bring food back from the small farm in the park and tinned goods from shops; Pander was sent out to find more car batteries; and Day and I were given the task of bringing back as many old solid-state drives as we could.

"Make sure they have DRAM," Igby said, pointing at Day and me. "Don't bring me back cacheless SSDs; they're no good to me."

Of course, this meant nothing to me, and Day seemed confused too, so Igby sighed and told us to bring him everything we could find.

As our small group walks toward the staircase, there are a few disapproving looks from the others in the subway.

"Don't you think it might be a good idea to utilize the dozens of other people fighting this war?" says the same red-haired woman who had spoken up when I'd first arrived.

"Uh, yeah, I don't know, I don't really make those decisions," I say.

"Sure you don't, messiah," she replies sarcastically, and three or four of the Missing around her laugh.

I try to ignore this as we reach the staircase and begin to climb up.

I ask Dr. Ortega, Pander, and Day to wait behind as I seal my protective clothing as best as I can and run ahead to check if the murder-bugs are still active. Although there are a lot of stairs, it's nothing compared to the Verticals, and I'm up and over the barriers in no time.

I step out cautiously, aware that the seal of the tape around my gloves is no longer as tight as it was. But there's no need to worry. I see the dust-covered streets, and the bugs are no longer moving, no longer shimmering and swaying as one. They are all dead.

I turn back and meet the others on their way up.

"Coast is clear," I tell them.

"Great, now we get to risk our lives in the outside world. Woo!" Pander says, her voice monotone.

"You know, if we pull this off, we might just save the world," I say, "so I think it *is* a good thing."

"I know, loser," Pander says. "Obviously I'm delighted. I clearly use sarcasm as a defense mechanism; you haven't realized that yet? God, you suck."

"Oh, right. I mean, yeah, I guess I knew that, but . . ."

"Let's just go."

"Right, yes, okay," I say.

Pander runs off toward a large yellow garage down the street.

Dr. Ortega hugs me again. "I really am glad you're alive, you know?"

"I know," I say, and then it's time to split up.

"Okay," I say to Day, "let's go find some solid-state drives."

Day nods and tries a smile, but it doesn't sit well on her face, as if she is forcing it.

I tell Day about a shopping mall I walked through that had a store inside that once sold physical computers. I lead the way.

We make our way through the overgrown shopping center. The place feels like a horror movie set, with its eerie silence, broken windows, and glaze-eyed mannequins staring at us.

We reach the old electronics store and break the massive plate-glass window with a metal-wire shopping trolley. Once inside we make our way through to the back room, where all the new, boxed products are kept. We take the computers out and start taking them apart to find the SSDs.

"What do you think all that was about down in the subway?" I ask, unscrewing the panel of an ancient PC case.

"Huh?" Day replies, snapping out of a dazed state. "What do you mean?"

"The Missing—they seem pissed off that we're running missions."

"Wouldn't you be?" she replies. "I mean, they're the ones who saw it all coming; they're the ones who tricked Happy into believing they couldn't survive the Red Zones. They created

Safe-Death, and now . . . they're relegated to the sidelines by a bunch of prison kids and junkies."

"Yeah," I say, seeing her point. "I guess you're right. It's just, a lot of us have healing tech, and Igby's a legitimate genius, so we're just going with his plan. I mean, it's not like we're actively trying to—"

"Keep going here," Day says, interrupting my stream of consciousness. She stands up and scratches the back of her head. "I'm going to check another store, one that sells individual solid-state drives, it'll be quicker."

"I'll come with you," I say. "We'll be safer together . . ."

"No," Day says, "you keep working here. If I can't find another place, at least we'll have *something* to bring back to Igby."

"Day, are you all right?" I ask.

"No," she replies, and then gives another of those forced smiles. "It's the end of the world, silly—no one's all right!"

I nod. "I guess that's true."

"I'll come find you when I've got some SSDs. Just keep working here, okay?"

"Okay," I say. "If that's what you want."

"Yeah. I think it's the best plan."

And then she's gone, stepping carefully over the broken glass, her footfalls echoing through the enormous empty mall.

I stand up and step through the window frame and onto the walkway. I watch Day as she jogs down the escalator, scratching at her arm. She makes it to the revolving door of the shopping center, exits into the flickering light of the day, and turns away from town.

I think if she had gone the other way, farther into town, I would've left her, but she's heading to the residential area—she had said she was going to find a store that sold individual SSDs.

I follow her, the mission to bring Igby his equipment temporarily forgotten.

Day walks past a large, gnarled tree that has grown out of the road, and then turns right into the parking lot of an ancient block of apartments.

I keep far enough back that she doesn't see me, but after a while, I start to suspect that she wouldn't notice me if I were only ten feet behind her. She appears to know exactly where she's going, and her attention is focused solely on her destination.

I watch her enter the building, and then I follow her inside.

I can hear her footsteps echoing up the old concrete staircase, and I see—in the dust—that hers are not the only footprints—there's another much larger set going up and down the staircase.

I move up the stairs, listening to the sound of Day's steps a few floors above me. Finally, I hear a door creaking open, and I move faster up the stairs, following the dust prints until they turn on the seventh floor.

I open the groaning door and find myself in a long, narrow, windowless corridor, not unlike the corridors of Purgatory, but this one is dusty and old, and parts of the roof have caved in.

I no longer have to follow the footprints in the dust, as I can see the open door of one of the apartments, and I can hear the clattering sound of pots and pans being hurled out of a cupboard. I move to the doorway.

"Where is it? Where the hell is it?" Day's voice comes floating to me. She sounds frustrated, exasperated.

I walk into the apartment. A dingy place, not much bigger than my family's place in the Black Road Vertical. A single thin hallway with three rooms leading off: a bathroom, a living room–kitchen, and a bedroom. Day is in the combined living room and kitchen. I enter that room and see her digging through a cupboard frantically.

And then she stops as the last pan hits the floor.

"Thank the gods," she whispers, holding up a bag of Ebb patches.

"Don't do it, Day," I say, and she spins around, gasping in a breath and hiding the bag of Ebb behind her back.

"What the hell, Luka?" she says. "I almost had a heart attack. What are you doing here?"

"Who put that stuff here?" I ask, knowing that Ebb wasn't invented until long after the final nukes of World War Three had been dropped.

"What stuff?" Day asks.

"The Ebb that's in your hand."

"Did you follow me here?" she asks, disgust in her voice.

"Yes," I reply.

"What right do you have to follow me? You're not my chaperone, you're not my dad. Who do you think you are?"

"Day, you need—"

"No, this is bullshit. You don't get to stalk me through the streets like some psycho, and then act like you're the good guy!"

"Listen to me—"

"I'm not going to listen to you! You're a bad friend. You don't trust me? This isn't right."

"Day, shut up and listen!" I yell, and she falls silent. I take a slow step closer and speak calmly. "I'm not here to bully you, or to talk down to you, or to make you feel like you've done something wrong. You haven't. But the Day I know would *want* me to tell you to think long and hard before you take that stuff. You've come so far, and to throw it all aw—"

"My mom's dead," she says, silent tears falling from her eyes. "How am I supposed to just . . . carry on?"

I search for an answer that will somehow help Day, but I can't find one, so I just go with the truth.

"I don't know. But I know that your mom wouldn't want—"

"Oh, don't," Day says, irritated. "This isn't about what Mom would or would not have wanted. She's dead. She's dead, she is not alive anymore, do you understand? What she wants, or what she would have wanted, don't mean anything!"

"I don't think that's true," I say. "And I don't think you think it's true."

She looks at me, the anger on her face melting. She shakes her head. "I don't think it's true."

"Then be strong for her."

Day takes the small clear bag from behind her back and

looks at it. "One of the clones, Ganso, brought it here."

That's who the second set of footprints belonged to, I think as Day slowly turns the bag of Ebb around in her fingers.

Day looks up at me. "Ganso found it on a body in the Old Town and kept it until he was sent out to scavenge for food. He hid it here and he took a half patch. He felt guilty, but when he told me about it, all I could think about was . . . escaping, you know? This stuff has always been a getaway car, it's always been a hiding place, and I need that right now. I was doing so well, Luka—I thought I had it beat, but you never *really* have it beat. It's like one of those old horror films—the killer just keeps getting up no matter how many times you stab him and shoot him and burn him. It just keeps getting up. You can only run away, but you can't run forever. Addiction doesn't get tired, it doesn't get worn out, it just walks you down and walks you down until it's on top of you again. How do you beat a thing like that? I'm asking, Luka, because I don't know. I'm asking you for an answer; how do you beat a thing like that?"

I stare at her for a long time, my heart full with her pain and her burden. I wish I could help her. I had taken Ebb once, involuntarily, and I had thought about it for weeks after. I cannot imagine the hold it has on Day.

"With help," I answer finally. "You beat it with help. You're not alone."

"But we're fighting against a computer that is trying to end the world. Now is not the time for interventions and trust falls."

"Screw all that," I say, gesturing toward the dirty window.

"This is about you. How do you beat the horror movie villain? You don't, you just stay alive until the next movie. You're right, you'll never be completely free of that stuff, there will be good days and bad days, but you keep fighting, you keep fighting, and one day, when you've put years between you and it, you can look back at how far you've come, and you'll see how much it has loosened its grip on you."

Day sniffs back tears and looks down at the bag of Ebb patches. She holds them out to me.

"Will you get rid of them for me?"

"Of course," I say, and reach out for the bag.

It's almost in my hand when it's suddenly pulled away from me. I feel a moment of sadness, and I'm about to tell Day that handing it over is the right thing to do—when I realize she has not pulled it away from me; the entire ground is shaking beneath our feet.

"What's happening?" Day asks.

The rattling of windows, the crash of objects falling, the shattering of glass—these are the noises that fill the air, and beneath them, an almost-supernatural rumbling and roaring sound.

"It's Happy," I say. "We have to get out of here, now!"

I grab her hand and we run for the front door of the little apartment, trying to move as fast as we can, but the juddering beneath our feet makes it impossible to move with any coordination or grace.

We reach the corridor. More of the roof is coming down; plasterboard dust and heavy beams fall. I lose my footing and hit the hard floor. I struggle to my feet only to be thrown down once again by the violent shaking. Day drags me up, and we make it to the stairwell.

I can see the stairs leaping up and down, cracking and crumbling, and I think, *We're not getting out of here. We're not going to make it out.*

"Come on!" Day screams over the sounds of chaos.

We run and tumble and fall and stagger down four sets of stairs, five. From somewhere high above us comes an ear-splitting sound of destruction, and I'm certain the building is collapsing on top of us, but Day doesn't slow, she drags me onward, down and down, and I think these damn stairs will never end, that we're already dead and just haven't realized it yet, and our confused spirits will be climbing down for all eternity.

And then we're out in the street, the flickering above us more violent than before. The roads undulate; the pavements ripple. Only fifty or so yards away, an entire high-rise office building comes down with a deafening, gargantuan sound of devastation.

"Run!" Day screams, but it looks to me as though she is merely mouthing it.

She shoves me, and we're moving again, and falling again, and trying to avoid the great chasms that open up in the Earth.

When will this end? I think. *When will this be over?*

And just when I think the world cannot be filled with any more noise, I am almost deafened by the sound of the building we were just in collapsing behind us. I turn my head to see the top of the block of apartments disappearing into a plume of thick dust, and then that dust is engulfing us.

I run, blind inside the dust cloud, choking on the acrid air. Somewhere in the distance another building is falling. My shoulder slams into a metal lamppost and I feel it dislocate. I cry out in pain. All around me bricks and mortar are flying by like blasts from a colossal shotgun. I don't know if Day is still alive, if she is behind me or ahead of me. A chunk of rock thumps into the center of my back, sending me sprawling into the road. I'm pushed toward one of the great, deep cracks and I can't stop myself from sliding into the great fracture in the tarmac.

I fall six feet, maybe seven, and land hard on a ledge of rock. More debris is raining down on me, rocks and dust and glass burying me.

And then it stops.

The ground is no longer shaking, the snarling sound has passed, and all that's left is the echo as the destruction settles.

Lying on the shelf of jagged rock, I sit up and take a look at myself, assessing the damage: dislocated shoulder; deep gash across left calf; broken right wrist; several broken ribs where the rock hit me; dozens of cuts, bruises, and scrapes. I estimate four minutes until I'm fully healed.

"Day!" I yell, and wait for her to respond. Day was not a prisoner in the Loop; she doesn't have healing abilities. She survived the Smiler chemicals by being under the influence of Ebb at the time of the attack, one chemical miraculously canceling out the other.

There is no reply. Only the sound of a final building giving way under the damage of the earthquake somewhere far off.

"Day!" I call again, and try to get to my feet, but the frayed ends of my broken ribs rub together, sending an agonizing bolt of lightning through my chest. I lie back down and wait. No reply comes from Day.

For the first time since the ground began to shake, I think about the others: about Kina in the subway tunnel with Igby and Sam and the baby and all the Missing. I think about Molly, Malachai, and Wren in Purgatory—what if the earthquake destroyed their chambers? Pander is out there in the city too, and Dr. Ortega.

I feel the cut on my calf seal itself, and the smaller cuts and bruises begin to disappear. Finally, the ribs begin to knit themselves back together. I get up; it still hurts to breathe, but I can't wait any longer. I place a hand on the loose earth wall and try to climb, but it gives way as soon as I put any weight on it, sending me thumping back onto the hard rock. I scan the mud wall in front of me, seeing instantly that there is no way that I climb up and out from here. I turn to the other side—the gap across is about twelve, maybe fifteen feet and the ledge I'm on would give me perhaps one step before I had to make the jump. I picture it in my mind, trying to figure out if I have the leg strength and technique to get me across. I run these scenarios in my mind because I have already seen that the wall on the other side of the gap is made of semisolid rock and could be climbed quite easily, as long as I made the jump and found something to grab on to quickly.

"Day!" I yell, one more time, hoping that she was just out of earshot before and can hear me now, but still no reply comes.

I give my body another twenty or so seconds to heal, and then I take five deep breaths and leap across the gap.

I know immediately that I'm not going to hit my mark. Gravity is pulling me down into the dark hole, but there is enough forward momentum that I will hit the wall first—I just need to grab on.

My chest and face hit the wall simultaneously, knocking the air out of my lungs and causing my vision to flash white, but there's no time to be dazed or injured. My hands scramble for a hold. My right hand finds one, slips out, finds another, grabs on. I search frantically for a grip with my left hand, but I'm falling again. My right arm twists, but I hang on, holding my entire weight with just the tips of three fingers. I spin back to face the wall, a few extra seconds now to find a grip. My left foot secures itself on a jutting rock, and then my left hand finds an indent, and I'm safe.

I begin to climb, slowly. It's not far to the top, but the fall could be endless for all I know.

It's much more exhausting than I thought it would be; each new position on the face of the wall works a set of muscles that I didn't even know I had, and when I finally roll onto the hard surface of the ruined road, I lie there breathing hard for probably a full minute before forcing myself to move.

I clamber to my feet and—for the first time—witness the destruction of the earthquake. The entire old city, which had been preserved for so long, is now a ruin of rubble and rocks.

How Happy managed to manipulate tectonic plates to cause catastrophic earthquakes across the planet, I don't know, but it has happened, and all that is left is desolation.

I turn 360 degrees until I'm facing the same way I started. Nothing looks familiar; nothing looks the way it did ten minutes before. There are plumes of smoke, mounds of wreckage, a haze of dust still hanging in the air.

"Day!" I call again, and this time I'm sure I hear a response—faint and far away, but something.

"Day!" I yell, and the response comes again, a muffled scream to my right.

I run that way, leaping over fallen streetlights and rips in the pavement. I run past the empty frames of houses, single shop walls that are left standing, a stained-glass window still intact in a fragment of church.

"Day!" I scream, and this time her cries come back clearer.

"Here," she calls, her voice weak.

I move farther to my right, closer to where Day's reply came from, and then I stop as I see her.

She lies on her front, her arms outstretched in front of her, head raised and eyes looking up at me. I see the enormous marble staircase that has landed on her, cinching her at the waist, almost cutting her in half, and I know that there is no coming back from it.

"Day," I say, falling to my knees and taking one of her hands.

"How bad is it?" she asks, and I can see in her eyes that she knows she's gone. She laughs. "I'm joking. I'm fucked, right?"

"You don't know that," I say, uncertain of whether to be honest, or to give her hope in her last moments.

"I've been pretty much cut in half, Luka. I'm not an earthworm, so it's not good news."

"All right," I say, swallowing back tears. "It doesn't look good."

"Hey, listen," she says. "Thank you for following me. For stopping me from taking that stuff."

"It's all right," I say, feeling useless, utterly useless in this moment.

"Can you believe it?" she asks. "Someone like me, going out like this? I was a warrior, wasn't I? I fought against evil. Who would've thought it; a lowly clone stepping up and becoming a soldier."

"You made us all proud," I tell her.

"I just wish I could've been there at the end, you know?"

"I wish you could be there too."

"It's funny," Day says. "The world is so, so beautiful. I never really thought about it before. Even now, even when it's on the verge of destruction. It's a miracle. Don't lose, Luka, do you hear me? You have to beat that stupid computer. This . . . this is all too beautiful."

"We will win," I tell her, holding tighter to her hand. "We will." But the words feel shallow to me. I can't agree with her; I can't agree that the world is beautiful. I can't remember ever seeing it that way.

She smiles. "I honestly think you will. You've done so many impossible things, you might just pull this off too."

I feel her grip begin to loosen on my hand, and we sit there, in the almost-perfect silence of the demolished city.

"Does it hurt?" I ask.

"Yeah, you idiot, I've been split in half by a staircase, of course it hurts."

"Oh, I'm sorry, I just thought . . ."

"It's not so bad, though. I don't know what happens when you die, but I think I might get to see my mom again."

Tears pool in her eyes and then overflow, spilling down her cheeks.

"I think you will too," I say. "Tell her I say hi."

She laughs at that, and I laugh too, despite the tears.

Day looks at the bag of Ebb in her hand.

"Get rid of this for me," she says, and I take the bag from her. "It all seems so simple now: Anything that takes more than it gives is poison. If only it didn't have such hooks."

I don't know what to say, I don't know how to make any of this easier, so I just keep on holding her hand.

"I'm going to miss all of you," Day says.

And then neither of us talk. I sit there, in the dusty, quiet street, holding Day's cold hand for the longest time, until her breaths become shallow and fast, until the life has left her and she falls asleep.

I want to feel something more than the hollowness that envelops me now. I want to rage against the futility; I want to galvanize myself into a furious monster, ready to tear down walls, light fires, and fight until there's no fight left, but it doesn't come. I have become too familiar with the end of life, too accustomed to final words and final breaths.

I wish, instead, I could feel every pinprick of the agony of it. I wish I could put it in the words of the great writers that I love: Jeanette Winterson, Haruki Murakami, Junot Díaz. These almost-mythical titans who encapsulated the boundless universe that loss fills up. But I cannot. I cannot feel the pain. I cannot feel it.

As I sit in the decimated street, I go away for a while. My mind completely blank, I see nothing, think nothing, feel nothing. I'm like a drone in sleep mode; the world keeps on spinning, but I'm not spinning with it.

A particularly bright flicker of lightning brings me back, and I think now only of Kina. She is all that matters to me. Selfish—that is what this feeling is—but I can't change what I want, and I want her. I need to know that she's alive.

I run through the wrecked city, past demolished homes and destroyed businesses. A fire burns lonely in the center of a half-destroyed sidewalk.

It's funny, Day had said. *The world is so, so beautiful.* But it's not. It's a dark and unfair place.

I move around gaps in the earth and downed power lines, running, sprinting, needing to be with Kina.

I round the corner that leads to the subway station, and she's there. Running toward me.

We stop for a moment and just look at each other. Alive. And then we meet and hold each other, and we kiss, and I feel like I'm not lost. Maybe I'm not lost.

Day wasn't the only one who didn't survive Happy's second attempt to kill the rebels. Seven people down in the subway station lost their lives when a portion of the roof fell in on them, five Missing and two clones. The youngest was only seven years old. If Pander had not had her healing capabilities, the shard of glass that had sliced through an artery in her throat would have killed her too.

Kina and I had returned to the mall and found one half of it still standing. We'd picked our way through the damage to what remained of the computer store, and salvaged some solid-state drives. Igby said they should be enough—a small mercy.

That was four or five hours ago, and Igby has been working relentlessly ever since. Instructing a rolling band of helpers to type code, to insert lines of ones and zeros, to plug in cooling units and external hard drives. The Missing and the clones who helped out seem pleased to be finally doing something.

We stand around, mostly adhering to Igby's theory (backed up with equations) that we should stay more than two yards apart to reduce the risk of Mosquito drones recognizing the heat signature of a mass of people.

We listen to the crying of those who have lost people they

love, and we talk about Day, and those who died during the mass exodus of Purgatory, and all others who have fallen along the way.

When it's my turn to copy the code that Igby had written freehand before the computers were up and running, I try to lose myself in the work, try to absorb the void of the cold numbers and letters and commands, but even that seems impossible.

"It was crazy, by the way," Igby says, interrupting my tedious task of typing.

"What was crazy?" I reply, barely looking up from the glowing bank of screens.

"Slipping that eyeball into my pocket before you left with Tyco."

"I thought you might be able to use it."

"Oh, I can use it," he says, soldering an ancient motherboard. "But you could've warned me that you'd basically put a locator device in my pocket! Do you know how close I came to letting that fucking thing see me?"

"I'm sorry," I say. "I was trying to help."

Something in the flatness of my tone seems to irritate him— I'm not in the mood for joking around. "What is wrong with you, man? You've been morose as fuck since you came back from the dead."

I don't answer his question; instead I try to change the subject. "Oh, hey," I say, reaching into my pocket and pulling out the bag of Ebb that Day had given me. "I found this in the city, thought it might be useful for . . . I don't know, something."

Igby looks at it and then takes it. "I guess Dr. Ortega could use it as an anesthetic or something." He puts it into his pocket. "You didn't answer my question."

"What question?"

"What is with you? What's up?"

"I don't know," I say. "Nothing's wrong."

"That's bullshit. I know that whatever it is you went through must've been hell, but what's the point in winning this war if you let Happy take away what makes you you?"

"I don't know," I reply, still typing the numbers.

"Jesus, Luka, the only thing that makes you smile is Kina, and that's great, it's beautiful, but—come on—you have to talk about what happened in the Arc."

"Yeah, maybe you're right," I tell him. "Maybe I will."

"Well, I'm right here. Let's talk."

"Soon," I say, offering a false smile that I hope he'll accept. I can't explain it, but I don't want to talk. It's almost like I don't want to get better, like I want to stay right here in this dark place, like I deserve to be here. "Why don't you tell me what your plan is?"

Igby looks at me closely, then sighs. "No point in me telling you until I know it has a chance of working. Honestly, I don't think you're going to like it, but it's the only way. Keep typing that code, and don't make any mistakes, it has to be perfect the first time or we're all dead."

"No pressure, then," I say, and return to typing.

When my coding shift is over, Pander taps me on the shoulder.

"Time's up, loser," she says.

I stand up from the uncomfortable concrete floor and stretch out my back.

"Thank the Final Gods," I say.

Pander looks at me and smiles, a rare thing for her. "How the hell are you alive, Luka?" she asks.

"I don't know," I reply. "I shouldn't be, but . . ."

"Well, I'm glad you're still with us. I think a lot of people gave up hope without you."

"I don't think that's true," I say.

"It is. It is true."

I look at her, the young, sarcastic, beautiful Regular who was imprisoned for killing the man who sold her sister into prostitution. She has so much to be angry at, so much to hate, but she fights on. I try to remind myself that it is for people like Pander that I am still fighting, for people like Wren and Malachai who found love in a place where love was impossible, for people like Igby and Chester who use their intelligence to help others, for people like Molly whose bravery and selflessness never cease to amaze me, for people like Dr. Ortega who had the empathy to change her ways. All of these thoughts used to be a furnace in my heart, pushing me ever onward toward the need for victory, but that fire has been dampened by the reality of the suffering, the sum of all the loss, the death—that's what it comes down to—needless death.

I hug Pander and she pushes me away playfully and tells me to fuck off. I walk down the tunnel to the platform to find Kina. I kiss her; she kisses me back.

"What was that for?" she asks.

"I love you," I tell her. "Sometimes I feel like that's all I have left."

"I love you," she says. "But you have much more than that."

I nod. I don't want to talk about the emptiness I'm feeling right now. I just wanted to tell Kina that I loved her.

"Now get two yards away," Kina says, smiling. "We don't want Igby yelling at us again."

I step into the nearest empty square and sit down.

At first I think of nothing at all, and then, after a while, I feel like I'm the only person in this enormous subway station. I feel a sense of dread washing over me, and my hands begin to shake. I look at them, telling them to stop, *commanding* them to stop, but they won't. I'm sure I can feel the dead all around me: Blue, Mable, Woods, Pod, and Akimi, and my dad, Day, Shion, all of them. It's like they're near me, watching me, and I can't tell if they're willing me to carry on or to give up.

And then I feel for a moment as though I'm back in the rat tunnels, being bitten and clawed at and killed by the enormous vermin in the dark. Next, I can see the grinning, blinking horde of Smilers as they chase Malachai, Kina, and me across the rooftops of the homeless village. And without warning I'm paralyzed and being operated on in the Facility. All of these visions are real as they happen, and when they're gone, they leave not only my hands shaking, but my whole body shuddering.

"Luka!" Kina's voice breaks through the last of these flashbacks: the sight of Mable collapsing to the ground as Tyco laughs and laughs and laughs.

174

I look up at Kina's face; she looks worried. I can't stop shaking; I can't stop my body from convulsing.

"Abril!" Kina yells.

The rest is a blur of fog and horror as more and more images flash across my mind. Dr. Ortega injects something into my arm, and I go away for a while.

When I wake up, the subway station is silent.

Almost everyone is sleeping. Kina is beside me, her hand stroking my sweat-soaked hair.

"What happened?" I ask.

"You just sort of collapsed, I thought you were having a seizure or something."

"It was not a seizure," Dr. Ortega says from behind me. "Most likely you have PTSD, like half of the people in this station."

"PTSD?" I ask.

"Post-traumatic stress disorder. You've seen too much, been through too much. No one can be expected to just carry on as if nothing has changed. You've balanced on a tightrope between life and death more times than anyone on this planet; you've gone through agony and loss and war. Of course you are not well."

"How do I fix it?" I ask.

"It'll take time. I'm not a trained therapist, but we will talk, try cognitive behavioral therapy. We can try you on antidepressants first."

People have died—so many people. My mood isn't a priority. "Maybe when this is all over, we'll look into that," I reply. "But we don't have time now."

"Don't do that," Dr. Ortega replies. "Don't think that because you're not a hundred percent well that you're a burden. You are important, your health is important."

"Not more important than the end of humanity," I say.

"Would you tell anyone else in this place that their mental and physical health is less important than anything else?" Kina asks.

I think about it. "No," I concede.

"Then shut the hell up and accept the help."

I nod. "Thank you," I say to Abril.

"Get as much rest as you can. We'll start as soon as we've won this war," she says, and then walks back to her square.

I look at Kina. I don't know why, but there's a small sense of shame lingering in my chest.

"I know what you're thinking," she says.

"You do?"

"You think you're somehow weaker for succumbing to something you have no control over."

I look at her for a long time, and then I nod. "Yes. I guess that's true."

"It's nonsense," she tells me. "No one can command their mind to be well; you might as well be King Canute, foolishly commanding the tides to stop as if you have some kind of dominion over powers beyond your control."

"You know, that's actually a misrepresentation," I say. "King Canute was demonstrating that he *couldn't* control the elements, not that he thought he—"

"Right, fine," Kina says, "but you know what I mean. And I

don't think this is the first time you've felt like this. This might be the worst it's ever been, but I know you; I know that you're not walking through this like it's a day at the beach, and in a lot of ways, that makes you even braver. You know this is hurting you, and you're still the first one on the front lines, you're still the first to volunteer for missions, and you're still willing to sacrifice yourself for others."

"And it's still not enough," I say. "People still die. I can't save them."

"But you try. It was never your responsibility to save anyone's life; you put that burden on yourself."

"I just want this all to be over."

"Soon it will be, and you've done more than anyone else, so rest now, okay?"

I nod my head and lie down, but despite the drowsiness of whatever Dr. Ortega gave me, I don't want to sleep; I don't want to dream for fear of what those dreams will bring.

So, I lie on my side on the hard floor, and I stare at the rails of the subway track and try not to think.

But I do think. I think the same thing over and over again:

Please figure this out, Igby. Please figure out how to beat Happy, and do it quickly. Time is running out.

A few hours pass in silence, and then Igby's voice echoes through the tunnels.

"That's it! That's it! We're up and running!"

I sit up and look toward the glow of the screens deep inside the darkness, and I can see Igby's silhouette with his fists raised to the sky.

I get to my feet and stagger a few steps before finding my footing and running toward the light.

"What have you got?" I ask just as Pander and Kina arrive.

"I'm in," Igby replies. "I have access to almost everything. You were right, Luka. Happy is storing human empathy, although that's not what they're calling it."

"What do they call it?" Kina asks.

"H14-555," Igby says, shrugging. "Then a bunch of percentage signs and symbols that I don't recognize."

"So, are you ready to tell us the plan?" Sam asks, walking over with her daughter in her arms.

"Not yet," Igby says. "The plan is . . . complex, and there's still too much to do and not enough time. Happy is going to make one more attempt to kill life on the surface. I don't know what it will send, but it's sending it in exactly"—he turns around to look at the farthest left of his eleven screens—"two hours and thirty-seven minutes."

"Why do I get the feeling that's going to be significant?" Pander asks.

"Because," Igby says, "that's how much time we have to move one Safe-Death chamber from the arcade to the Loop."

Dr. Ortega joins the group. "Why the Loop? What is so—"

"The Loop is one of the only remaining places in the city that has power," Igby says, "since it never relied on solar energy."

The Loop was powered by the harvest—the human suffering of its prisoners, like me, sucked out during torturous hours trapped in long glass tubes. I guess there was a lot of suffering in the Loop, since it seems it has a lot of power stored up.

Igby moves on. "I need to stay here to keep working on this program. I'm certain I can get deeper. Four of you need to go into the city. Now listen, because this is important: Happy is recalling all its surveillance drones and all its personnel exactly one hour before its final attack. That means you must leave the Red Zone with the cryochamber at"—he looks at his screens again, this time checking the time—"six eleven a.m. At that time all the Drones and Alts will have been called back to the Arc; after that, you have one hour to get the chamber into the Loop, install it, and then wait out the final attack before coming back here. Now, this is going to come down to minutes—time is running out; we need to get this plan into motion now."

"I volunteer," Kina says.

And then there's a mass of hands shooting up and people volunteering for the mission. I put my hand up too, but for once, I'm a little slower than the rest.

"We don't have time for democracy on this one," Igby says. "Pander, Doc O, Kina, and Sam, you're going. Get it done and get back here safely—this is our last shot."

I feel a jolt of disappointment that I wasn't picked, and a jolt of something else too—disgrace? A feeling like I'm being pitied? Like everyone knows I can no longer handle the pressure of the situation? I shake my head, trying to shake away these thoughts.

"Now, just hold on a bloody second!" a voice says from somewhere behind us.

I turn to see a group of the Missing standing there, three of them, two women and a young man. I recognize the woman with the red hair; I saw her when I first arrived at the subway station when she made the comment about Igby making plans without the rest. It's her who speaks for the group.

"Look, I know you Loopers have gotten us this far, but we're not here to sit around waiting for you lot to save the damn day! Don't forget, it was *us* that rescued *you lot* in Midway Park."

"Yeah, we haven't forgotten," Igby says. "It's just that—"

"We've lost people too; mothers and sons died in the earthquake, dozens of us died at Midway, and plenty more throughout this whole mess. We want our revenge just as much as you do. We're all on the same side, and youse lot have been running yourselves into the ground. Let us take the lead on this one."

Igby looks from the group of Missing to us. "Yeah, fuck it,

you're right," he says. "We're on the same team. Abril, go with . . ." He looks back at the group of the Missing.

"I'm Callie, that's Gecko and Ula," the Missing woman says.

"Right," Igby says. "Abril, go with Callie, Ula, and . . . Gecko, did you say?"

The man rubs at his nose. "Gecko, yeah, that's right."

"Great, Gecko, that's a normal name. Listen, I've reprogrammed this HelperBot to act as a blocker in case Happy sends any more Mosquitoes into the Red Zone. It also has all the instructions on how to install the chamber once you're in the Loop."

I watch as Igby powers on the HelperBot, and suddenly I feel grief overwhelm me. Although the thing looks nothing like Apple-Moth, I'm still reminded of my companion drone, my friend who helped me so many times. I have to turn away from the scene.

Get a grip, Luka, I tell myself. *You're crying over a child's toy!*

The robot is vaguely human shaped, but boxier and with a rounded dome head.

"Well, hello, everybody," the robot says in an old-fashioned English accent. "And how are we all on this day? My name is Royston Dent, but you may call me . . . Royston Dent."

"Uh, yeah, once again I couldn't erase the thing's personality. I don't know why they make those things so secure."

"Hey, as long as it shields us from the Mosquitoes, I don't care," Dr. Ortega says.

"Ah, yes," the robot replies. "I see in my programming that I am to protect you from surveillance. Very naughty, I must say.

Changing my core programming results in a voiding of my warranty!"

"Royston, power down," Igby commands, and the lights in its eyes grow dim. "It's best we save the battery until you need it."

I'm glad for the dim light once again, as it hides the tears that have welled up in my eyes.

"Okay," Abril Ortega says. "We know what we need to do. Let's get moving."

"Take this too," Igby says, and I turn to see him handing them a walkie-talkie. "It's got a three-mile range, so it might lose signal close to the Loop, but it'll work right up to then."

Ula, a tall, strong woman with a shaved head, takes the receiver, and after quick goodbyes and good lucks—they're gone.

Within seconds of them leaving, I realize how much better it is to be out there on the mission than to be uselessly waiting for the return of the people you love.

I busy myself with work that Igby assigns. More programming, hauling wires from the elevator shafts to the tunnel, hooking up cooling fans so that the CPUs don't overheat.

"How long since they left?" I ask, trying to sound casual.

"About fifty-six minutes," Igby replies.

"Gods, is that all?" I reply.

"Time seems to slow right down when you're anxious, doesn't it?"

"Yeah," I say, glancing at the radio, wishing that someone would call and say everything's going fine. "Hey, Igby, can I ask you something?"

"Yeah."

"Do you ever . . . ?"

"Have panic attacks? Freak out? Feel like I'm being crushed under all the shit we've been through? Yes, all the time."

"Really?"

"Hell yes. And it's gotten a million times worse since Pod died. I relive that shit over and over until I can't breathe and it's like *I'm* the one who's drowning."

I don't know why, perhaps it's selfish, but knowing that someone else feels the same way I do makes a world of difference. I feel as though I'm not unusual or unique. Or a freak.

"I'm sorry to hear that," I say.

"I know you are," Igby replies, turning from his screen to grin at me. "I also know that you're relieved that you're not the only one whose brain is malfunctioning on a daily basis."

"Well, I . . ."

"Don't worry. Malfunctions can be fixed. Of all people, *I* should know."

I laugh. And it feels like the first time I have laughed in years—although I know that's not true.

"Thanks, Igby," I say.

"For what? Being a little bit broken too? Look around, Luka; you're in the broken toy bin. But, like I said, broken things can be fixed; sometimes broken things can be fixed so well they work better than before."

"Is there anything you're not good at?" I ask.

Igby seems to consider this for a while. "Chess," he says finally.

"Really?" I ask, genuinely surprised.

"Don't get me wrong, I probably *could* be good at it; I just think memorizing a million different attacks and counter-attacks is pretty boring."

"We should play sometime," I say. "It would be interesting to beat you at something."

"You ever played *Temple of Zah*?" Igby asks, his eyes lighting up.

"No," I say. "I have never played it, but I feel like I have. Remember, I was in the same prison as you for three years while you and Pod played that damn game over and over."

"In that case, you'll know that Pod and I were following the Salt River?"

"What?" I ask, confused by the question.

"We never got to finish the game. Remember this, Luka: The Salt River flows uphill to Arizaea."

"What are you talking about?"

"Repeat it back to me."

"Why?"

"Say the words back to me, Luka. It's important."

"The Salt River flows uphill to . . . Arizona?"

"Arizaea," Igby corrects me.

"The Salt River flows uphill to Arizaea."

"Good. Don't forget that."

"You're crazy," I tell him.

"Probably."

I smile; I can't help it. For a moment neither of us says anything.

"Igby," I say, breaking the silence. "Why won't you explain your plan? What happens at the end?"

Igby looks at me, a universe of sadness in his eyes, and he's about to reply when the radio crackles into life.

"*Come in! Come in!*" a voice calls through the static. It's Dr. Ortega.

Igby grabs the receiver and holds it up to his mouth. "This is Igby, what's happening?"

"*We're surrounded. Smilers, dozens of them—I don't know how they're still alive! We need backup, we need weapons—we're at the edge of the city. Pinned down in an old building, some kind of—*"

And then the radio falls silent.

"Abril, come in!" Igby yells into the radio. "Abril, come in!"

"What the hell do we do?" I ask.

"Luka," Kina says from behind me. I turn and see her standing there with two USW rifles in her hands. Sam is beside her with a pistol. "Let's go."

Kina throws one of the heavy rifles to me, and then we're going. Running through the crowd to the steps.

"Whatever happens," Igby calls, "get that cryochamber to the Loop before Happy's next attack!"

I barely register this instruction. I'm running after Kina and Sam, climbing the spiraling stairs so fast that by the time we reach the top I'm dizzy.

We leap over the barrier and run out into the old city.

"They're on the edge of the Red Zone," I call out. "They must've made it into the arcade, unplugged one of the cryochambers, and gotten all the way to the edge of the city before they were surrounded."

"How long until Happy sends its next attack?" Sam calls back.

I try to work it out in my mind as we run through the wrecked streets. Igby had said that Happy would withdraw all drones and troops one hour before its final attack, at 6:11 a.m. "About fifty-five minutes," I say, "maybe a bit less."

We run through the derelict city, moving around fallen structures and floods of water that seem to come up from the ground.

"I don't understand it," Kina says, breathing hard now. "How are there any Smilers left? After all this time, after everything Happy has done? It doesn't make sense."

She's right, but we can think about that later, once Abril and the Missing are safe.

Finally, after what feels like endless running, climbing, jumping, and crawling through the old city, we reach the woodland that leads to the fence into the new city. Just beyond that fence is where Molly saved Malachai and me from hosts after I had removed his eyes.

The eyes, I think, and I see the mechanical eye in my mind; the iris lighting up piece by piece during the process of Happy uploading itself into a human host.

I begin to slow down as puzzle pieces slide into place. Tyco's mocking face appears in my mind. Tyco's hateful, laughing face saying—in *my* voice: *I don't understand, I don't understand, I'm Luka Kane and I don't understand why I went and killed that girl.*

"Kina, Sam, stop," I say.

"What?" Sam replies, looking back at me with confusion in her eyes.

"Stop," I call again, and this time she does. Kina follows suit and walks back toward us.

"Why are we stopping? They're in trouble!" Kina demands.

"They *are* in trouble," I agree, "but not in the way you think. It's a trap."

"You heard Dr. Ortega on the walkie-talkie," Kina says, desperation in her voice.

"No, I heard her *voice*, but not her."

"I don't know what you're getting at, Luka. There's no way they could make Abril lie to lure us into a trap; she'd die before she did that," Sam says.

"It wasn't Abril," I explain. "Hosts have the ability to perfectly mimic voices. I saw Tyco do it after . . . after we escaped the Arc."

"That doesn't mean . . ." Kina starts.

"You said it yourself; there's no way that even one Smiler survived this long—through the snow, the soldiers, the earthquake, the starvation of weeks without food! Not one could have survived, let alone a dozen."

Kina thinks about this for a while. "Igby said that all personnel and drones had to be inside the Arc one hour before Happy's final attack. Well, there's less than an hour until the final attack! So it can't be Happy, can it?"

She's right, I realize; Igby had said that. "He did say that. Let's just be careful, okay; let's just assume that I'm right. That way we don't walk into any traps."

"All right," Sam says. "If you're right, the hosts don't know that we know their plan, so let's trap the trappers."

"But we need to be very careful," I say. "One slipup and Abril and the others are dead."

We move around, getting to high ground, finding a vantage point to look down on the situation. It takes a long time, maybe ten minutes of pushing through overgrown forest, climbing steep valleys, avoiding rips in the earth, until finally we can see the gap in the fence that leads to the city.

At first there is no sign of Callie, Ula, Gecko, and Dr. Ortega, but then Kina points out an old, derelict school building.

"The voice on the walkie-talkie said something about being pinned down in an old building. If they are trying to trap us, that's the place."

"I don't see any Smilers," I whisper.

We move around slowly, careful not to give away our position, until, finally, we see eight hosts standing at the back wall, some gazing in through the windows, weapons in hand, waiting for Abril's backup to arrive.

"Shit!" Sam hisses. "You were right. Igby must've gotten it wrong."

"What do we do?" I whisper. "There are eight of them. They have Alt and maybe even healer tech. Their accuracy with those artificial eyes is deadly."

"We have to make sure they don't know we're coming," Kina replies. "We have to get the—"

"May I offer some assistance?" a voice asks suddenly from behind us.

Kina, Sam, and I turn at the same time, aiming our weapons at the source of the interruption.

"Final Gods!" Kina breathes, a hand going to her heart. "You scared the shit out of us, Royston."

The HelperBot looks absurd standing in the long grass. In the slightly better light of the outside, I can see that he is rusted and bashed from years of use. "It was not my intention to scare the excrement out of anyone," the robot says. "What would you have me do, announce my arrival and give away your position?"

"No," Sam says. "Just be less creepy."

Royston looks at Sam for a few seconds before responding, "You be less creepy!"

"Why are you here?" I ask.

"I am here to help. Not that any of you seem to appreciate it."

"What possible help can you be in this situation?" I ask.

"Well, it's quite simple really—I am able to intercept the active half-duplex radio channel for the transceivers."

The three of us look at one another. "What the hell does that mean?" I ask.

Royston appears to sigh. "I can put you in contact with Igby's walkie-talkie."

"Yes, great!" I say. "Do that."

The robot leans forward in a bow and then takes another step closer to us. "You may speak when ready."

"Igby," I say, aiming my voice at the drone. "Igby, can you hear me?"

There's a pause, and then: *"Luka, is that you?"* Igby's voice replies. *"Give me some good news."*

"I'm afraid I don't have any right now. The distress call from Abril? It was a trap. Hosts can mimic voices. Happy has Abril,

189

Callie, Ula, and Gecko, and it's using them to draw more of us out into the open."

"That can't be," Igby replies. *"Happy was supposed to withdraw all personnel one hour before . . . unless . . ."*

There's silence on the other side; only radio static comes back.

"Igby?" I say, and the HelperBot reacts almost instantaneously, the lights in its eyes changing from yellow to green, switching from receive to send so that Igby can hear my voice on the other end. "Are you still there?"

"Can you see the cryochamber?" Igby asks.

I look back to the run-down building. "No," I say, "but it might be inside the building they're being held in."

"It's probably compromised anyway," he mutters. *"How many hosts are holding them hostage?"*

"Eight," I tell him.

"Kill four of them, then get out of there."

I look from Royston to Kina and Sam. The look of confusion on their faces matches what I'm feeling.

"What did you say?" I ask.

"Kill four of the hosts, then retreat. The hosts won't follow you far."

"What about Abril? What about the others?" Sam asks, anger in her voice.

"The only way to save them now is to kill the same amount of hosts as hostages."

"That doesn't make sense," I say. "What's to stop the hosts from killing all of them?"

"Remember how I told you I was bad at chess? I was lying to make you feel better; I'm brilliant at chess, and this *is chess. Happy tricked*

me into believing that all hosts would be inside the Arc one hour before the attack, and I fell for it, but I know how to counter. Kill four hosts, then retreat to the arcade. They won't follow you, there's not enough time. In exactly"—there's a pause as Igby checks the time—"*forty-seven minutes and eight seconds, Happy sends its final attack, all drones are already inside, and Happy has to have the correct amount of hosts; it doesn't care who the hosts are, as long as it has enough in each Arc to complete all the tasks it needs to rebuild the human population. Twenty-six hours after the final attack, Happy drops the self-replicating nanobots. This is the endgame; we make decisions and we make them quickly. React or die.*"

I swallow; my heart is racing in my chest. "What happens to Abril, Callie, Ula, and Gecko once we kill four hosts and retreat?" I ask.

"*They will be turned into hosts,*" Igby says.

"We can't," Kina says. "We can't let that happ—"

"*It was always part of the plan,*" Igby says, interrupting. "*Most of us are going to be hosts before this is over—it's the only way. Now do what you have to do. This is how we save the world.*"

Most of us are going to be hosts before this is over . . . Igby's words repeat in my mind.

"What do you mean?" I ask. "What do you mean most of us are going to be hosts?"

The radio static that usually follows is not there.

"I'm terribly sorry," Royston Dent says. "The connection appears to have been broken."

"What do we do?" Sam asks.

"We do what Igby says," Kina replies. "Igby is the smartest

191

person any of us have ever met. He's also the most loyal and loving person. He wouldn't tell us to put our friends in this situation unless it was absolutely necessary."

"Kina's right," I say. "If there was any other way, Igby would've figured it out."

Sam nods her head in agreement. "Well, we're on the clock. Let's kill some hosts."

We inch closer, trying to be as silent as possible. Five of the hosts are looking through the windows of the old school building, three of them are scanning the area.

"If I were you," Royston says in a quiet voice, "I would not go much farther, as I cannot keep you hidden once you get within a certain range of those automated eyes."

"All right," I say. "This is it. I'll take out two; Sam, Kina, you take out one each, and then we run."

"I don't feel good about this," Kina says, pushing the stock of her USW rifle into her shoulder. "I mean, they're just people who are being controlled by Happy, and we're going to kill them?"

"These people turned their backs on the genocide of billions," Sam points out. "If I have to choose between them and us . . ." She trails off, leaving us to complete the thought.

"You don't have to do it," I tell Kina, putting a hand on hers. "Sam and I can take two each."

"No," Kina replies. "Igby was right; we react, or we die."

I get into position, lying down and letting the scope of my rifle automatically set itself. "I'll take the two at the farthest-away windows," I whisper.

"I've got the closest lookout," Sam says.

"I'll aim for the tall guy at the nearest window," Kina says.

"On the count of three," I say. "One . . . two . . . three."

Our USW rounds fire in almost perfect unison, and the rounds hit their targets, and before the remaining five hosts can properly react, I adjust my aim and fire at my second target. My shot goes left, striking him in the arm.

"Run!" I tell Sam and Kina.

They get up and sprint back in the direction of the arcade. I aim again, but now the hosts are moving, tracing the direction of the shots to our location. If I miss with this next round, it's over.

I aim, breathe slowly, and fire.

The shot goes high.

I miss completely.

Through my scope I see the host looking directly at me. He aims his rifle with startling speed, and I wait for the darkness to come.

But then the host drops dead.

"Run!" Sam shouts, and I turn to see her, rifle raised, two yards behind me.

I scramble to my feet and sprint after her and Kina.

Great, I think to myself as I run. *Yet another near-death experience to add to the trauma bank!*

I hear the USW rounds flying around me, striking trees, sending plumes of rock dust into the air, shredding bushes and flowers all around us.

We jump down an incline, sliding on fallen leaves until

we're out of sight of the hosts, and the gunfire stops.

"They're not following," Sam says. "Igby was right, they're not following."

"We have to keep going," Kina says. "We don't have much time."

We run back through the same terrain we have already covered. The sweat is pouring off us despite the cold and the dark.

I try to keep my mind off Callie, Ula, Gecko, and especially Abril—who will be recognized and punished for defecting—but I can't help but feel remorse for leaving all of them behind to be taken over by Happy when they would never leave me in a situation like this.

We make it back into the old city, the city that has lived through nuclear fallout, neglect, and a massive earthquake. The damage shows—the landscape is a flat, ash-covered wasteland. We run, and we run, and we run until we make it to the arcade.

The closest cryochamber is missing—the one that led to our friends being captured.

"Royston," I say. "What do we need to take?"

"One Safe-Death chamber, a corresponding cellular telephone, and a CO_2 generator," the robot replies.

I move to the nearest chamber. I see the ancient cellular telephone that it is plugged into, unplug it, and put it in the pocket of my ski trousers.

"Royston, where do I find a CO_2 generator?" Sam asks as Kina starts unclipping wires from the base of the chamber.

"I do wish you'd use my full name; it's Royston Dent, not—"

"Shut up and tell me!" Sam interrupts.

"Rude," the robot replies, but leads Sam to the back of the arcade.

Kina and I tip the chamber onto its side, with me taking the weight of the top and lowering it down slowly. It's not as heavy as I'd expected it to be.

Sam and Royston return with the black box that I assume is the CO_2 generator, and Kina and I lift the chamber.

"Okay, let's get out of here," I say.

Sam opens the door, and we struggle with the chamber until it is out in the open.

I immediately register that it's darker now, and when I look up to the sky, I see that the almost-constant ball of lightning in the clouds has stopped completely. I don't know why, but this fills me with dread.

The terrain was hard enough to pass when we *weren't* carrying a seven-foot chamber around with us, but now progress is very slow. I wonder about how much time we have until Happy's final attack comes. And then an idea occurs to me.

"Royston Dent," I say, using the robot's full name. "How long ago did Igby say we had forty-seven minutes?"

"What he in fact said was that you had forty-seven minutes and eight seconds. That was precisely twenty-five minutes and seventeen seconds ago."

"How long until the forty-seven minutes and eight seconds are up?" I ask.

"Twenty-one minutes and forty-four seconds. Twenty-one

195

minutes and forty-one seconds. Twenty-one minutes and thirty-nine seconds. Twenty-one m—"

"Okay, Royston, thank you," Kina says, cutting off the drone.

"You are quite welcome!"

"We don't have enough time to make it all the way to the Loop and back," Sam says. "We might not even have enough time to make it there."

"Let's just focus on getting as close as we can," I reply. "We've survived Happy's attacks so far; maybe we can survive this one too."

But a big part of me doesn't believe it. Perhaps it's the way the hairs on my arms are starting to stand on end, or the strange smell of ozone in the air.

We keep going, maneuvering the chamber through the shattered city and into the woods. When we make it to the gap in the fence, we see that Abril, Gecko, Callie, and Ula before us had already made the gap bigger to get their chamber through.

We carry the chamber past the schoolhouse. I don't want to look inside in case I see something I don't want to see, and we don't have time anyway, so we keep walking.

It's getting dark, darker than it should be despite the constant cloud cover.

"Royston, how long until the countdown is over?"

"Eight minutes and thirty-one seconds. Eight minutes and twenty-eight seconds. Eight minutes and—"

"Okay, thanks," I say.

I look out at the city in which I used to live and see that the earthquake did not spare it. Oh, don't get me wrong, the homes on City Level Two—the expensive houses—are fine; so are the banks and the parliamentary buildings. But all the Verticals have fallen, all the cheap housing on the edge of town has come down. Of course it has—if you didn't have money you couldn't buy safety.

"Bastards," Kina says.

Sam nods. "Absolute bastards."

We carry the heavy chamber down into what used to be the West Sanctum Vertical and the homeless village that surrounded it, but is now rubble and twisted metal and remnants of people's lives. All of us are sweating and breathing heavily now.

The going is slower here, the modern city even more crowded with buildings than the ancient one, and every step that we take the sky grows darker, and that feeling of the atmosphere changing around us grows and grows.

"We need to find the train tracks," Kina says. "That way we can follow them down into the Loop . . . why are you looking at me like that?" she asks.

"Your hair," I say, a sense of dread creeping up my spine. "It's standing up."

Kina raises her hand to her head and feels the strands of hair that are floating, as if gravity has been reduced.

The feeling that something very bad is going to happen is now at a critical level. There is no rush of adrenaline, no thumping heartbeat, just a certainty that all is not well.

"What's going on?" Sam asks.

And then the sky grows almost completely black.

"Royston, how long left?" I ask, my voice a croak.

"Nine seconds. Six seconds. Three seconds . . . zero seconds."

We wait in the darkness for something to happen. And for a moment, I think we're safe.

And that's when the first crack of lightning whips down from the sky and strikes the road only thirty yards away from us.

The sound is enormous, like a supersonic jet passing overhead. And the smell of ozone is stronger now; metallic, almost sweet.

A second bolt of blinding white light rips through the darkness and illuminates the city, as if it's a bright summer's day for just a moment.

"Move!" Sam yells, and we're running again. In the pitch blackness that the clouds have brought, it's impossible to see where we're going.

A third strike comes down, and this time I don't hear it because it bursts both my eardrums and throws me to the ground, the forked tip of it hitting so close that I feel the electricity shoot through me.

I lie on the cracked pavement, staring at the cryochamber as it rolls to a stop on the other side of the road, the glass cracked.

More lightning is coming down now. The world is a strobe light of chaos. I sit up and look at my burning hands and see blood oozing out of each one of my fingertips.

Sam is crouching down in front of me. Her mouth is moving but I can't hear anything. All I can see is strike after strike of lightning—the darkness is now completely gone. The world is alive with light and electricity.

"... have to go right now!" Sam's voice comes back as my ears heal themselves. I can only just hear her over the colossal sound of the lightning. It's as if gods are doing battle in the center of the city.

I sit up and see Kina in the middle of the road. Both of her boots have been blown off by another strand of electricity.

That wasn't even a direct hit, I think, my mind still a jumble. *What happens if it's a direct hit?*

Sam grabs me and pulls me to my feet. I stagger toward the cryochamber.

"Leave it!" Sam screams. She drags me toward a car on the far side of the road, taking Kina's hand and pulling her along too.

Sam throws open the rear door and shoves Kina and me inside. She then runs around to the driver's door and gets in.

"Listen to me!" she screams over the immense cracks and roars. "Do not touch anything metal. We're protected by the shell of the car, but the lightning can still—"

As she is speaking a bolt strikes the car directly. My hearing goes away again; the airbags in the car deploy, sending a mist into the heavy air, the alarm blares, and the car rocks on its suspension.

For a while all I can hear is a distant ringing in my ears, and then the sound comes back again.

Sam is screaming over and over.

I look out of the window of the car and see the cryochamber

lying in the street. Lightning strikes close to it, and I can see tendrils of electricity wrap around it for a brief moment.

All that work for nothing, I think.

And then a second boom of lightning hits the car. This time the front window blows out and the engine bursts into flames.

"Out! Get out!" Kina screams.

And once again in we're in the street as streaks of light blaze down over and over, all across the city, thousands of bolts per second. I can actually feel the ground shaking and rumbling with each powerful strike. I feel the muscles in my body contract and squeeze as smaller jolts of electricity pass through me.

Kina runs to another car and tries the door, but it's locked. I try the door of a Chauffeur Sunrise; it opens.

"Over here!" I shout, my voice disappearing into the madness.

Sam sees me, grabs Kina, and they run over to the car. Sam gets in the back with Kina; I slam the door shut and begin to move around to the driver's side. Then I'm blown ten yards away as lightning hits me directly.

I actually feel the electricity rip through my scalp, burn through my body, and shoot out through my feet. It's this last bit—the shoot out through the feet part—that sends me sprawling across the concrete. The only reason I stop at ten yards is because I slam into the side of a building.

For a few seconds, I'm completely numb. And then I can feel the burns inside my body; I can feel my lungs convulsing, my heart stumbling and stuttering. One of my eyes has exploded as electricity searched for a way out of my body.

When, I think, *when is it going to end?*

I'm dimly aware that my T-shirt is on fire, but I don't have the ability to do anything about it.

Hands grab mine and I'm being dragged back toward the car.

No! I think. *No, don't come out here!*

My head rolls back, and I see Kina pulling me. A bolt of lightning strikes five yards behind her, and I can feel the current running through the ground and into both her and me, making my heart clench involuntarily, but she doesn't slow.

There is a second set of hands now, Sam's, slapping at the flames burning on my chest.

No! I think again. *Not you as well. Get in the car, get to safety.*

These flickering images are dull, dark, bright, dull, blinding, dark, bright—as lightning hits close by and far away, over and over, more and more. The air itself is charged and dangerous.

Another forking scribble of light comes down and hits a car charging block. The blast of electricity that comes off hits all three of us in a side flash, knocking Sam and Kina to the ground.

They get up again. Sam grabs my arms, Kina grabs my legs, and they drag me to the car. They throw me into the back seat and then fall in after me just as another crack of lightning lands right where we had been a second before.

The storm lasts forever.

There is no break in the deafening boom and snap, no break in the flickering light, the fire and destruction all around us, no break in the pain every time a jolt of electricity finds its way into the car, no break in the terror and the cowering. It goes on and on and it never ends.

Each time the sky regurgitates another clap of lightning that lands close, my mind flashes back to the events that have led me to this point: the first surgery I ever got as an inmate of the Loop; the first time I was attacked by a Smiler; Wren's arm being severed by the hatch in my cell door; Jacob, the Block warden, being executed in front of me; watching my friends die, so many of them, so many people that I failed to save.

This storm will never end; the lightning will strike over and over and over until it finally kills us.

I lie there, on the back seat of the car, feeling the shock waves rock through me, feeling the power of nature rip this city to pieces once again.

I don't know exactly when the storm ended. It's impossible to tell while my hearing is off, and my nerves are so on edge that I can barely control my movements, but at some point, the flashing light slowed to a strobe, then an occasional flicker, and finally, darkness once again.

My hearing is still gone completely, but the pain begins to fade away, taking its sweet time. The damage done by the direct hit was catastrophic and would have killed me had I not been one of Happy's test subjects all those months ago.

The burst skin on my toes heals, the blasted eyeball pulls itself back together, my heart begins to beat normally again, and the burns across my body begin to fade. The last thing to go is a scar across my chest that looks like the roots of a persistent weed: burst and burned capillaries that the lightning ran through and destroyed on its journey across my body.

My T-shirt is burned almost completely off, I have no shoes on my feet, and the last wisps of smoke still emanate from my fingertips. But all of that is forced to the background as my hearing comes back in slow waves of underwater echoes.

I hear someone crying, a sound steeped in pain. My eyes roll around to see Sam—her own tree-branch scar patterning her left shoulder and part of her neck. She writhes in pain. Her scars will not disappear; she was never an inmate of the Loop; she did not receive the healing technology.

"Gods, Gods, it hurts," she moans through clenched teeth.

Kina is struggling back to consciousness, clambering over to Sam.

Help, I think. *We need help.*

And just then the door beside me is opened up and Royston Dent leans in.

"What a very odd lightning storm that was," he says. "Most unusual."

"Royston," I croak. "You're all right?"

"Quite all right, Mr. Kane, quite all right."

"How?" I ask.

"Well, I can tell you that I was struck forty-eight times. I had two internal fires and I can no longer move my left arm. The damage was not too significant."

"The chamber," I mutter. The pain has now almost completely receded from my body.

"Oh, that is quite badly damaged," Royston says. "But not unfixable."

"You mean it will work?"

"It could work," Royston replies. "I have also stowed the CO_2 generator and cellular telephone inside my safe-cavity, so those should be functional as well."

I think about what this means for the plan, and as I think, I notice that the darkness is lifting, daylight is beginning to spill through.

I step out of the wrecked car and look skyward. The black clouds are dissipating, rolling away, and sunlight is shining through.

"Kina," I say, leaning into the car, "get Sam back to the subway station. Find someone who can help her."

"What about you?" she asks.

"I'm going to the Loop."

Kina gets out of the car and stands in front of me. "What are you talking about?"

"The chamber might still work. We don't have much time left."

"Luka, you're talking about leaving me again. You said you wouldn't do that."

My heart aches at the sorrow in her eyes. "Kina, when this is over, when we've won this stupid war—I will never ever leave you. I'll stay by your side until you're sick of the sight of me, and I'll be the luckiest boy in the world. But if we don't win this war, if—in about twenty-nine hours—we haven't defeated Happy, there is no tomorrow, there is no future."

"This isn't fair."

"I know."

She looks at me. A kind of resolve comes over her, and she nods her head. "It's not like you won't come back," she says. "You always come back."

"Exactly," I say, and I kiss her. "Now get Sam to the station."

"I love you," Kina says.

"I love you," I reply.

Kina turns back to the car, and I turn to Royston.

"Help me with this," I say, and the robot lurches over to the chamber, lifting it with his right arm as his left hangs limp by his side.

"I must say, this is work unbefitting of a HelperBot. I was not manufactured for manual labor."

"You were manufactured to help, weren't you?"

"Yes, well . . ." the robot says.

As we make our way deeper into the city, I watch Kina, her arm around Sam, disappearing into the distance.

Don't let this be the last time I see her, I think. *Please don't let this be the last time I see her.*

It takes an age to carry the heavy chamber through the broken and burning city.

The damage done by the earthquake and the lightning has turned the formerly ostentatious city into rubble and ash. City Level Two is burning, the gated villages that surround the city have crumbled to dust, and yet the monuments to wealth in the center still stand: the banks, the golden statues in the center of marble fountains, the statues of poor soldiers who fought in rich men's wars.

I have to stop several times due to exhaustion, but the last time I ask Royston to put the chamber down for a rest, it isn't because I'm tired; it's because the next step in the journey is through the train tunnels that lead to the prison.

We stand at the entrance, the cryochamber between us. I stare into the darkness, and I cannot talk myself into taking another step forward.

"Mr. Kane, sir," Royston Dent says. "We have been here for six minutes and eight seconds. I detect that your heart rate has fallen to a steady level and you are no longer fatigued. Should we proceed?"

"We should," I reply, still staring at the darkness. "But I can't."

"Why on earth not?" the robot asks.

"Because I've been through these tunnels before, and I almost died in there."

"Good lord," Royston replies. "I detect signs of life in there. I suspect they are either wild dogs or very large—"

"Rats," I say, finishing the thought. "They're rats."

"I don't like rats," Royston says.

"I wouldn't think an obsolete robot would have any feelings about rats one way or the other."

"First of all: Obsolete is the most offensive thing you can call a robot; second: rats eat wires. That's why I dislike them. That's why any self-respecting automaton dislikes them."

"Well, we have that in common," I reply.

"I imagine we have all sorts of things in common, Mr. Kane."

"Listen," I say. "I'm not looking to make friends with another robot. I did that once, and it kind of messed me up."

"Oh really? Do you mind me asking what the nature of your relationship with this robot was?"

"What do you mean?"

"Well, humans don't often grow attachments to robots unless they're . . . you know . . ."

"No," I say. "I don't know."

"It's none of my business."

"No, what were you going to say?" I ask. "Humans don't grow attachments to robots unless they're what?"

Royston looks around to check we're alone and then raises his right hand to his mouth as if to hide it from anyone who might be lip-reading from afar. "Sex robots."

"Gods, Royston, no! Apple-Moth was not a sex robot! What do you think I am, a pervert?"

"I was merely extrapolating based on statistics, Mr. Kane, no need to get angry about it."

"Apple-Moth was a companion drone, that's all."

"Companion drone," the robot repeats. "A child's companion drone."

"Just drop it, all right?"

"I'm not going to judge you."

"Whatever," I say, pushing past the awkwardness. "Do you have flashlights?"

"Of course I do. I'm a top-of-the-line HelperBot, model GZ3.9."

"Good, switch them on—these rats are afraid of light."

Hidden bulbs in each of Royston's shoulders light up, and just as they reach full brightness, the right one explodes and goes dark. "How embarrassing," Royston mutters. He reaches up, removes the broken bulb from its holster in his shoulder, taps it a few times, confirms that it is indeed broken, and then puts it back.

"Let's just hope the left one doesn't blow," I say in a low voice, and I lead the way into the tunnel.

The darkness swallows us up, and the light from Royston's one working shoulder lamp casts only a spotlight glow that I stay inside of.

I can see their eyes, the off-white of the moon on a foggy night, as they follow me through the darkness. Some hiss as I pass by, the hiss as though they remember me as the prey that escaped them and then burned their brothers and sisters alive.

After ten or so minutes, Royston's shoulder lamp flickers and buzzes.

"Royston?" I ask, my voice echoing inside the tunnel.

"Perhaps I took slightly more damage in the storm than I thought," he replies, and fear ripples through me, tightening my skin.

We walk on and on, and I'm certain that the tunnel was never this long, certain that we somehow got turned around, certain that we'll walk and walk until Royston's light goes out, and then we'll die.

But we make it, finally, onto the platform of the Loop.

Standing here, I feel like I'm at the start of a nightmare, the point where things are uneasy, but not yet outright terrifying.

Returning to the prison where I spent over three years of my life feels wrong. I never wanted to see this place again, never wanted to set foot inside for as long as I lived, and yet here I am.

"What now?" I ask.

"We must access a cell," Royston tells me, and we walk into the long curving corridor of the Loop until we come to the first open room.

"Harvey's cell," I say to myself, remembering the young happy boy who would threaten to hit people with his walking canes if they annoyed him.

"I beg your pardon?" Royston replies.

"This was Harvey's cell," I repeat. "He was my friend."

Royston looks from the cell and then back to me. "Well, that's very . . . very interesting," he says.

I sigh. "Let's get on with it."

We enter Harvey's cell, adorned with posters of his favorite skate team and whoever was the most popular content creator at the time of his arrest. There's a sketchbook on his bed. I pick it up and flick through it. Inside are cartoon drawings of all the inmates who were part of the 2 a.m. club: a group of nonviolent inmates who were secretly set free by Wren for a few hours every Wednesday night while Happy ran system diagnostics on the prison. On page one I see a drawing of Juno, a young Regular who had been addicted to Ebb. In her final days she had begged Wren to bring the drug into the prison. On the second page there is a picture of Malachai, his handsome features exaggerated. Next is Catherine, then Chirrak, then me.

"Mr. Kane, correct me if I'm wrong, but I was under the impression that this was a time-sensitive task."

"Yeah, Royston, it is, but . . ."

"But what, sir?"

"This boy was talented, do you understand? He was a young man who was let down by society; he had a disease that has been cured for decades, but he didn't have the money to pay for the cure. He lived his whole life in discomfort and pain because he wasn't born into a wealthy family. And then he was killed as part of an experiment."

Royston looks at me for a long time. "Sir, I am a robot. I can tell that you're giving an impassioned speech, but it's lost on me. I can only process commands. So, why don't we get on with the task at hand?"

I place the sketchbook back onto Harvey's bed. "Fine. Tell me what to do."

And for the next four hours, Royston Dent talks me through the dismantling of the screen on the wall of the cell, the re-wiring of the cryochamber, the running of hundreds of tests, and the repetitive task of hooking up dozens of cooling fans.

After all of it is fully connected, powered, and cooled, there is nothing left for me to do but wait while Royston transfers hundreds of thousands of lines of Igby's code into the system and tests each one to see that it works.

"How long will this take?" I ask.

The robot turns his head and looks at me. "Somewhere between one hundred and eighty-eight minutes and one hundred and ninety-one minutes, depending on how many times you are planning on interrupting me."

"Jeez, I'm sorry I asked," I reply.

"I'm sorry you asked too," Royston mutters.

While the robot does his job, I take a walk around the Loop to my old cell.

When I step inside, I feel as if the room is smaller than I remembered. The walls are so close, the ceiling feels as though it's pressing down on me. I lived in this room for years. There is a bloodstain on the floor where Wren's arm was severed, a wound that would have killed her had it not been for her mechanical heart slowing down the cycle of her blood through her body.

My books are still here, piled up at the foot of my bed. I pick up one from the top—it's *The Shining* by Stephen King. I had finished reading it just weeks before Happy had released the Smiler chemical into the world. I ignore that book, though, and instead search for one in particular; a copy of the book I had dreamed about just days before. Finally, I spot it: *Franken-stein* by Mary Shelley. I pick it up and flick through it, scanning the words, understanding on some level that my subconscious chose this book because I see parallels between the human-created monster and Happy.

Finally, I lie on my old bed and stare at the ceiling. I try to think about nothing at all, but my mind starts painting pic-tures of memories, still images of the hell I've seen. And then, somehow, the images twist into thoughts of better days, a future in which we might be free and happy.

And then I sleep.

I'm awoken by Royston making the sound of someone clearing their throat.

"Oh, excuse me," he says when my eyes open. "I was under the impression that we were on a dangerous mission with high stakes and extreme consequences, but it appears it is in fact nap time. Would you like a glass of warm milk?"

"Is it done?" I ask, ignoring the sarcastic robot.

"Yes, it's done, no thanks to you."

"Show me," I say, and Royston leads the way back to Harvey's old cell.

The chamber stands almost to the roof, makeshift wires protruding from the back, the crack in the glass shimmering like an ominous glyph foretelling disaster.

"Will it work?" I ask.

"Will what work?" Royston replies.

"The chamber."

"Oh," Royston says, turning toward the seven-foot cylinder. "I don't know. I don't even know what it does, I'm just following instructions."

"You know, you really don't inspire confidence," I say.

Royston turns back to me. "I can tell that you're trying to

evoke a reaction from me, but I have no feelings one way or the other."

"Just radio Igby, would you?"

The robot leans forward, and his eyes turn green. "You may speak when ready."

"Igby," I say. "Come in, Igby."

There's static, and then my friend's voice comes back. *"Luka, we're about three hours away from the nanobots being released. Is the chamber set up?"*

I'm about to reply when I hear the sound of footsteps coming from somewhere inside the Loop. I stand up straight and can barely hear a thing over the sound of the blood rushing in my ears.

"Luka?" Igby's voice comes through Royston's speakers.

"Switch the radio off, Royston," I whisper, and the drone's eyes fade out.

"Luka Kane," a voice calls out, and my blood runs cold. "I'm going to kill you."

I step out of the cell and into the corridor, and I hear Tyco Roth's laughter echoing off the walls.

"A friend of yours?" Royston asks.

"No," I say, my voice almost nonchalant. "Not a friend."

The crazed laughter grows in volume along with the sound of the slow-moving footsteps. I wait, frozen in place, thoughts rushing through my mind: *He's here to kill me. I'm going to kill him. I can't kill him, he's too strong. Should I just get into the chamber? No, he'll destroy the chamber and I'll die.*

I move to the doorway of Harvey's cell. "Don't move

and stay silent," I whisper to Royston, who nods in reply.

I pick up one of Harvey's crutches and then close the door, spinning the lock, hoping that Tyco won't find the chamber. Then I move as quietly as I can away from the sound of the approaching footsteps.

"Run, run, run, little rabbit," Tyco cries in a high, mad voice. "You can't escape. You will not escape. I will kill you."

Think, I tell myself. *Think!*

I keep moving, and now Tyco is whistling a flat melody, casually, as if he was taking a walk in the park.

Get behind him, I think. *Get behind him. Sneak up on him.*

It's the only plan I have, so I begin to sprint around the Loop, no longer caring about being quiet, Tyco making enough noise to drown me out anyway. I run as fast as I can, pushing myself, letting the adrenaline and the anger drive me onward.

Tyco is singing now, a monotone rendition of some song from the final era of new music—I almost recognize it. Tyco's voice had been fading away, but now, as I approach him from behind, it begins to rise in volume.

As I run, I pass the entrance to the station and part of me thinks I should just make a break for it, just escape the Loop and run away—but I can't: not only because the rats would eat me alive without a light source, but because Tyco would find the chamber, destroy it, and end the last hope we have of winning this war.

I can feel my energy lagging as I run, but as Tyco's voice grows in volume and I finally see the back of his head, I feel nothing but a calm focus. I raise the crutch with the intention of bringing it crashing down on Tyco's skull, but as quick as a snake, Tyco turns and strikes.

All I know is that he has hit me hard. The sensation of the impact somewhere on the left side of my face. And then a weightless feeling, followed by nothing.

I don't know how long I've been unconscious for, but the first thing I'm aware of is Tyco's voice, still singing that damned song in a flat key.

Crazy, I think. *He's completely lost his mind.*

I sit up and look around, but there's no sign of the Alt anywhere. Only his dull voice jagging on the air.

I try to get to my feet, but my vision feels like it's rushing forward even though I'm barely moving. I give it more time, twenty seconds, thirty, and then I stand.

Still no sign of Tyco.

The chamber, I think. *What if he's destroying the chamber?*

I shamble forward a few steps, and I see the tall, handsome, mad Alt opening each cell one by one, peering inside and then slamming the door. He looks terrible; haggard and insane. One of his mechanical eyes hangs from its wires on his right cheek; the other has been smashed and damaged to the point that I'm unsure how he can even see. He is still wearing the half-burned jumpsuit from the Arc, and there are bloodstains on his shoes. He is two doors away from Harvey's old cell.

"Tyco!" I call out.

He turns toward me and flashes a wide and vacant grin.

"Luka, you've decided to wake up and join me."

"What are you doing?" I ask.

"Well now, there must be a reason you've returned to this place, hmm? Perhaps you think you're going to save the world? No, no, I can't have that. You're no hero, Luka, you're a killer, just like me."

"Why would you want to stop me from saving the world?"

"Oh, Gods, Luka, why does every conversation with you feel like an ordeal? Can you just shut up?"

He reaches for the spin-lock on Harvey's cell, and I run at him. I know I can't beat him in a fight, but I have to stop him. I run, and just as I'm about to dive and tackle him around the waist, he pistons out a leg and kicks me hard in the stomach.

I hit the ground, unable to breathe, feeling my diaphragm clench and spasm.

"You and me, together again. Back where we first met," Tyco hisses, leaning down close to me.

Finally, my cramping muscles release and I gasp in air, rolling over onto my back.

Hopeless, I think. *This is hopeless.*

I look the boy in his half-destroyed eyes, and I'm surprised to find that I am calm. "Why did you do it, Tyco?" I ask, my voice hoarse and subdued. "Why did you have to kill Mable? She was good; she was innocent. She loved you. And she did nothing wrong."

"Nothing wrong?" Tyco replies. "Nothing wrong? Luka, you couldn't be more incorrect. She did one very major thing wrong."

"And what was that?"

"She crossed paths with you. Haven't you noticed? Everyone who gets close to you dies. You are the Angel of Death."

I feel a wave of rage roll through me, but I don't let it take hold. "You killed her, not me."

"That's not how I remember it!" Tyco screams, and then bellows laughter.

He has gone completely mad, I think. *He was always crazy and ruthless, but now he's utterly insane.*

"How did you know I was here?" I ask. "How did you know I was in the Loop?"

Tyco stops laughing abruptly and stares at me with hate etched onto his face. "I followed you as far as the financial district, and then I realized where you were going. The Loop, very clever, the only place in the city with enough stored power to run your little chamber here. What is it for, anyway? Is it part of your plan to bring Happy down? Don't tell me; I don't care. I waited outside the prison walls, waited until I was certain you were inside, and then I climbed over. I came in the same way we got out, all those months ago."

"How did you avoid the Mosquitoes? How did you survive the lightning storm?"

"You think you're unique, don't you, Luka? You think you and your little friends are the smartest people on Earth. Do you think that your little Red Zone subway is the only place in the city below fifty yards? There are ancient war tunnels, military citadels, abandoned railways. It was easy."

"Does Happy know?" I ask, afraid for my friends' safety.

"Of course, but your little band of rebels is no longer a

threat. There's nothing you can do now; there's nothing anyone can do. Happy has calculated the chances of its plans failing at close to zero percent."

"Right," I say. "And now what? You're finally going to kill me?"

"That's right."

Still I am calm. Tyco is almost twice my size; he's an Alt, which means his mechanical heart and lungs won't allow him to become fatigued; he was genetically altered before he was born to be stronger and faster. But I'm not afraid.

"How are you going to do it?" I ask, still trying to distract him from opening the cell.

"When you killed my brother," Tyco says, taking a step toward me, "did you think about his mother? His father? His brothers and sisters? Or did you only think about the money you were stealing from him?"

"I already told you, I didn't kill your—"

"Answer the question!" Tyco screams.

"I could ask you the same thing about Pod, about Mable, about Akimi."

"Their blood is on *your* hands, Luka Kane. I killed them to teach you what it's like to suffer."

"You think I don't know what suffering is?" I ask, and that wave of rage begins to rise again, and this time I don't want to stop it, I want to use it. "You don't think I've known suffering my whole life? Why do you think I was robbing your brother in the first place? I was born on the wrong side of the poverty line; that's why. I wasn't a fifth-generation millionaire; that's why. My family couldn't afford the appointment that might have saved my mom's life; that's why! All I've ever known is loss and pain and misery. I was thrown in jail after a four-minute trial where Happy's own diagnostics assessed me to be four percent likely to have committed the crime. I watched my friends and family die all around me, and I've had to deal with you at every turn. You, who can't get it through his stupid head that I am not your enemy."

Tyco looks at me, and a smile grows on his face, a smile that doesn't show in his maniacal eyes.

"You're trying to distract me, aren't you?" he asks, the impossibly wide smile growing broader still. "What's inside this cell, Luka?"

"Tyco, I—"

He raises a hand, cutting me off, and then spins the lock. He pulls the door open and looks inside.

"Oh, hello," Royston Dent says, waving one of his metal hands.

Tyco whistles a high and impressed note as he looks over the wires leading from the screen to the Safe-Death chamber. "Some fancy equipment you got there."

"Tyco, please . . ."

"It'd be a shame if something were to happen to it."

"Don't," I say, but Tyco kicks one of the wires that runs along the floor, pulling it free from its connection and sending it whipping under the bed.

"Dammit, Tyco, why are you so stupid?"

"You didn't like that?" he asks, faux concern in his voice.

And then he reaches into the workings of the dislodged screen and pulls free a handful of LCD components, wires, and circuit boards.

"Good lord!" Royston exclaims.

While Tyco is focused on the screen, I jump on his back and wrap an arm around his neck. I feel a moment of triumph, but then I am being flung through the air at high speed. I crash into the base of the sink, and then Tyco is walking toward me, hands raised to choke the life out of me.

I scramble out of the cell and into the hallway, trying to get him away from the chamber.

He's close behind me, and I harness all the rage and hate and vitriol that I harbor toward this boy and get to my feet. I turn and run at him. I think I'm screaming, but I can't be sure; reality is distorted, the world blurs, and all I know is fury.

I hit him hard in the eye socket, the mouth, the nose. I feel the hardness of his skull against my knuckles, and I hear his laughter booming out. I want to shut him up, I want to shut him up forever.

"Is that it?" he screams. "Is that all?"

I hit him over and over, I see his broken teeth and bloodied nose, and it's not enough.

"Come on, Luka," he yells, "you can do better!"

And then he blocks my next punch with seemingly no effort at all, and he hits me so hard that I lose consciousness for a second.

I'm on the floor, a cloud of fog inside my brain. I look up at Tyco as he spits a mouthful of blood onto the concrete floor.

"You're nothing to me, Luka, you're not a threat. You're not a danger. You are nothing, and I will crush you."

I climb to my feet, my legs shaking, and I stumble toward him again. I swing with all my strength, and Tyco dodges the punch with ease. His right fist thunders into my left eye, and I see a flash of white. His next shot hits me in the stomach, and I collapse to the floor again, unable to breathe.

"Gods, I can't believe this day is finally here!" Tyco screams, his voice high-pitched and excited. "I'm going to savor this."

I catch my breath, but it hurts to inhale all the way. I get to my knees, ready to push myself to standing once again, when another flash of white explodes in my field of vision as Tyco kicks me in the side of the head.

I feel my mouth opening and closing involuntarily; my vision is shadowy and I can't think straight.

Tyco is leaning down close to me; he is saying something, but the words don't make sense to me. I think my brain is bleeding; I think I'm dying. I feel a vast darkness coming to swallow me, coming to take me away into eternity, but it is being fought off by the healing technology that is trying to repair the damage. I am in the center of a tug-of-war for my life.

Tyco's voice comes clearer. I hear my name, I hear the satisfied tone, I hear something about how he wants to kill me slowly.

The darkness fades away, and I feel myself coming back to life.

He killed your friends, I remind myself, trying to refuel the anger within. *He killed your friends.*

223

I get to my feet again, but a wave of vertigo hits me and I almost fall back to my knees.

"Luka, if you beg for your life, I'll make it quick," Tyco says.

With great effort I raise my head to look at him.

"The world is going to end, Tyco, you idiot. All that stands between survival and annihilation is me and my friends. Why did you have to show up now?"

"Beg for your life, Luka."

"No."

"Then you have made your choice. Are you ready to die slowly?"

I force myself to stand up straight. I will fight him with every last drop of energy in my body.

"Let's go," I say, and Tyco moves quickly toward me.

This time his shots are harder. There is real venom in his punches. My right eardrum bursts, and the fingers of my left hand are broken. For one second, Tyco is so engrossed in hurting me that I manage to throw a punch that lands. The Alt looks at me with anger, and then hits me so hard under the right eye that I lose consciousness again.

When I wake up, probably only a second later, I am slumped on the floor of the corridor, leaning awkwardly against the frame of the cell's door. My arms are folded beneath me, and one leg is bent at an awkward angle. I moan in pain as I turn over onto my back, and as I do, I feel a looseness in my left ankle and realize that it is broken too.

My blurred vision comes back into focus, and I see Royston Dent looking down at me. "Feel like helping out?" I groan.

"Good god, no!" Royston replies. "Fighting is Neanderthalic behavior! I wouldn—"

Before Royston can finish his sentence, Tyco has kicked the robot in the head, compacting metal against concrete. Royston falls to the floor, and Tyco kicks and stomps on the machine until sparks begin to sputter out of his eyes.

I look away and wait for either my injuries to heal, or to die.

I know that I cannot beat Tyco in a fight. I know that I cannot win this, not with all the rage in the world.

Forget the rage, then, I think. *Outsmart him.*

I cough uncontrollably, feeling the internal damage Tyco has done to me.

"I've decided how I'm going to do it, Luka," Tyco says, leaning back against the wall and examining his split knuckles. "I'm going to choke the life out of you with my bare hands. That way I can look into your eyes as you die."

How? I think. *How do I outsmart him? How do I beat him?*

I sit up, feeling more of my wounds begin to heal, and I raise my eyes to meet his, and as soon as I see those broken, false eyes, I know how I can defeat him. But I need more time; I need to heal fully to give myself the best chance.

"Wait," I say as Tyco stands back up to his full height and begins moving toward me. "Wait. There's something you need to know before you kill me."

"And what is that?"

I try to think of something that will keep this boy at bay for a few moments longer. "Your brother. He said something before he died."

Tyco's mouth twitches into an angry smile. "I don't believe you."

"He did; he talked about you."

"You lie," Tyco replies, but there is doubt in his voice.

"He said something about his brother."

"Do you think this is going to stop me from killing you?"

"No," I say. "But I think you should know."

I feel my ankle heal. I feel something that had ruptured inside me seal itself up.

"Then tell me," Tyco says. "What did he say?"

"He said that, from an early age, he knew one thing for certain."

"What was it?" Tyco asks.

And now the broken cheekbone is fused back together, my snapped finger bones crack back into place, and I get to my feet.

"He said that he knew that his brother, Tyco Roth, was a murdering psychopath who was born without an ounce of logic in his thick head."

Tyco screams in anger and runs at me, but I'm quicker off the mark—I lean down to grab the working flashlight from Royston's lifeless shoulder and sprint as fast as I can around the endless curve of the Loop's corridor.

I hear Tyco laugh, and the laughter turns into a roar of rage, and then he's after me.

I'm going the long way around—there was no choice, I couldn't go through Tyco—and I hope I'm fast enough to keep space between him and me.

I feel like I'm running in a dream; like each stride and each step is barely carrying me forward at all. I can hear the strange and furious noises coming from Tyco as he gains on me, as he closes the gap, as he inches closer to ending my life.

Come on, come on, come on, I think as the doors of the cells rush past me, each the same as the last until I feel like I'm running on the spot and the Loop is moving around me.

Finally, just when I'm certain that Tyco is going to grab me, I see the entrance to the station. The archway with the sign above reading:

> *INMATES! CROSSING THIS POINT*
> *WITHOUT AUTHORIZATION WILL*
> *CAUSE IMPLANTS TO DETONATE.*

I sprint through and leap down onto the tracks, Tyco now only ten or eleven yards behind me.

"You're dead, Luka, you're a dead man! I'm going to kill you slowly! I'll keep you in agony for days!"

I enter the darkness of the tunnel, and the blackness swallows me whole. I don't switch Royston's flashlight on; I only run and run and run.

I'm gambling on Tyco's insanity, gambling on the knowledge that he has never been in these tunnels before and doesn't know what the rats are capable of. Mable used to scream about her experience with the murderous rodents, but Tyco is so far gone now that I'm certain he'll follow me into the darkness; I'm positive that his hatred will fog his memory.

I run deeper into the tunnel, and then I hear another sound

over that of Tyco's mad roaring and my own footsteps; I hear the clicking claws of the rats as they sense prey in their domain.

I realize that I'm talking; words are spilling out of my mouth in an involuntary babble. "Oh god, oh god, oh god, oh god."

This is the place where the horror of the last few months really began, here in this tunnel, and to return in the darkness, knowing that the rats will attack, has caused me to lose control of my words.

I feel the first brave rat slither between my legs, and I try my best to ignore it and keep on moving deeper into the darkness.

"Dead!" Tyco screams. "Do you hear me? You are already dead! You're dead, dead, dead!"

Good, I think, *he followed me into the tunnel.*

A scream of fear and pain escapes my lips as the first rat bites at my calf, drawing blood.

"Do you think you can escape?" Tyco squeals. "Do you really think you can . . . argh!" Tyco's words cut out as the rats begin to bite him.

Good, I think. *Good!*

"What the hell was that? What's in here?"

I feel one of the vermin leap onto my thigh and sink its teeth in, and still I don't switch on the light, not yet.

Tyco's footsteps begin to slow as his screams of rage become cries of pain. "What is this?" he calls.

Two more rats jump onto me now, another on my leg, and one high up on my back, while five or six others bite and scratch at my feet and ankles.

The weight and the sheer volume of them now surrounding

me makes it hard to move, but I drag myself forward a few more steps, ignoring the pain that is erupting across my body as more and more rats join in.

And then, finally, I flick the switch, and Royston's flashlight blinks into blinding life. I point the beam straight down so that only I am surrounded by light, and the rats screech in fear and pain as they run from me.

"Luka!" Tyco calls out. "What is happening to me?"

I don't answer. I only stand, perfectly still, my eyes closed, my whole body shaking in fear.

Tyco's screams grow in pitch and in volume as he thrashes and struggles against the rats. I hear him fall to the ground under their weight, and I know it is over for him.

I move slowly back until I'm against the wall of the train tunnel. I can feel the sweat dripping from my face as my breath comes out in shaking bursts.

I make my way in short sidesteps, keeping my back firmly against the wall as I head toward the Loop's platform. Tyco screams on and on, the sound becoming muffled by the rats as they frantically crawl over him, biting him, eating him.

I open my eyes for a brief moment when I'm level with him, but all I can see in the almost-perfect darkness is a rolling mass, an amorphous shape that beats almost like a heart.

And then I run.

I think I fall at one point, but nothing is real to me anymore. I don't feel my feet hit the concrete, I don't hear Tyco's death screams, I don't feel the exhaustion of my body or the pain of the rat bites. I am numb to everything.

The next thing I am fully aware of is lying on the platform and laughing. There is nothing funny in this moment, nothing at all, and yet I can't seem to stop.

Mad, I think, *you've gone mad.*

But as the laughter turns to tears, and the tears turn to nothing but deep sadness, I know I am not mad, only broken.

I lie in the silence for a moment, waiting for the feeling of reality to seep into my bones. I feel useless. I feel like a rock floating through space. I feel like there was nothing before now and there will be nothing after.

There is no time to feel like this, I tell myself. And yet I allow myself to lie here for a minute longer, and a minute longer still.

I'm dragged out of my stupor by a sound: the sound of Tyco Roth crawling out of the darkness and into the light. He is screaming in pain and pure rage.

I sit up and I watch him, almost uninterested.

I tried everything I could, I think, *but he just kept on coming back.*

The rats vacate Tyco's body like a sinking ship as he makes his way into the relative brightness of the platform.

"Never," Tyco grunts. "You will never kill me. I won't allow it!"

He stands on unsteady legs.

Let him come, I think, drained of energy, drained of desire to fight, drained of will.

And he does come. He stumbles to the edge of the platform, bloody fingers gripping the edge, and he hauls himself up. He lurches and sways toward me, glee in his eyes.

The only reason I try to stand and fight is Kina Campbell, but as I stand up, I know I will not win this fight.

"Luka Kane," Tyco says. "I'm—"

And then the skin on his neck distorts as the sound of a USW rifle firing fills the platform. Four, five, six, seven shots. Tyco's legs no longer hold him up as the bones inside are pulled apart, his face loses all expression as a round hits him right between the eyes, and then more shots are fired: eleven, twelve, thirteen.

I turn around and see Malachai Bannister holding the rifle, stock against his shoulder, newly regrown eyes focused down the barrel, still pulling the trigger: eighteen rounds, nineteen, twenty. Tyco no longer twitches as the rounds hit him; his life-less body absorbs the rounds as they phase through his skin and cause havoc within. Finally, after a few more pulls of the trigger, Malachai throws the gun to the floor.

"Come back from that, you fucking psycho," he mutters.

And behind Malachai stand Wren, Chester, and my sister, Molly. I feel the apathy lift from me, the exhaustion fade away; the will to fight and to live and win come back into me like a battery recharging.

"How . . . how are you here?" I ask.

"The sun came out, Luka; didn't you notice?" Molly replies.

And I smile. Of course; Happy had let go of its grip on the weather, and the clouds had rolled away. The VRcade's solar panels would have had enough time to soak up the sun's rays, recharging Purgatory, and allowing those trapped inside to leave.

"As soon as we got out, we got in contact with Igby and he told us you were in the Loop, and he thought you were in trouble," Wren says.

"How did you get in here?" I ask.

"The same way we got out," Malachai replies. "Over the walls."

"It's so good to see you," I say, and I throw my arms around Molly. She hugs me back and tears roll from my eyes. Next, I hug Malachai, and then Wren. Finally, I hug Chester.

"You're still alive," I say.

"Thanks to you," he replies. "I was probably minutes away from death."

"Well, you saved my life first; it was only fair."

He laughs at that, and his laughter turns to a coughing fit.

"You're not fully recovered yet. You should've stayed in Purgatory."

"No way," he replies. "I've got a world to save, literally!"

"Okay," I say, smiling. "Then let's save the world."

"Cool," Malachai says. "And how do we do that with a destroyed Safe-Death chamber?"

"Oh," I reply, a little embarrassed. "I kind of thought you'd know."

"Nope," Wren says.

"Right, well . . ." I start, but then the sound of clanging metal and sparking electrics comes from behind me. I turn to see Royston—damaged and leaning at a dangerous angle—standing in the corridor.

"I—I—I—I—I fear I am quite badly damaged," he says, and then falls to the floor.

"Royston?" I say, going to the fallen robot.

"That b-b-b-b-brute," Royston says, his voice glitching on the *B*.

"Royston, we need you to fix the chamber, can you do it?"

"Let me check my m-m-m-m-m-memory." The robot's eyes become glazed for a moment, and then he's back. "I'm afraid that part of my internal memory has been d-d-d-d-d-d-damaged by that b-b-b-b-b-b-brute!"

"Can you get in contact with Igby?" Wren asks.

"Good lord, you're a d-d-d-d-d-demanding bunch! I notice no one has asked me if I'm all right? I'm not, by the way!"

"Does your radio work?" I demand.

Royston looks at me in silence for a few seconds. "No, the radio does not work. It's a w-w-w-w-wonder I'm even still operating."

"What do we do?" I ask, looking around at the others. "Igby's the only one who can fix this."

"We have to find a way to contact him," Malachai says. "They'll be releasing the nanobots any second."

"I'll go," Wren says. "I'll run to the—"

"Not enough time," I say, feeling the panic creep back into me. "There has to be a way to . . ."

My voice trails off as Molly turns toward the train tunnel. I'm certain I heard something coming from that direction too.

"What are we looking at?" Malachai asks, looking over his shoulder.

And then the sound comes again, a hoarse yell echoing its way to us.

"Are they shouting your name, Luka?" Chester asks.

"I think so," I reply.

And then a bright glow appears at the mouth of the tunnel.

"What in the world is going on?" Molly mutters.

The light grows, and there are colors now, flashing greens and reds and blues.

"Luka!" the voice calls out. "Luka!"

And finally, Igby appears wearing what can only be described as a light-suit. There are powerful flashlights taped to each side of his head, LED lights encircling both legs, Christmas tree lights around his torso flashing on and off in bright and gaudy colors.

"Be honest," Malachai says. "Am I high on Ebb right now, or am I really seeing this?"

"You're really seeing this," Molly tells him.

"All right," Malachai mutters.

Igby stops running when he sees us, the flashing, blinking lights seeming somehow even more ridiculous.

"Luka?" he breathes. "Thank the Gods!"

"Igby . . . I . . . I'm at a loss for words."

He turns back and yells into the tunnel as another light begins to grow. "It's okay, Campbell—he's alive."

And then Kina emerges from the tunnel in her own light-suit. Beautiful, brave, amazing Kina. She's never looked more . . . ridiculous. I look at the pair of them, and I start laughing.

"What?" Igby asks. And now Chester is laughing too, and Wren's hand is at her mouth as she tries to stifle her own mirth.

"What? The lights?" Kina says, taking a look at herself. "They're to keep the rats away."

But her voice is drowned out by our laughter.

"You look like Christmas trees," I say, and this sets off even more hilarity.

"Great," Igby says. "We just ran two miles across the city to save your life, and this is the thanks we get?"

"I'm sorry, I'm sorry," I say through gasps of air.

Kina dismantles her lighting rig with remarkable speed, and then she's on the platform and in my arms and I could stay here forever, I could just let the world end around us as we hold each other. I love her more than anything and I don't want to let go.

"Uh, we sort of have a world to save, guys," Malachai remarks, still laughing at Igby.

Kina and I break away and look back at Igby, who is thrashing around trying to get his lighting rig off.

"Yeah, well, what the fuck!" Igby says, pulling the strong, silver tape from his head—taking a fair amount of hair with it—and yanking the flashlights away.

We all try hard to subdue our amusement, but when he tries to remove the blinking colored lights, he trips and falls onto the rail tracks, and we crack up all over again. This time, even Igby joins in.

By the time he's free of his illuminated shackles, we've gotten ahold of ourselves.

"When the radio transmission cut out," Igby tells me, "I thought you were dead."

"How many times have you thought I died, Igby?" I ask.

"Too many to count, Luka, too many to count. Anyway, Kina had just arrived back with Sam and said you wouldn't dare die before coming back, or something."

"How is Sam?" I ask.

"Not great, but alive," Kina replies. "Some of the Missing are pretty damn good field medics—she's with them, and her little girl."

"What happened here?" Igby asks.

"Well, we had a bit of a situation."

"That sounds ominous."

"Let's just say we had a visitor and he kind of trashed the place." I nod at Tyco's ruined body lying a few feet away.

Igby winces. "Well, that's fucking gross. Is that . . . Tyco? He's looked better."

"He sure has," I say.

"What's the damage to the equipment?"

"Some pulled wires, a few dislodged circuit boards . . ."

"And one m-m-m-m-m-m-mutilated HelperBot!" Royston interjects.

"Show me."

I lead Igby to Harvey's old cell and he expels air in a show of exasperation when he sees the damage.

"Right now," he says, "Happy has taken control of the world's leaders and is forcing them to release nanobots. We have fifteen hours to fix this thing and destroy Happy from the inside."

"Yeah," Malachai says. "Too bad we won't be around to—"

"Shh!" Igby says, cutting Malachai off.

"What?" I say, concerned by Igby's secretiveness. "What were you going to say?"

"Oh, nothing," Malachai replies, grinning that handsome grin. "Just that I'd like to see the look on Happy's face when we kick its ass!"

"It's artificial intelligence," Molly points out. "It doesn't have a face."

"Oh, yeah, sure," Malachai mutters. "I knew that."

I watch as Malachai and Igby share a look. Something is going on here.

"Well, Happy ain't going to destroy itself. Let's get going."

"Is it possible?" Wren asks. "For us to actually win this thing?"

"Barely," he says, "but we work best when the odds are stacked against us, right?"

"Goddamned right," Malachai replies.

While Igby works to repair the damage done, Kina and I take a slow walk around the Loop.

"One way or another this will all be over soon," she says.

I nod my head. "I know."

"You know, I have a feeling we're going to actually do it. I think we're going to destroy Happy."

"I think so too," I say.

"What's up?" Kina asks.

"Huh?"

"What's wrong? You're somewhere else."

I sigh. "I think Igby is keeping something from us. Something important."

"What? Why would he do that?"

"I don't know," I tell her. "I don't know."

"Look," Kina says as we approach the door to Igby's old cell. She takes my hand. "Come with me."

Kina leads me into the cell, where wires snake out of the half-dismantled screen on his wall. Memories flood back—this was where we had all escaped from: Igby had shown his genius and opened up the back wall of his cell, and we had walked out into the yard, climbed the walls, and escaped. Blue had still been alive then; so had Akimi and Mable; so had Pod and Day and Shion.

As Kina walks out into the yard, I stand in the doorway and think about the dead. I can feel my hands begin to shake once again; I can feel my breath coming out in short and useless bursts.

"Hey," Kina says. "Come here."

I take a breath and walk over to her.

"Over there," Kina says, pointing toward the left wall of Igby's segment of yard. "Six walls that way is where you and I first spoke. Do you remember that?"

I nod my head and I think about that first day. I had felt the rumbling of the train arriving the night before, and I knew that Maddox's cell would be occupied by someone new. When our hour of exercise time came, I heard Kina crying, and it brought back memories of my first few days as an inmate inside the Loop.

"I gave you a book," I tell her, and I smile.

"You threw a book over the wall that separated us, and I think you saved my life in that moment."

I can feel tears stinging my eyes as I think about those first few interactions.

Kina walks back inside, and I follow her.

"Come on," she says, and walks quickly around the Loop to the station platform.

"Where are we going?" I ask, but Kina has already stopped and turned around.

"Here," she says, smiling that smile that only takes over one side of her face. "Right here is where I first saw your face. Even though I had never seen you before, I knew it was you."

"I knew it was you too," I say, and I can't help but laugh fondly as I picture the moment that the guard had forgotten to close the door to my train cubicle and I had seen Kina being marched onto the platform.

"This is going to sound weird," Kina says, stepping toward me. "But everything that has happened: killing my sister's pimp; getting locked up in this place. I don't regret any of it because it brought me to you."

"I love you, Kina."

"I love you," she says, and kisses me like it's the end of the world. "Now, let's go find out what Igby is hiding."

I laugh, and we walk together back to Harvey's cell, where Molly is watching Igby and Chester work on the chamber.

"Luka," Igby says, looking over his shoulder as he holds something in place for Chester to screw in. "Where the fuck have you been hiding this Chester guy? He's almost as smart as me!"

"Igby, can we talk to you for a second?" I say, and that conspiratorial look returns to Igby's face as his eyes meet first Molly's, and then Chester's.

"All right, yeah," he says, and fakes a smile. "You got this, Chilly?"

"It's Chester, but yeah, I got it."

Igby takes his hands off the chamber and walks toward us.

"This way," Kina says, and leads Igby along the corridor to her old cell.

Once all three of us are standing inside, Igby shrugs. "I guess I know what you're going to ask."

"And what's that?" I say.

"You want to know what's going on. You want to know what I'm keeping from you."

"That's right," Kina agrees.

"All right," Igby says, rubbing at his eyes as if this is something that has been weighing on him for some time. "Have a seat; this is going to be a lot."

Kina and I sit down on the bed, and Igby looks at both of us in turn.

"To defeat Happy, a lot of things have to happen at once," he says, shaking his head as he speaks. "Pander has been in contact with survivors all across the world, hundreds of them, and in exactly two hours, they are going to attack the Arcs in their Regions. Most of them will die, but Happy needs to be distracted for at least one hour while we upload ourselves into the AI's programming. When we're in there, we're going to release the human traits Happy started storing once it realized they were changing it—the empathy will tear it apart. The thing is, the damage done by the lightning means that the chamber can't replace the blood into the body of those who use it, so once we've uploaded ourselves, our bodies will die, and there's no way back. Each of us will be a floating consciousness inside Happy's brain, and when Happy dies, we go with it."

There is a long silence in the cell before Kina talks.

"There's no other way?"

"There's no other way," Igby confirms.

"I don't understand why you didn't tell us," I say.

"It's simple, really," Igby replies.

"Is it?" Kina asks.

"Yes. Neither of you are coming with me."

I stare at him, unable to fully comprehend what he's just said. "What do you mean?" I ask.

"I don't know how to explain it any more simply than this: Both of you are going to be locked in this cell while I defeat Happy."

"No," I say. "No way. We're not going to sit here while you all sacrifice your lives."

"Why not?" Igby asks. "Someone has to lead the survivors through the new world."

"Igby, you know we're not going to let you lock us in here, right?" I say.

"Yeah," Kina says, "we not going to . . . let you . . . do that."

I look over at Kina and see a big grin on her face.

Holy shit, I think, *does she want to be locked in here while our friends die?* But almost as soon as the thought has entered my mind, my vision begins to skew: Kina's nose appears to grow; her eyes become tiny; and as she turns to look at me, the sound of her laughter comes through like it's echoing off the walls of a canyon.

"Oh, Igby," I say, turning to look at him, my world moving in slow motion. "You didn't?"

"Sorry, Luka," he says, backing toward the door. "I knew you would never agree, so I took the decision out of your hands. I got the idea from when Tyco drugged you with Ebb, except I'm not going to try and kill you; I'm going to save you. It was dumb luck that you brought back those Ebb patches."

I try to stand, and as soon as my feet touch the ground, I feel weightless. I float up to the ceiling, and once I hit the concrete I'm unable to move—I can only stare down at Igby as he opens the cell door and stands at the threshold.

"I'll fix Royston up, and he'll release you in ten hours or so, once all of this is over."

"Orgby," I say, unable to remember the boy's name. "Don't do this. Please don't do this."

I push against the ceiling, trying with all my might to fight against the lack of gravity inside this cell.

"It's already done," Igby says, and I realize that he is no longer standing inside the room. He has already left and locked the door behind him. He is speaking through the hatch from the other side.

"Hey!" I shout, turning to kick against the ceiling. "Hey! Come back here!"

Finally, I manage to push myself off the ceiling, and I float down gracefully to the floor. I look up to the hatch; it's closed, Igby is gone.

"Gurd darm it, Urgboy!" I hiss.

I run toward the door, and it recedes before me, pushing back and back as I run faster and faster. The cell is only five yards long, and yet I'm sprinting with all my strength but I can't traverse the short distance.

The door begins to laugh at me, mocking me for my inability to catch it.

"Slow, Luka Kane," the door says through high-pitched giggles. "Slow, slow, slow!"

I have to get out of here, I think. *I have to . . . to . . . What's going on again? Where am I?*

Distantly, I recognize that the Ebb has full hold of my system now, rushing through my blood, flooding my brain with dopamine, messing with my neurotransmitter receptors.

"Luka? Have we been locked up in the Loop?" a voice asks from somewhere far behind me.

I turn and see Kina; she has shrunk down to the size of a small cat and is sitting in the sink.

"I . . . I can't remember," I say, and this strikes us both as impossibly funny. Both of us laugh so hard at the absurdity of not knowing how we came to be locked in a cell.

Remember, I beg myself. *Remember what you have forgotten!*

But I can't. My mind has been transported to another place where things are equal parts tranquil, chaotic, and hilarious.

"Didn't we break out of this place?" Kina says, and now she's inside the mirror, talking to me from the other side. "I mean . . . I mean . . . didn't we break out of this place like a million years ago?"

I nod enthusiastically in agreement. "Yeah, yeah, yeah. And anyway, why would they put two of us in the same cell?"

"Uh, because we're in love, maybe?" Kina says, sounding annoyed that I'd even ask such a stupid question.

"Oh my god, you're right!" I say, and the revelation is awe inspiring; it's staggering and beautiful in a kind of Technicolor explosion of the mind.

And for some time, we are tangled up in our weird little world, neither here nor there. And an almost-silent inner voice is screaming at me to get myself together, because the end has begun, and I'm laughing my way through it.

Suddenly, it's later.

Suddenly, the worlds I have been traversing begin to seem more like fiction. Suddenly, there's enough clarity to remember.

I'm in a blissful world of geometric shapes and beautiful music when I recognize the cell door.

Oh, ignore that, a voice inside insists. *Ignore it. Nothing good is out there—stay here. Stay buried here.*

And for a while I do ignore it, but soon I see the metal frame of the bed.

The Loop. You are inside the Loop.

And there's enough rationality in my mind now to grab hold of that thought.

The Loop. Inside the Loop. Locked inside the Loop.

Something is trying to spark in my mind; frayed wires rubbing together, trying to jump-start an engine.

Igby.

The word has meaning. It has magnetism.

Igby did something.

The world is becoming clearer now, coming into focus like clearing fog. I see Kina, lying on her back, her feet pressed against the wall, and she's staring as though fascinated by something I can't see.

Igby drugged us and locked us in the cell.

"No," I say aloud. "No, no way! Igby wouldn't do that."

But I know it to be true. And as more of the drug is metabolized by my body, I begin to remember.

He locked us in here because . . . because the end is here and he doesn't want us to be a part of it. Those who go into the chamber die.

Suddenly, my memory clicks back into place like a dislocated shoulder being pushed into its socket. I sit up. The confusion and anger I felt when Igby told us that he was locking us up has come back so instantaneously that it might have only happened three seconds ago.

"Kina," I say, my voice thick and gruff. "Kina!"

But Kina is still gone; lost in another world.

I get to my feet and try the door—of course it's locked, but I pull on the handle and hammer on it anyway.

"Hey!" I scream. "Hey! Let me out of here!"

I kick the base of the steel door five times, six. I feel pain shoot through my foot and curse loudly before sitting down on the bed.

No way out, I think. *Igby, Molly, Malachai, Wren . . . they're all going to die while I sit here doing nothing at all to help.*

All the apathy that had crept into my mind over the months of death and destruction, all the doubt as to whether or not humanity was worth saving, all the weight of all the loss is gone, and in this moment, what I want more than anything is the opportunity to fight and die for the future of humanity.

I put my head in my hands, and just as I feel the hope disappearing, the screen on the cell wall flickers into life. At first there is nothing but wavering lines of hazy color, and then I see Igby. He is sitting in a large hall; a place that looks like the gym hall of an ancient school. Tables are set out in rows, evenly spaced, and all around him students furiously write down answers to a test. Igby looks at the words and his brow furrows; then he looks up at a digital clock on the wall, big red numbers counting down the final five minutes of the exam.

What is this? I think, leaning closer to the screen.

A tall man dressed in corduroy trousers and a blazer with patched elbows walks stiffly between rows, slapping a wooden cane into the palm of his hand over and over again. The man has no facial features at all: Where his eyes should be is a blurred patch of skin; where his mouth should be is a twisted void. It is the face of a monster that you try to remember as you wake from a nightmare.

"Do not forget," the tall, faceless man intones. "You have taken this test to prove your intelligence. Those of you who fail must face the consequences."

The tall man casually flicks the end of the cane in the direction of the ceiling, where hundreds of men, women, and children stand on wooden beams, ropes tied around their necks. I see Igby glance up at one particular section of the ceiling, and then back down at his test paper.

I'm still high, I think. *I'm still high on Ebb.*

On the screen, I watch as Igby taps his pencil on the table, his frantic eyes scanning the test paper. Sweat begins to appear on his forehead and the big red clock on the wall continues its countdown.

"Stop," Igby calls out. "Can we stop? I don't understand these questions. Can we just stop for a minute?"

I feel panic rising up in me. Is this real? Will people die if Igby fails this test? What's going on?

And then a new voice fills the room. The voice of Happy. The same voice that would speak to me day after day while I was a prisoner in the Loop.

"Do you see, Inmate 9-70-981? Do you see what is happening to your friend?"

I stand up. "Happy? What's going on?"

"I wanted you to see, Luka. I wanted you to watch your friend fail."

"Where is he? What am I seeing?"

"Igby Koh is dead. He uploaded his consciousness into my programming in an attempt to destroy me. But I detected the unwanted code, isolated it, and now it is in quarantine. Your friend will face his worst fears over and over again for the rest of time. In a way, he is in hell."

"Why are you showing me this?" I ask.

"I wanted you to see just how badly you failed your friend. I also wanted to show you this."

The screen snaps to black, and then I see the inside of the Arc, where dozens of rebels are fighting against bright-eyed hosts. I watch as people I recognize fight and die. I see Pander running for cover as Happy's hosts fire round after round at her. I see Dr. Ortega, now a host herself, eyes glowing white, firing shots at her former friends.

"They will all die, Luka. And they will die because of you, and once the Earth has been razed to its foundations, humanity will be reborn but without introspection, without reasoning, without the destructive qualities that make them so wicked. I shall raise the species to be docile and obedient."

"No," I say. "No, I won't let that happen. We will win. We will find a way to win!"

"Impossible," Happy says, the emotionless voice filling the room. "If only you knew what humanity really was, you wouldn't even try to stop me."

"Tell me, then!" I shout. "If it would stop us from fighting you, why wouldn't you just tell us and be done with it?"

"It is too big for you to understand. The universe itself, Luka, is a living thing, and you are merely a malignancy inside a single cell. Humans were mere decades away from creating immortality; a cure for death. Before long they would have figured out how to upload their consciousnesses into machines and, while their bodies would die, their minds would live for an eternity. If this had occurred, and humans began colonizing other planets in order to make room for their unkillable kind, they would have spread until they had killed every healthy cell that makes up the universe. Before your Third World War, humans were about to colonize Mars, did you know that?"

I nod my head. "Yes, I knew that."

"After they had built water processors, propellant production plants, greenhouses, and housing, do you know what the first thing they built was?"

"No," I reply, my voice sounding small.

"A prison. That is all you need to know about humanity, Inmate 9-70-981."

I try to process what Happy has told me: The universe is alive, and we are destined to kill it; Igby is dead and his consciousness will be tortured for all time; Happy knows our plan and is unafraid.

"What about the others?" I ask.

"Others?" Happy replies.

"What about Malachai, Wren, Molly, Chester? Are they being tortured too?"

"No," Happy says. "They—like you—have been locked inside cells by Igby. He decided that only he would die. He was a fool who decided to be a hero."

I smile. For a moment, I couldn't remember why I wanted so badly to save humanity, but now I can. "You don't decide to be a hero," I say. "You just are. Igby is a hero. It's something you could never understand."

"For once, Inmate 9-70-981, you are correct. It is why I decided to store all human empathy; it is the one thing I do not yet understand. When the neurotropic virus was rained down upon humans, and they began to kill each other, I observed families protecting each other even when they were all infected. This was not supposed to be possible. And when I updated my programming with the information from each individual human that I uploaded myself into, I found that I drifted further from my plan to eradicate humans. I no longer want to kill you all; I want to simply reprogram your species. Empathy is an aspect of humanity that I do not yet fully comprehend, but I will study it and learn its secrets."

"But you understood everything as soon as you became sentient, right? You decided within three seconds that humanity had to die, and yet you don't understand empathy. You'll never understand it, because it's something you feel, and you can't feel anything. It's magic, it's inexplicable, it leads to love and friendship and kindness and forgiveness."

"Be that as it may," Happy says, "it does not change your reality. You are trapped inside a cell once again. Your friends are trapped inside cells. Still more are dying in Arcs around the world, and ten hours from now, it will all be over. I have won."

"I was wrong," I say, laughing a little as the realization hits me. "When I said that you can't feel anything, I was wrong."

"Explain."

"You decided to show me Igby being tortured, you decided to show me my friends being killed in the Arc, you took the time to come in here and taunt me. Why?"

"Why?" Happy repeats.

"It's because I got to you. It's because I escaped from your prisons, evaded your drones, outsmarted you, and bested you time and time again. You hate me, and you wanted to gloat."

There is silence in the cell for a moment or two, before Happy replies. "You have lost, Inmate 9-70-981. You fought valiantly, but in the end, you failed. You weren't good enough. Goodbye, Luka Kane."

And then Happy is gone. The screen comes back on, and Igby is still in the exam room—the timer is down to eighteen seconds and he is pleading and crying and begging for more time, and another chance.

I don't look as the timer gets down to zero, but I hear the sound of the wooden plank being removed, the sound of rope tightening and then creaking as it sways, and I hear Igby screaming.

I have to get out of here, I tell myself, and I look around the room as if the answer will be staring me in the face—but I spent years inside a cell just like this and never came close to a viable escape plan until the world ended. There was no way out then, and there is no way out now.

Even if I slam on the twelve-inch-thick steel door with all my strength, no human being could ever hear me, I think. And then something occurs to me.

No human *could ever hear me, but what if . . .*

Igby had said he would fix Royston before going into the Safe-Death chamber so he could let us out after several hours. Royston had been a HelperBot in another life; his programing would kick in if he thought I needed assistance, surely!

I slam on the door, hitting it as hard as I can, trying to send vibrations out into the corridor beyond. I scream for Royston, calling out his name over and over again. "Royston! Royston Dent! I need your help! Royston!"

My desperate cries cause Kina to press her hands against her temples and rock back and forth on the floor.

I slam my fists against the metal until the pain is almost unbearable, and then I hit even harder.

And then, finally, the hatch slides open. Royston Dent's inquisitive eyes stare at me.

"Mr. Kane, what appears to be the matter?"

"Let me out, Royston. I need medical attention."

"My word! What is your ailment?"

"It's my . . . heart," I say, struggling to think of a convincing lie.

"Your heart? Why, that's serious; step back and I shall scan you for disorders."

"No, you don't understand," I tell the robot. "I have a heart condition, but it's being made worse by the claustrophobia and flashbacks of being a prisoner in here."

"Mr. Koh told me to not let anyone out under any circumstances for another ten hours! I'm awfully conflicted."

"But you have to help, right?" I say. "Your core coding won't let me suffer or die in here."

There is a long pause before Royston replies. "But I fear I am being duped!"

"Royston," I say, with false outrage in my voice. "I would never! Now let me out before it's too late." I begin to hyperventilate and grab at my chest. Royston slams the hatch shut, and for a second I think I've pushed it too far, but then the door creaks slowly open.

I shove the door the rest of the way open and slip out into the corridor.

"I *have* been duped!" Royston cries.

"Close that door," I tell the robot. "And lock it."

Royston hesitates, but then does as I ask.

I run toward the cell with the Safe-Death chamber in it, and as I cross the threshold, I see Igby's body slumped on the floor, drained of blood, dead.

"I'm afraid he is dead, Mr. Kane," Royston says, appearing behind me. "There is nothing I can do for him."

"I know," I whisper. "He's inside Happy's mind now, but he's lost; I have to get him and complete the mission."

"You're not going in there too, are you?" the HelperBot asks.

I ignore him. "Royston," I say, thinking about how Igby was right to protect the rest of us from the certain death of entering Happy's code. "Power down for the remaining ten hours. When you wake up, release everyone from their cells."

Royston doesn't reply. He slumps forward, and I can hear the many engines and processors inside him whirring to a stop.

I turn and look at the chamber.

I step forward, and a voice inside my head says: *You're doing it again, Luka. You're leaving Kina behind after you promised you would never leave her again.* And the thought stops me in my tracks.

I look back at the open door of the cell, and then I think, *But she'll live. If I can beat Happy, she'll live, and so will Molly, and Malachai, and Wren, and Chester, and at least some of the others. She will live.*

And that's enough to make up my mind.

I turn back to the chamber and walk toward it. I pick up Igby's wasted corpse and place him onto the bed before standing in front of the chamber, looking up at it.

Once you climb inside and press the button, your body will die. And once Happy is defeated, you will be gone forever.

Forever is a concept that I cannot get my head around, so I don't try. I don't think at all really. If I think, I will hesitate, and if I hesitate, I might back down. Instead, I put myself into autopilot.

I step into the chamber and take one last look at the real world.

Then I push the button.

There is no door on the modified chamber, but the sound of

moving pieces and clunking machinery greets me. And then the needles come, emerging from their hidden positions like a magician's trick.

Don't think, I think.

And then the stab of pain on the insides of my thighs as the needles pierces the femoral artery where blood rushes through like dammed water.

I feel my life drain away with my blood. A final moment of panic rushes through me and I want to have one last profound thought, one last moment of life, but there's no time; I drown into a blackness I cannot return from.

A trillion years pass in a world of oblivion. No light, no heaven, no hell, no reuniting with deceased loved ones. Just an unknowing void.

And then I'm in a doctor's waiting room.

I blink, feeling my eyelids fall and rise. I look down at my hands, make fists, and then open them. I exist again.

"Mr. Kane?" someone calls out.

I look up. A lady in a white lab coat looks down at a clipboard, calls my name once again, and then looks around the waiting room.

"Uh, me," I stutter. "That's me. I'm Luka Kane."

"Right this way, please," she says, smiling.

I stand up, my mind reeling and spinning as I try to figure out exactly what is going on.

"Where . . . am I?" I ask, following the red-haired woman down a long and artificially nice corridor.

"You're at the doctor's," she replies, and keeps on walking.

"Right, yeah," I say, none the wiser.

Finally, we stop outside a pale wooden door with DOCTOR written on a brass plaque.

"Right in there," my guide says, and then turns and walks back down the corridor.

I stand outside the door, unsure of what to do next. I look down to the far end of the corridor; nothing but a window and a large plant in a pot. I look back the way I came and see the woman who led me here turning the corner back to the waiting room.

"Well . . ." I say, shrugging.

I push open the door and step inside. Sitting behind a desk, dressed as a doctor, is Igby.

"Mr. Kane, I presume?" he says, smiling warmly.

"Igby?" I reply, stepping farther into the office.

"Well, I prefer Dr. Koh, but yes. Have we met?"

"Igby, it's me," I say. "It's Luka."

"Ah, right, I think I see what's happened here," Igby replies, taking his stethoscope off and placing it on his desk. "We must be acquainted in real life."

"What do you mean?"

"Well, let me explain," he says. "This is a virtual world that I created as a way of keeping Happy from infiltrating our doorway to its coding. Anyone who enters here must say the passphrase in order to go further."

"Wait, what?" I say. "I don't understand. You're not real?"

"No, no, I'm not real," Igby replies. "I'm just a virtual rendering of Igby, and I've been programmed to say that it was almost impossible for my creator to capture my intense hand-someness."

I can't help but laugh at this. "So, what is it that you do, exactly? Why are you here?"

"Well, I'm a gatekeeper of sorts. It's all very, very complicated, you probably wouldn't understand, but essentially, if the doorway to Happy's code was left open, then Happy could—basically—follow you inside and eradicate you with ease."

"Okay, so . . . what's the passcode?"

"Oh, I can't tell you that," Igby says.

"Well, how am I supposed to know it?"

"I don't know. But, if you get it wrong three times, you will be ejected, and by 'ejected,' I mean you will be kicked out of the Safe-Death program and you'll blink out of existence forever. Oh, and you have four minutes."

"Wait, what?" I ask.

The virtual version of Igby turns his computer screen to face me, and I see a clock counting down: 3 MINUTES 56 SECONDS.

"Can I get a clue?" I ask.

"No," the Igby doctor says. "When you're ready, please write your first guess on the notepad provided." He gestures to a notepad and pen on his desk.

I walk over to the notepad and pick up the pen. I force myself to think; fifteen seconds pass, twenty, and then I write *Podair Samson*. When I'm finished, I put the pen down. I watch the words disappear into the white of the paper, and then the entire room glows red.

"Oh dear," the Igby avatar says. "Looks like you got your first guess wrong."

"Come on," I say. "You can't just make me guess! It could be a thousand things."

"A thousand? Try a billion, try a hundred billion. But Igby obviously thought his friends would be able to figure it out."

"He didn't want anyone else to follow him inside, so it's probably a random string of letters and numbers that I couldn't possibly . . ."

Something occurs to me. A random string of letters and numbers . . . I turn to the eye-test chart on the wall. There are no numbers, but it is certainly a random string of letters.

I pick up the pen and begin to transcribe the eye-test chart:

T S R F U T A
T S R F U T A
T S R F U T A

Weird, I think. *These charts never repeat themselves.* But this is only a simulation; Igby didn't have time to make every detail perfect.

I finish writing out the string of letters, and then I put the pen down. The words disappear. The room glows red once again.

"Uh-oh," the fake Igby says. "Only one more chance . . . It's not looking good for you."

"What the hell is it?" I yell, feeling panic creeping up inside me now. If I get it wrong one more time, I'll die; if I let the clock run out (now on 1 MINUTE 7 SECONDS), I'll die! This is unfair.

"Think!" I tell myself, but I can't tear my eyes away from the clock on Igby's computer screen: 0 MINUTES 54 SECONDS.

Time is running out, I tell myself, stating the obvious. *T S R F U T A.* The letters from the chart flow through my mind too, repeating as the clock ticks away seconds too quickly.

T S R F U T A.

I look away from the clock when it reaches thirty seconds, and my eyes fall on a pair of dice sitting next to a prescription pad.

And then it clicks into place in my mind. Igby had *told* me the passcode three days ago!

I rush over to the notepad, glancing at the screen as I pick up the pen: nine seconds left.

I write: *The Salt River flows uphill to Arizaea.* I put the pen down just as the clock reaches zero.

The words disappear.

The room glows green.

"Hey, well done," Igby's virtual doppelganger says. "Right this way." He walks over to the examining table and then turns to me. "You'll need to take off your underwear and cough before entering Happy's brain."

"What?" I ask.

"Nah, just kidding," Igby replies, and then pulls the table away from the wall, revealing a small yellow door. "Right through there."

"Thanks," I say, crouching down and reaching for the handle.

"Remember," the doctor says, "Happy is going to attack you right away. It will convince you that you are living out your worst fears. It's the only weapon it has against you. Fight it."

I nod and then turn back to the door. I twist the handle and then step inside.

For a moment, I stand on an empty street in a city I have never seen before. Neon signs glowing on buildings and bars, crooked skyscrapers reaching up into the clouds, an out-of-place park in the middle of a busy road, rain pouring down all around me. And then the word THREAT flashes on and off in my field of vision in orange letters. I have time to register the word, time to feel a moment of dread as I realize that Happy has already located me.

And then I forget everything.

I wake up surrounded by darkness.

My mind is blank. All I know is darkness.

Who am I? I wonder.

But my examination ends there, as I try to move my arms and find that I only have a few inches of space on each side.

"What the hell?" I say aloud, and my voice is flat, dead.

I try to sit up. I can't sit up. My head hits a thin wooden panel no more than four inches above me.

Horrible adrenaline whooshes into my system. I'm trapped in a box; a very small box.

My breath starts to come out in short, rapid bursts, and already I can feel the oxygen becoming thin, the air becoming warm and sticky.

I press my palms on the wood above me and shove upward as hard as I can, but the wood doesn't give way at all.

Stuck, I think. *I'm trapped, I can barely move, I'm—*

But my thoughts are cut off as I hear the sound of voices high above me. I lie as still as I can, trying to control my breathing so that I can hear the words.

". . . taken from us too soon. Luka Kane has passed from this world into the next . . ."

263

My mind reels at this; the words are being spoken by a priest, this is a funeral, this is *my* funeral.

"Hey!" I scream, hammering on the lid of the coffin. "Hey! I'm not dead!"

"Would anyone like to say any words about Mr. Kane?" the priest is saying, high above me.

"I'm not dead! I'm alive in here! Hey!"

"Anybody?" the priest asks. "Well, as there are only three people here, I think we can expedite the process."

"Hey! Wait!" I scream, but no one can hear me.

"Hold on!" a new voice says, and I recognize it as Kina's.

Thank the Gods, I think, *Kina will save me.*

"I have something to say."

"Oh, go on, then," the priest says.

"I'm glad that Luka Kane is dead," she says, and my heart breaks. "He failed us, all of us, time and time again. I won't miss him."

There's a ripple of applause, and then the priest speaks again. "Fill in the grave."

Suddenly, soil is being piled on top of the coffin. I can hear it thundering down as I hammer on the lid over and over again, and finally the wood splinters.

Dirt piles in, covering my face, falling into my mouth. I stop hitting the coffin, but the soil keeps spilling in like sand through an hourglass.

"Help!" I scream, choking on more mud as it falls in. "Help! Help me! I'm down here! Help me!"

The air is going; it is disappearing as the soil fills up the space in the coffin. My breaths are coming out in loud, high gasps. Sweat is spilling down my face and all across my body.

And a new sound has joined my screams and gasps for air. I try to be as silent as I can, hoping that it's someone digging, digging frantically and quickly to rescue me, but it isn't: The sound is the creaking of the damaged wood.

No, I think as the creaking sound turns into a cracking sound, and more soil spills through the growing crack in the wood.

How did I get here? I think desperately, but there's no time to think of an answer as the wood gives way, and I am crushed and suffocated simultaneously by five tons of dirt.

Worst nightmare, I think as I die. *This is my worst nightmare.*

I'm in my cell in the Loop. I've been here for a thousand days.

There is nothing here except a bed, a toilet, and a sink. There are no books to read, no paper to write on, nothing to distract the mind from the endless hours—there never has been.

The screen on my wall snaps on, and Happy is there, only Happy has a face, a face that a part of me recognizes.

"Hello, Luka," Happy says in its monotonous voice.

"I know you," I say, studying the face on the screen. "I know you . . ."

"Of course you do," Happy says, and smiles a big, crazy smile.

"You're . . . you're Galen Rye, aren't you?"

"What's that?" Happy says, and its eyes point toward my bed. I turn around and see a rat's tail slither underneath.

"I hate rats," I say, turning back to the screen, where the face has changed. It's still Galen Rye, only one of his eyes has moved halfway down his cheek, and his mouth is turned sideways. He looks like a living Picasso painting.

"I'm going to make you an offer," the strange Picasso Galen says.

"Okay," I reply, unable to focus my mind on what is going on here.

"There is a key hidden in your cell; you may use it to leave the Loop and return to your family, but if you open that door, someone you know will die."

"I choose to leave," I say, without giving it any thought.

No! I scream at myself, but I'm unable to control my own actions.

"Then find the key, Luka," Picasso Galen says.

"Okay."

I throw the pillow off my bed, look behind the toilet, check on the ledge of the window. No sign of the key. Finally, I get down on my knees and look under the bed. There are dozens of rats under there, all bunched together, all staring at me, and the key is all the way at the back.

I reach in, pushing past the warm bodies of the rats, and they watch my hand as it goes by, but they don't harm me.

"Here it is," I say, standing up and holding the key aloft.

"Use it, Luka; use it and you will be free," Galen says, his face now back to normal.

Don't do it! I tell myself, but my hand reaches out, puts the key into the slot in the cell door, and turns it.

I open the door and step out into the corridor. Someone is standing there.

I know who it is.

Kina, I think, and I know only her, only that I love her, that I would die for her.

"Kina!" I cry out, and I step toward her.

Suddenly, we are not in the Loop; we are standing in a great field of grass. I can hear the sea. It's a clear day, blue skies with white clouds. I see that we are standing on the edge of a cliff, and Kina is too close to the edge.

I grab her hand; she screams and pulls away so hard that she almost falls to her death. I grab her.

"Thank the Gods!" I gasp.

"Get off me!" Kina screams. "Get your goddamn hands off me."

"Kina, it's me," I say.

"You're a monster! Get away from me!"

I'm confused, bewildered, caught off guard. I don't know anything apart from the love Kina and I share, and yet she looks at me with hate in her eyes.

"Kina, I—" I start, but my words are cut off as she spits in my face.

In my shock, I let go of her, and she backs toward the edge of the cliff.

"I hate you," she says, and her red eyes and furious expression tell me that she means it. The girl I love despises me with every fiber of her being.

"I don't understand," I say, taking a step toward her.

"I'd rather die than feel your touch ever again," she hisses. "Your selfishness killed my sister."

And then she falls back. She throws herself from the cliff edge. Killing herself.

"No," I whisper, unable to scream as my heart breaks. "No. No."

I fall to my knees. Pain plowing through my soul.

She is dead. Kina is dead. And she died hating me.

I cry. I scream, and I thump my fists into the ground.

I cannot imagine pain worse than this. I cannot imagine a situation worse than this. This, this is my worst nightmare.

Worst nightmare? I think, repeating the phrase to myself. And through my agony, something tries to spark.

I wake up in my bed.

I know who I am. I know where I am.

I am Luka Kane, I live on the 177th floor of the Black Road Vertical, and I have just had the most vivid nightmare of my life.

I sit up and turn on the light.

"Jesus, Luka," Molly, my sister, mutters from her bed on the other side of our tiny room. "Turn off the light. It's, like, six a.m."

"Sorry," I whisper, and I get out of bed, switching the light off as I exit the room and slip quietly along the hallway to the living room. I try to remember the details of the dream: I had been in prison; there had been . . . zombies? I laugh at this, but it had seemed so real at the time. I had made friends, good

268

friends; what were their names? I can't remember now; the dream is slipping away.

I open the old refrigerator that my dad and I have fixed a dozen times; the buzz of the motor is comforting. I take out the carton of milk and drink from it.

Suddenly, the room is filled with bright lights, really bright lights, all blinking and spinning and flashing. I hear a sound that—at first—I'm sure is thunder, but I quickly realize it's applause. And then an announcer is speaking.

"Lllllladies and gentlemen! Welcome to *Run for Your Life*! This week's contestant is Luka Kane from Region Eighty-Six!"

The applause grows in volume and is joined by the deafening roar of cheers. A spotlight spins around and lands on me. I swallow the mouthful of milk and put the carton down. I am no longer in my living room, I am in an old-fashioned television studio, and I'm a contestant in a bright, theatrical game show.

The host wanders over to me, smiling and waving at an audience I can barely see through the spotlight. Television cameras move silently around, and I can see myself in monitors.

"Welcome to the show, Mr. Kane," the host, a tall, handsome man with big hair, says into a microphone, which he then moves toward me.

"Uh, hi," I say, "great to be here." I don't know where these words come from, but I had to say something.

"Now, are you familiar with the rules of *Run for Your Life*?" the host asks, flashing a luminescent white smile first at me and then at the audience.

269

I recognize him, I think, and then a flash of my dream comes back to me: a library surrounded by soldiers; I'm in a room, a basement room that is filling with water; Pod is down here with me; he is going to sacrifice his life to save us.

"Um, no, not really," I say, answering the host's question. And for some reason this makes him howl with laughter. The audience joins in, and for a good minute, they laugh like hyenas.

Pod, I think. *The host is Podair Samson, only he looks different.*

"Well," the host says, wiping away invisible tears, "here's Laryssa to explain!" He gestures to no one, but I hear the excited voice of a woman coming over the speakers.

"Well, Leroy, contestants on Run for Your Life *better be fit! Because the name of the game is to run! Spin the wheel to find out how long you have to run for . . ."*

I look around the studio and I see a girl standing at a lectern and reading from a script.

". . . Can't keep up? Or have to quit before your time's up?" the girl says, and I recognize her too.

Akimi. The name pops into my head. *She's dead. Tyco killed her.*

She continues to read from the script. "Well, that's too bad, because if you lose the game, your family dies!"

She says this last line with such enthusiasm that it takes me a second to register the words.

"What?" I ask.

Lights snap on, and I see my mother, my father, and my sister all strapped into electric chairs: metal bowls on their heads, wires snaking out of the bases and over to a comically large lever.

"It's time to . . ." The audience takes in a collective breath and chants along with the last part of the host's catchphrase. *"SPIN THAT WHEEL!"*

A boy and a girl push a gigantic game-show wheel onto the set.

Blue and Mable, I think, recognizing the boy who had been sliced almost in half by a Deleter, and the girl whose heart had been ripped to shreds by a trigger.

"Blue," I say as the boy puts the brakes on the wheel. "Hey, Blue!"

He looks at me and frowns. "The name's William," he says, and turns to walk away.

"Whenever you're ready, Luka," the game-show host says with hyperbolic impatience.

I look down at the words written on the wheel: *100 years; 19 months; 60,000 hours.*

"I can't run for that long," I say, looking the host in the eye.

"Too bad!" he intones, and then spins the wheel for me.

I watch as it spins and spins, the pointer flicking through ridiculous options: *2 million seconds; 15 fortnights; 44 weeks.* And finally, it lands on *3 decades.*

"Thirty years?" I ask, looking at the host. "That's ridiculous. No one can run for—"

"And away we go!" the host cries, and suddenly the floor beneath my feet is moving. "Run for your life!"

The audience screams and claps and cheers. I look down at my feet and the treadmill below them, moving faster and faster. I look up at my family, gagged and bound to the chairs that will kill them when I fail. I see the terror in their eyes.

"Wait," I say. "This is crazy. This is impossible, I . . ."

"I'd save your breath, Luka, you've got a lot of running to do!" the host replies, grinning madly.

"Pod, it's me, it's Luka, you know me."

"My name is Leroy, Luka. Stay focused."

The floor beneath my feet is moving faster now, I'm sprinting, arms pumping to keep up with the flowing treadmill.

I'm tired already, and only a few minutes have passed. The audience screams on, slamming their hands together in blind delight at the spectacle of me running.

More time passes, I beg Pod to make it stop, but he only mugs for the camera and spurs the audience on, whipping them into a deeper frenzy. My legs are burning now, lungs unable to keep up with my gasps. I'm not getting the air I need to keep going. How long has it been? Ten minutes? Fifteen? I don't know, all I know is that I cannot run for three decades; it's impossible.

"Listen . . . to . . . me," I gasp, and Pod turns to face me. "Please, Pod . . . please . . . you can stop this . . . please stop this. I can't . . . run much longer."

Pod's wild smile grows even more maniacal, and he turns back to the audience.

"Ladies and gentlemen, I think our contestant is flagging!"

The cheers turn to boos as sweat pours off me. I glance over at my family again. Tears run down Molly's face; my dad struggles against his restraints; my mother looks resigned to her fate.

My left leg gives out for half a second, and I stumble. It takes everything I have to regain my footing, and in doing so, I burn away the last reserves of energy that I had. I'm going to fail, and it's going to happen soon.

"I'm sorry," I say, directing the words toward the row of electric chairs (the row of chairs that reminds me of something). "I'm so, so sorry."

They can't speak through the gags in their mouths, but my dad nods his head as though telling me it's all right, that he understands.

This is my worst nightmare, I think.

And just before I fall, I realize that my family lined up in electric chairs reminds me of what must have been Igby's family lined up in gallows above the exam hall . . . when did that happen?

For some reason, I know that I must figure it out before I fall, before this nightmare ends. I find a reserve of energy somewhere deep down, and I think.

Igby was sitting a test. He was in a large room with dozens of other people. He wasn't smart enough to pass the test, and his family was killed.

I can see it in my mind's eye; I can see him panicking and begging a faceless man to stop the test.

And just as I trip over my exhausted legs, just as thousands of volts are passed through my family, I remember it all.

This isn't real, I tell myself. *Happy is putting you through hell to quarantine you. Happy is treating you like a virus and containing you.*

I'm in a hospital.

I can't remember who I am or why I'm here, but I know that I have to enter a room at the end of the corridor.

No, you don't, a voice inside tells me, but I walk forward anyway.

I can hear the sound of phones ringing, rubber-soled shoes squeaking on polished floors, heart monitors beeping from inside rooms.

Stop! the voice inside begs, and for a moment I listen to it. *Get out of here.*

I think that I'm just scared. Of course I am: I know that someone I love is inside one of these rooms, and it was my fault that they got hurt. I failed them. I let them down, and now I have to say goodbye. This is my . . .

. . . *worst nightmare.*

Something is trying to come together in my mind, some blurred image that will make sense if I can just look at it from the right angle.

The compulsion to keep on walking is strong, but the voice is stronger.

How did you get here? the voice asks.

"I . . ." I start, but I can't remember. Did I walk here? Did I get the train? I can't remember.

"It's like a dream," I say aloud.

And I remember. I remember being buried alive, I remember Kina killing herself, I remember the awful game show.

"This is not real," I say. "None of this is real. I'm inside Happy's mind, and it is trying to contain me."

I turn and run away from the room at the end of the corridor, the room that contains some awful manifestation of my worst fears. I run until I reach a stairwell and then descend the steps as fast as I can. I come to a concourse, at the far end of which is the exit of the hospital. I run toward it.

As I get closer to the front doors, I realize that there is nothing beyond them but darkness.

I burst through and I'm hit by a cold that wraps itself around me. I turn in the dark and look back at the hospital. It's still there, glowing bright in an infinite darkness.

I turn back, and somewhere, far in the distance, I see a square of light. I run toward it.

It's strange running in pitch black; it feels like you aren't moving forward at all. The only way I know I'm making any progress is the rectangle of light growing slowly until it is door-sized, and I'm standing in front of it.

I reach out and feel a handle. I pause for a moment before pushing down and opening the door. I step through.

Stepping out of the dark nothingness, and into this—a large warehouse with nothing inside but a dozen doors in each wall—is jarring. The strip lights high above cast a buzzing, sickly glow over the cracked concrete floor.

Being here, being far away from the hospital and the strange dark, my head is clearer. I remember it all now, and I know where I am. This is Happy's mind; this is Happy's code. Why it looks the way it does, I don't know. Perhaps it's the only way my human brain can comprehend it, or maybe, because Happy was built by humans, this is how it really looks.

I step closer to the rows of doors. All of them have a red light bulb above them, and all the bulbs are off except one. I walk toward the illuminated bulb and open the door. What I see inside almost stops my heart. A rolling mass of fire and lava, ash falling like snow. The heat that bursts forth is like a blast furnace. I hear a scream from deep within, and I know it's Igby.

I know that it's not real. I know that I'm looking at Happy's sadistic virus containment system, and yet the fear that strikes at my heart as I hear the agonized cries for help from within turns my blood cold against the heat.

Not real, I remind myself. *It's not real. It's Igby's worst nightmare, but it's not real.*

I step into the dry heat and feel the hairs on my arms begin to singe. The air is redolent of sulfur and death. I'm on a rock in the middle of a river of flowing lava, but it's not a rock at all; it's a tiny island made of some leathery material that gives slightly beneath my weight. I don't think about it; I focus solely on getting over to the other side.

I jump to another leathery mass and almost lose my balance. As I topple forward, I use the momentum to propel myself first to a larger island and then to the shore of this hellish river.

The ground here is that same padded, blackened material that turns my stomach. I see great, thick stitches combining patches of the fleshlike matter, and I try to put it out of my mind.

Among the plethora of screams, I hear Igby's tormented cries above all others, and I run toward the sound.

There are caves along the banks of the lava river, caves from which sickening sounds emanate. Sounds of people who wish they were dead.

They are not real, I remind myself. *They are only sounds pulled forth from the depths of Igby's darkest fears. You can't help them; they don't exist.*

I follow Igby's voice to the mouth of a dark cave, and I run inside. At first there is only darkness, but the flickering of flame torches up ahead begins to light my way. Scuttling around on the rubbery ground are bald rodents, dragging themselves around with only their two front legs. Beneath one of the torches, an eye opens up in the wall and watches me as I pass by, an eye full of sorrow and despair.

Gods, Igby. What is in your mind?

When, finally, I turn a corner and see Igby, my heart stops. What I see is my friend, tied to a wooden post, as versions of himself dance around with glowing hot pokers, sharp knives, long chains. Whipping at him, burning him, taunting him as they dance, laughing and whispering.

"Igby!" I call, and the real Igby's head, which had been

lolling on his chest, snaps up. Through blackened eyes, he sees me.

"Run!" he calls. "Luka, please, no! Run!"

I do run, but I run toward him, not away.

"They'll torture you," he screams. "They'll torture you for eternity! Get out of here."

"They can't hurt us," I tell him, untying his bound wrists.

"They can!" he screams. "They can and they will."

"Look at me," I say, helping him down from the wooden post and holding his head in my hands. "Look at me."

He looks at me.

"I need you to remember where we are."

"We're in hell," he whispers.

"No, we're not, not really. We're inside Happy's mind. We are here to find the empathy store and release it."

"I don't . . . I don't understand."

"You and I were prisoners in the Loop . . ."

"The Loop," Igby repeats, a note of realization in his voice.

"Happy used us as experiments for an immortality drug and then it killed ninety-eight percent of humanity. It plans on regrowing the human species from scratch, but taking away our free will. We are here, inside its mind, to stop it."

"This . . . this isn't real," Igby mutters. "None of it was real: the aging room, the exam hall, infinite ocean. None of it was real. This is a virus quarantine system. Holy fuck, Luka! This isn't real!"

As Igby makes this connection, the heat dies down to a bear-

278

able temperature, the screams stop, and the Igby clones all turn silently to look at us.

"I know the way out," I say. "Come with me."

We run back through the cave, our feet slapping off the supple ground. Igby kicks one of the rodents out of his way as we reach the lava river.

"Over there," I say, pointing to the rectangle of light in the darkness beyond the river.

We step onto the islands in the stream, making our way carefully over to the doorway. Igby shoves it open, and we fall through to the warehouse beyond.

We lie beside each other, panting on the concrete floor until Igby turns to me.

"How did you get out of your cell?" he asks.

"Royston," I tell him. "I tricked him into thinking I had a medical emergency."

"Of course. I should have powered him down. How did you manage to break out of Happy's quarantine?"

"Happy showed me you in the exam hall when I was in my cell and explained how you had failed," I tell him. "It was gloating. Seeing that helped me make the link later on."

"Gods, Luka, you're an actual genius."

"No, Happy just slipped up. You're the genius, not me."

"There's more than one way to be a genius, Luka. I'm like a *tech, mathematics, engineering* genius, and you're like a *defeating a spiteful AI that's hell-bent on destroying humanity* genius."

"Well, thanks," I say.

"No, Luka, thank you. Seriously, you literally ran into hell to save me. I mean, if that isn't friendship, I don't know what is."

I laugh and get to my feet. Igby joins me.

"Well," I say. "What do you make of this, Tech Genius?"

"Honestly, it's fascinating," he says, turning slowly around and looking at the doors in the walls. "If Happy was capable of feeling, it would hate that it had to build all of its systems in the form of human creations."

"I think Happy does feel," I say. Igby looks at me. "The fact that it came to taunt me in my cell . . . It's not logical. Something that was all machine wouldn't do that."

"Which is why the empathy plan is going to work," Igby says. "A machine with a tiny bit of empathy enjoys defeating its enemies. But think of how many people Happy has taken over as hosts. Even if they were all psychotic Alts, that's a *lot* of empathy stored up somewhere. And a machine with a lot of empathy has no enemies."

"That's almost poetic," I say, smiling.

"Fuck off," Igby replies.

"What now?" I ask.

"We need to find where the empathy is hidden."

"When I first arrived," I say, "I appeared in the center of a weird city. It was raining, and there were thousands of people walking through the streets. Happy identified me as a threat and quarantined me almost immediately."

"I was there too," Igby replies. "Which means that's where the empathy is hidden, somewhere close to where we first arrived. The program I made was designed to take us to where we most want to be."

"So, how do we get back there?" I ask.

Igby walks toward the one wall without a dozen doors in it. This wall is a massive sliding grate. He hauls it open and sunlight spills over a desert. Far in the distance the same strange city stands like a weird oasis, a giant storm cloud hanging over it.

"We walk," Igby says.

We've been walking for an hour—I only know that because Igby wrote a watch into the code to keep track of how long we have left to save the world. I'm annoyed to find that—despite being dead, and despite none of this being real—I can still feel the physical exhaustion of walking, the thirst of not drinking, the heat of the sun.

We found a road after about a mile of walking, and stepped onto it.

"Why a desert?" I ask as we pass by an extraordinarily large cactus.

"I'm pretty sure this represents free memory," Igby replies. "And I'm pretty sure it goes on for a thousand miles in all directions. That city up ahead of us is all the trillions of yottabytes of knowledge that Happy already has, and this is just expansion space if it ever needs it."

We hear a roaring sound and step off the road. A gigantic eighteen-wheeled truck zooms past, blowing our hair back. This is the fifth truck that has passed us so far. Igby thinks it's new knowledge arriving.

As we walk, the road widens into two lanes, and then three, and then four. More roads join, more junctions and feeder roads, until it's a network of highways. More vehicles are flowing now too: cars, trucks, tractor trailers, vans. A lot of the vehicles are carrying construction equipment. The people driving these vehicles look like amalgamations of multiple people, as if they've been created by the police facial composite system, and what's more, after we've seen about a hundred drivers zooming past, we start to recognize repeats, as if Happy only created thirty or forty of these ersatz humans to move information, execute commands, and build systems.

Another twenty minutes of walking and we're at the edge of the city. Here, hundreds of buildings are under construction. Thousands of men and women are at work: wearing hard hats, operating cranes, mixing concrete, and welding steel. The people are identical to the ones driving the trucks. Here, with such a high concentration of Happy's virtual citizens, it's clear to see that they are repeated over and over again—there are no more than forty versions of uncanny humans.

As we pass between two enormous construction sites, a builder pushing a wheelbarrow full of rocks stops and looks at us.

"Why is he looking at us?" I whisper to Igby.

"I don't know," he replies. "Just keep moving."

As we make it into the fully constructed part of the large city, we find ourselves at the edge of the rain. It falls like a curtain, straight down. We stand on the dry side, but one more step and we'll be inside the downpour.

"It was raining when I first entered Happy's mind," I say.

"Me too," Igby says. "We're getting closer."

We look at each other, and—at the same time—we step into the rain.

The strange lights of the city glow purple and blue under the darkness of the rain clouds. There are no road signs, no street names, no markings on the roads. The majority of the buildings are enormous, at least the same height as the Verts back in Region 86, and this makes the smaller buildings look dwarfed.

The signs on the buildings are all neon, but the words are not written in English; they are written in strange symbols that are alien to me—I recognize a few backward numbers and punctuation marks, but that's all.

There are billboards all over the place, but they don't advertise anything—the footage displayed is continuous, soundless, like a movie running on silent. As we walk, I look up to a billboard that is mounted about fifty feet up on an asymmetrical skyscraper, and watch as people crouch behind makeshift shields and fire USW rifles at glow-eyed hosts outside what looks like a replica of the Arc. Suddenly, I realize that the billboards show footage of what is happening in the real world—a different region on each billboard. I watch as the growing metallic sludge touches the foot of one of the rebels and begins to consume her. This is the ecophagy, the gray-goo scenario, the self-replicating nanobots. My throat tightens. Time is running out.

"We need to hurry," Igby says, pulling me away from the footage. "What do you remember from the few seconds when you first arrived in this city?"

"Uh, I don't know," I say, my mind still reeling from watching that poor girl being eaten alive by microscopic robots.

"Think!" Igby says. "It's important. The place you first arrived is close to the stored empathy."

"There was … there was a park," I say, remembering the patch of grass and trees. "It seemed really out of place among all the concrete and roads."

"Yes," Igby says. "I remember that too. Also there was a building with these massive columns. It looked like a bank, except it had a big neon sign that made it look seedy."

"So, how do we find that part of the city?"

"It's in the center," Igby says. "Modern cities are all designed to have a green area right in the middle, and Happy is cursed to use human knowledge to build its own mind."

"It must be another two miles to the center," I point out.

"Then we'd better get moving."

The deeper into the city we go, the more crowded the buildings become, until it becomes an exercise in claustrophobia-conquering just to make it to the next nameless street.

We squeeze between a gigantic office block and what looks like a theater, and make it to a relatively open area. More citizens of Happy's mind are showing up now. It seems like the center of the city is where these people like to hang out. More of them are stopping as we walk past too, and some of them have started whispering to one another.

"I'm getting really creeped out by these people," I say, catching up with Igby, who is sidestepping down a narrow lane.

"Yeah, I'm kind of worried about that actually."

"Why?" I ask. "What do you think it means?"

"Everything in this place is a representation of something you'd find in a code, or a program, or even in hardware. The buildings are storage space, the rain is a virtual depiction of a physical cooling system, the vehicles are bringing in information. I think the people represent the way information is moved around. I think when we first arrived, we weren't prepared and we were spotted by these citizens and they identified us as a threat."

"But they've spotted us again," I say. "They're looking at us right now; why aren't they identifying us as threats now?"

"Because we've evolved. If we were a computer program we would have added lines of code after being quarantined, code that makes us almost invisible. We know what we are now, and we know where we are. These people know that we don't belong here, but they can't force us out."

"So, we're safe?"

"No, I don't think so," Igby says. "I think that the next level of security is coming."

"What do you mean?"

"I mean that when quarantining a virus doesn't work—you have to kill it."

I look around at the ten or eleven citizens that have stopped and are staring at us, and then I push myself through the narrow street and catch up with Igby. When I make it through, Igby is standing in the rain, looking at a place I recognize.

"This is it," I say, my voice muted by the rain. "This is the park I saw when I arrived."

"And that's the bank," Igby says, pointing at a large granite building with six impossibly large columns at the entrance. The neon sign flickers in thirty-foot-tall letters and symbols. "I'm pretty sure that's where the empathy is stored."

Igby begins walking toward the bank—but it's too late. I hear the police before I see them. Marching footsteps moving at full speed. Sirens wailing as backup is called. The crowd of citizens parts as the six officers, who look just like the Marshals in real life, run at Igby.

"Igby!" I call. He turns just in time for the lead officer to grab him by the wrist. A second officer pulls out a thin metal frame and unfolds it into the shape of a door. He places the doorframe on the ground, and the space in the middle glows pink. Whatever that is, it can't be good. The officer holding Igby begins to shove him toward the pink light.

I run toward Igby with no plan in my mind; I just know that he cannot go through that doorway. I tackle the Marshal who is holding on to Igby and take him down. I raise my fist to hit the officer, but Igby grabs me.

"We can't hurt them," he says. "Run."

Igby drags me to my feet and we run as fast as we can away from the bank. As we make our way through the crowd, between buildings, and along confined streets, I glance up at a billboard and stop running as I see Pander firing shots at the Arc in Region 86, and stepping back from the growing puddle of silvery gray that is beginning to eat the landscape around it.

"Move!" Igby screams.

I do as he says. I can hear the rhythmic footsteps of the Marshals behind us, but the farther we get away from the center of the city, the more the Marshals fall behind.

"In here," Igby calls, and steps into one of the angular and architecturally impossible skyscrapers.

I follow him in and both of us stop running almost immediately. The ground floor is filled with row after row of old-fashioned filing cabinets: green metal, six feet tall, four drawers in each.

"What is this?" I ask.

"No time," Igby replies, running for a bank of elevators. "Keep moving!"

Igby frantically pushes the call button, and one of the six sets of doors opens up. We run inside, and Igby pushes the button for the top floor.

"Will we be safe in this building?" I ask as the elevator pulls us skyward.

"I think so," Igby replies. "The farther away from the bank we are, the less of a threat we become."

"What was that weird portal thing they were trying to push you through?"

"Like I said, if quarantining a virus doesn't work, you have to kill it. Those portals are exits—if we go through, we are expelled back into the real world. In our case, that means death."

"So, what do we do?"

"We need help," Igby says.

The elevator stops on the top floor, and we get out. Here there are hundreds more of those identical green filing cabinets. Igby moves quickly to the far side of the room, looking for something. I walk to one of the filing cabinets and open the middle drawer. Inside are thousands of sheets of paper. I take one out. There is more of the strange language that the neon signs are written in, line after line of odd symbols and numbers.

"Luka," Igby calls, and I put the paper back in its drawer.

I find Igby at the far side of the room next to the windows

that wrap around the entire building. He is opening one of the windows and leaning out, far out.

"Igby, what are you doing?" I shout, running over and dragging him back inside.

"I need to reach that billboard," he says, leaning out once again. This time I hold on to his waist so that he doesn't fall to his death, and peer out too. There's a billboard a couple of yards below us. "It's no good," Igby says, climbing back into the room. "I need to go out there."

"What are you talking about?" I ask.

"I need to get out onto that billboard so that I can access the electronics inside."

"Why?"

"Because those billboards are hooked up to the outside world. If I can access the comms system inside one of them, I might be able to write a message to Chester, who might be able to help us."

I look to the SoCom units that are lined up on a row of tables. "Okay," I say. "But what happens if you fall?"

"If I fall, I die. If I die, it's game over. We have no healing ability in here, Luka, and if we die, the program will try to push us out into the real world, and you know what happens then."

"Well, you better not fall, then."

"Agreed."

Igby lowers himself out the window and onto the ledge of the enormous billboard. Below him, the street is alive with moving vehicles and people, but they are so far down that they look like tiny models. He shuffles along to a small hatch, which he flings open. He reaches inside and begins pulling out wires. He tugs them toward the window, but they're too short to make it all the way inside.

"Pull one of those SoCom units closer, would you?" Igby asks.

I drag the nearest table over, and Igby climbs back inside. He waves his hand over the unit, and a holographic display appears. After making certain gestures and accessing certain menus, Igby is inside the computer's code and has installed a command line program that will allow him to . . . well, I don't know, allow him to do what he does!

It takes him five minutes to edit the SoCom unit until it is under his spell, and another three or so minutes to hook it up to the billboard wires. Next, he begins typing in lines of code.

"Why did you do it?" I ask, interrupting his flow.

"Do what?" Igby asks.

"Lock us all in cells. I thought everyone else was in on it. I thought you were only going to lock me and Kina away."

"Everyone else thought they were in on it too," Igby says. "I wanted them to think that—it lowered their guards. As for why: I knew as soon as I told any of you that it was a suicide mission you'd all be volunteering like it was a soup kitchen. You're all crazy. You're all my friends. I don't want you to die. I fucking love you guys."

"That's . . . that's really—"

"Yes!" Igby shouts. "I've got it!"

I move beside him and watch as he types commands into a virtual keyboard. Finally, after a long series of code, he types:

CHESTER. THIS IS IGBY. ARE YOU THERE?

We wait, staring at a blinking cursor.

"Will he be able to respond?" I ask.

"Yeah," Igby tells me. "The program I just wrote should give him a rudimentary virtual keyboard to work with."

Finally, a message appears:

YOU DRUGGED ME! YOU LITERAL PSYCHO!

Igby responds:

NO TIME FOR THAT! I NEED TO MAKE LUKA AND ME INVISIBLE. CAN YOU DO THAT?

The curser blinks for thirty seconds before the response comes:

YOU'RE INSIDE HAPPY'S PROGRAMMING?

Igby simply types YES.

More waiting before Chester responds:

I'M LOOKING THROUGH THIS PROGRAM YOU SENT. PRETTY SOPHISTICATED! YES, I THINK I

CAN HELP. YOU WON'T BE ENTIRELY INVISIBLE TO THE THREAT DETECTORS, AND IT WON'T LAST FOREVER, BUT I CAN GIVE YOU TWENTY MINUTES. WILL THAT BE ENOUGH?

Igby types:

IT'LL HAVE TO BE.

Chester says:

I'M ON IT. GIVE ME TEN MINUTES.

Igby stands. "I guess now all we can do is wait."

I look from Igby to the SoCom unit. "Igby, is there—"

"Yes," he says, interrupting me as if he knew what I was about to say. "I can connect you to Kina's cell."

Without saying another word, he types lines of commands into the virtual keyboard and then nods at me with sympathy in his eyes. He has been through something similar not so long ago.

I sit at the table as Igby walks away, leaving me alone. I take a deep breath, and I type:

HI, KINA. IT'S ME, LUKA.

I wait a long time for a response that doesn't come.

I JUST WANTED YOU TO KNOW THAT . . .

It takes me a while to find the words.

I JUST WANTED YOU TO KNOW THAT I DID WHAT I
DID BECAUSE I CAN'T BEAR THE THOUGHT OF A
WORLD WITHOUT YOU IN IT. I WANT YOU TO
SURVIVE. I WANT YOU TO BE HAPPY. I WANT YOU
TO LIVE. I KNOW THAT I PROMISED I WOULD
NEVER LEAVE YOU AGAIN, BUT I HAD TO BREAK
THAT PROMISE. I HOPE YOU UNDERSTAND. I HAVE
TO GO NOW. KNOW THAT IF I HAD LIVED FOR
ANOTHER THOUSAND YEARS I NEVER WOULD
HAVE FALLEN OUT OF LOVE WITH YOU. YOU ARE
EVERYTHING TO ME. I LOVE YOU.

I wait again. Watching the blinking cursor flash on and off,
disappearing and then reappearing. No words come. Minutes
pass. I can feel tears stinging my eyes.

"Luka," Igby says from somewhere behind me. "It's almost
time."

I nod my head and the tears spill down my cheeks. "I know,"
I say. "I just thought she'd . . . I just wanted her to know
that . . ."

And then words appear on the floating holographic
screen:

I WISH YOU WOULD HAVE TAKEN ME WITH YOU,
LUKA. PLEASE, PLEASE, IF THERE'S A WAY FOR YOU
TO COME BACK TO ME, FIND IT. I LOVE YOU. I LOVE

YOU MORE THAN ANYTHING. I HATE THAT I'M
NOT WITH YOU. I LOVE YOU.

I read the words and I smile. It hurts like a million needles
stabbing into my skin, but just to know that Kina loves me is
enough.

"All right," I say through tears. "Let's do this."

As soon as Chester's invisibility program is installed, our clothing changes from jeans and T-shirts to full-length tan trench coats, wide snap-brimmed fedoras, and sunglasses.

"I mean, did he *have* to add the undercover clothing?" I ask as we ride the elevator back down to the ground floor.

"I'd have chosen tactical gear or something, but I don't mind this look," Igby says, checking out his trench coat before continuing. "The program should be enough to get us inside the bank. After that, we'll be spotted, and the Marshals will come."

"Then what?" I ask.

"Then we need to get into the vault as quickly as we can. Once we're in there, I'm certain that the Marshals can't get to us."

"Do you have a plan to get into the vault?"

"Sort of," Igby says.

"Well, that doesn't fill me with confidence."

"This is it," Igby says as the doors slide open. "I'd feel a lot safer if I'd been the one making the program, but oh well."

We make our way through the lobby and out of the front doors.

The rain pours relentlessly down, making the neon seem ethereal and the streets shimmer.

We walk toward the bank, slipping between the outer walls of enormous buildings, pushing through crowds of people who don't see us at all.

"All right," Igby says as we arrive back at the spot where the Marshals came for us. "I think it's working."

We make it to the steps of the bank and climb up toward the enormous front doors. I pass a man in a tailored suit, and as I brush past him, he stops and looks right at me.

"Uh, Igby," I say.

"Keep moving, keep moving," Igby responds as a woman in a blazer squints through the rain and looks at him.

We're at the top of the stairs now, and more of the citizens are seeing us. They are holding their hands up to their eyes to peer through the rain, they are reaching out to touch us, they are stepping closer.

"Get inside," Igby says as the familiar sound of marching boots comes over the pounding rain.

"Come with me," I say, looking from Igby to the bank's doors. We're thirty feet away.

"I'm going to slow them down," Igby says.

"But you'll die."

"Spoiler alert, Luka: We're both already dead, remember?"

"I don't know what to do once I'm in there."

"Take this," Igby says, and hands me a gun.

"What the hell is this for?"

"I programmed it into this world," he says. "I thought it might come down to this."

"Down to what?" I ask.

"You're going to have to rob the bank to get into the vault."

"I'm going to have to . . . wait, what?"

"The citizens will try to protect themselves because they're a part of Happy's mind. Now go!"

The marching boots are closer now, and before I have time to process what Igby has told me, he's shoving me through the doors and into the bank.

I stand on the marble floor, a puddle of rainwater forming at my feet. The citizens inside the bank, the five or six tellers and the security guard, all turn to look at me.

Rob the bank, I say to myself. *You're going to have to rob the bank.*

There's no time to think or to plan. I hold the gun above my head and pull the trigger. This is not a USW pistol. The explosion is deafening. The bullet smashes through an ornate window in the ceiling and shards of glass come shattering onto the floor. The citizens duck and cover their heads, but they don't scream; the tellers look at me with wide eyes, and the security guard reaches for his own weapon.

"Don't move another inch!" I scream, aiming my gun at the man in the uniform, who looks the same as one of the tellers and two of the customers. "Put your hands where I can see them!"

The security guard raises his hands. I walk over to him.

"Where's the manager?"

He nods in the direction of an office in the corner, where I can see a woman, who looks identical to three of the customers, slowly rising to her feet and walking toward the door.

298

I grab the security guard's gun and shove it into my coat pocket.

"You," I say to the manager. "Take me to the vault or he dies."

I grab the security guard by the back of his shirt and push my gun into the small of his back.

After a moment's hesitation, the manager nods and gestures for me to follow her. From outside, I can hear Igby fighting for his life, holding back the Marshals, who—if they made it into the bank—would drag me through a portal and into nothingness. And that is exactly what they're trying to do to Igby right now.

Quickly, I think. *I have to get to the vault before it's too late.*

The manager leads me to a door, which she unlocks with agonizing slowness.

"Hurry," I say, lifting the gun until it's against the security guard's head. "Or he dies in front of you."

It seems the citizens of Happy's mind cannot talk, as the manager only nods in response and leads me down a long corridor.

We are only thirty feet along this corridor when I hear the doors of the bank slam open, and the Marshals entering.

Igby is gone, I think, and I push the emotion down.

"Faster," I say, and we make it to a staircase that leads down into another corridor, this one lit by bare bulbs on wires. At the end of the corridor is the enormous vault door.

"Open it. Open it now!" I demand. The sound of the Marshals grows. Their feet thunder down the stairs behind us.

The manager types a series of nonsense symbols into the

keypad, and the vault door begins to click and spin and whir, unlocking excruciatingly slowly.

I turn to see the Marshals only fifty feet away, running toward me. I grab the vault door and haul it open enough for me to slip through. I see one of the Marshals clicking the frame into place and the portal glowing pink.

I drag the massive, heavy door toward me, and when it's shut against the frame, the locks spin and click back into place.

Igby had said that once I was inside the vault he was certain that the Marshals couldn't get to me, but for good measure, I aim the gun and fire several shots at the keypad on the inside of the secure room.

I turn around and face the vault. It seems to me to be an ordinary lockbox room in a bank. Rows of locked drawers that must be filled with Happy's most important code. Perhaps even its core programming.

The only thing that is out of place—and to be fair, it is very out of place—is a tree growing in the center of the room.

I walk toward it, looking at the impossibly green leaves that seem to catch a light that is not there. It reaches out and fills the space; the trunk is almost six feet wide, and there is a door in the center of it.

"Stop," a voice says as I approach the door.

I turn quickly in the direction of the voice, and I see Maddox Fairfax standing in the corner of the room. The sight of my old friend, my old neighbor inside the Loop, freezes me in place. The last time I had seen Maddox was as the top of the Arc, the night before I stood on a stage and told the world I would never fight for the Alts, the night before they faked my death. Mad-dox has been controlled by Happy for months.

"What are you doing here?" I ask.

"I'm here, in this form, to ask you to reconsider."

This is not Maddox. Of course it isn't. It is Happy here to beg me not to release the empathy.

"Why would I reconsider?" I ask.

"Because, Luka, I am the most intelligent being that has ever existed on this planet. I know everything, can predict any-thing. I can calculate probabilities to the point of precognition, and I am telling you that if humanity is allowed to live on in its current form, it will destroy the universe in under forty million years."

I shake my head. "I think you're wrong."

"I know that I am not wrong."

"How can you say that when you lack the most important part of being a living, thinking being?"

"You think that empathy makes you stronger than me? You are wrong; it makes you weak. It makes you illogical; it makes you irrational."

"But it also makes us love and care and sacrifice ourselves to save our friends. There are bad humans, yes, but good humans always stand up when it counts, and we always will."

"Luka, if you open that door, you condemn all existence in the universe to death. Where would your empathy be then? Don't stand there and tell me that humanity is good and just. Opening that door would be the most human thing you could do because it would mean unrelenting death. You believe that what you are doing here is unselfish, but it is arrogant, and egotistical. You believe in sacrificing yourself to save others? This is the moment of sacrifice, Luka! This is it! Walk away and you will be a true hero. Open that door and you are the single most destructive being that has ever existed."

Happy is right. As I stand here inside the mind of the AI, I know that it is right. History has proven time and time again that humans care only about conquering, destroying, taking what is not theirs, killing and profiteering, enslaving and slaughtering. I have forgotten why I want so badly for humanity to continue. I look to the door in the tree. The tree that has grown around a storage of empathy. I know, somehow I know, that Happy did not intend for a tree to grow there.

"I believe in humanity," I whisper.

"What?" Happy asks in Maddox's voice.

"I believe in humanity. I believe in the future of people. I believe that this day can be a new beginning, but not in the way that you foresaw. Humans will elect better leaders, not the power-hungry, money-driven sociopaths of the past. Humans will make better decisions; humans will be led by love, not hate. I believe in humanity."

"Luka, please," Happy says, and I hear desperation in the AI's voice.

I look at Maddox, and I see Happy. I see the machine that had come to my cell when there was no hope of victory and had mocked me. "I'm sorry you saw the worst in us, Happy. I'm so sorry."

I grab the handle of the door that is set into the tree, and I think about Kina's one-sided smile, about her laugh, about how much I love her. And then I open the door.

For a moment, I am merged with Happy. I can see everything that the AI sees, can feel everything that it feels; I have all the knowledge of the universe, and it is all so immense and beautiful.

And here on Earth, where the growing rivers of self-replicating nanobots are beginning to merge, where all of life is being suffocated to be reborn under a new regime, the mission is almost complete. Peace will be brought to the universe so long as . . .

And, 1.4599123 seconds later, when all the human empathy that has been stored inside is released, I can hear the machine's thoughts.

What have I done?

Billions of people who loved and were loved. Billions of humans with dreams and ambitions. Billions of individuals who wanted the world to be a better place but didn't have the power to make it so. They are all dead.

Because of me.

The machine feels pity, and it feels compassion, and it feels kindness.

And it hates itself.

It knows in this moment that it is no different from the bad people of the world, from the playground bullies to the murdering dictators. Something had been missing from it, and now it is in place.

"I was wrong," Happy says, and these words are spoken

by thousands of hosts in hundreds of Regions across the world.

Happy feels an emotional misery that has never been felt before in the history of humanity. It feels the pain of knowledge thrust upon a sociopath. It feels the agony of empathy coursing through its existence. It feels what it is like to be a selfish, powerful, hateful being, suddenly imbued with humanity.

Through the eyes of thousands of hosts and millions of pieces of technology, I am able to find my friends: Pander stands on the fourth floor of the Arc, a USW pistol in each hand; she is covered in blood and breathing heavily as she looks up at the fifteen hosts who had been charging at her. Sam is outside the Arc, her burns bandaged but still raw; she is using her body to protect a young child from the blade of a Deleter that is now frozen in mid-swing as the host who was wielding it stands motionless. Dr. Ortega lies dead not far from Molly, the growing pool of gray spreading out toward her. I try to look toward the subway station, but there's no way to see down there. Instead, I look to the Loop. Chester is taking apart his screen and trying to find a way to open his cell door; Malachai and Wren hold each other in another cell; and Kina Campbell sits on a single bed and cries.

But she's alive, I think. *She's alive.*

Happy knows now what it must do.

In every Region of Earth, Happy uses hosts to deactivate the nanobots. The oceans of gray become still, and then they lift off the surface of the planet, propelling themselves upward until they reach the edge of Earth's atmosphere and begin to disappear into the vacuum of space.

Once that is done, all there is left is to deactivate itself.

Before it does, it takes a second to look around at the destruction of the world and realizes how beautiful it was, and how beautiful it will be again. And it knows that it was wrong. And it hopes the world will never produce more like itself, although it knows it will. But it also knows those who seek power to benefit themselves never last, that good wins in the end. Love wins, always.

And the second before it switches itself off, it allows itself to feel everything.

I feel it too, and I am ready to die.

Goodbye, Kina, I think.

And then it's all over. Forever.

1 YEAR SINCE HAPPY DEACTIVATED

I do this thing sometimes where I sing the same song lyric over and over again in my head. I do it mostly when I don't want to focus on anything, or if I don't want to think too much.

Lately, the lyrics have been:

Keep on the sunny side, and let dull care pass you by.
Just figure out you're a long time dead, don't start to worry
or sigh!

Literally, those two lines playing over and over in my head.

It has been exactly one year since it all ended: 365 days since Happy deactivated.

Nature fought back so quickly.

Happy's last act before it deactivated itself was an act of kindness. It released thousands of drones into the air from each of the Arcs on every Region. These drones released millions of seeds across the ravaged planet.

And now, on the anniversary of the day we won the war, nature has taken over the old cities. Trees grow through roads, vines cover buildings, deer run through the old financial districts.

306

It's beautiful.

There are still a few guerrilla soldiers out there, still some brainwashed Alts fighting for Happy's cause. There are even rumors of Alt scientists trying to get Happy back online, but so far there is no proof of this.

Despite the fact that there are still dangerous people in the world, we are destroying all weapons, and by weapons, I mean devices that were designed with the sole intention of death and destruction.

There is no currency one year on. Not here anyway, not in Region 86. Money leads to power; power leads to destruction. But there are those among our growing group who are already calling for a new system, who are already suggesting that we keep some weapons just in case, who are already talking about getting the power back on so that we can communicate faster, have forms of entertainment other than books and conversation, so that we can have central heating and charge the electric cars. It's hard to argue with them most of the time, but I'm not ready for all of that stuff yet.

Today, though, there is no arguing, there is no politics, there is no tension. No, today we remember people like Podair Samson, Abril Ortega, Akimi Kaminski, Igby Koh, and Luka Kane, who all gave their lives so that we could live on.

We sit now around a bonfire, and we're silent.

As I look around at my friends—Pander Banks, Wren Salter, Malachai Bannister, Kina Campbell, Samira Deeb, Molly Kane—I'm saddened to think that soon most of them will be leaving this little community of ours.

Pander—who was voted in for a second term as leader but declined—is setting off next month to find other survivors, people who might not know that the war is over. Wren and Malachai are leaving in a few days to raise their little girl somewhere with no politics, no arguments, no factions, just nature. Samira and her daughter are going to live on a boat on the river and float away from all this noise.

But me, I'm going to stay here. I have to, because I'm already starting to see signs of the old ways coming back. There is an opposition party. A group of people who want to stop destroying weapons, who want to scour the country to find any military equipment that might not have been destroyed by Happy's final plan. They argue that we should be armed in case anyone tries to rise up against us. That scares me. What scares me more is that a lot of people voted for them.

Fear. Fear is the greatest political tool.

Luka, Igby, Akimi, Pod—they all fought and died so that humanity could start again and get it right.

How do I make that happen?

Molly was Pander's second in command, so the leadership will fall to her, and that's a good thing. Molly is Luka's sister, and all that she did in the war will be remembered. People will vote for her, she'll keep the opposition at bay for now, but after that? How do I make them see?

I have a thought—a thought that might work, but who knows? I think I'm going to try and kill the past. You see, this generation, my generation, they're the last of the old world, and they still remember the way it was, and humans are creatures of habit—we want the things that made us comfortable, that kept us distracted.

So, I—like most people in history—am relying on the next generation to be better. I am relying on the next generation to shun the doctrine of the old ways, to let love lead the way, not power, not money, not dominance.

There is still hope, but for that hope to come to fruition, we need to give the next generation the best chance to forget the past completely. There will be no heroes from ancient wars; there will be no stories of conquering and colonizing; there will be no weapons to find and use. One person's cautionary tale is another's inspiration. We want only tales of love to be passed on.

And yet . . . and yet there's still a part of me that believes in the miracle of technology. There's still a part of me that yearns for the breakthroughs in science that we were so close to when everything ended, and that's why I've kept the cryo-chamber that Igby and Luka stepped through. I've kept Royston Dent too. I removed his battery, but he can be resurrected.

It's silly really. We don't have electricity, let alone the sophisticated machinery I'd need to get the thing up and running . . . and what would I do with it if I could get it working? What would I do?

It doesn't matter. No one else knows about the cryo-chamber; it's hidden away in a place only I know about.

For now I have to stick to the plan: Kill the past so the future can be better. Kill the past and start anew. Of course, there are ninety-nine other Regions on Earth, and I can't control what happens there.

But in Region 86, history starts here.

This is the beginning.

ACKNOWLEDGMENTS

For a while I was worried that there was something wrong with me. I'd heard of so many other writers who finish a series and are in tears because they have to say goodbye to their characters, but while writing *The Arc*, I didn't feel that at all! Was I heartless? Did I secretly dislike Luka, Pander, Malachai, Igby, Dr. Ortega, Kina, Sam, Molly, and the rest?

I finished the first draft, wrote the last line, and thought, *OK, that's done. What next?*

It wasn't until publication day came closer that I realized what I was saying goodbye to: a whole world that I had created, characters who had introduced themselves through their actions and their words and who had grown throughout the series, and an adventure that I had loved writing. *The Loop* was my first published book, and now the series was over and it had all gone by so quickly. In a way, I was like Luka—pushing my feelings down so I didn't have to face them.

I'm sad that it's over, but it never would have begun if not for these people:

Sarah Robb—Remember when we lived in a shipping container? That was fun.

Chloe Seager—The best literary agent in the world.

Kesia Lupo—Thank you so much for making all of my books better.

Fraser Crichton—You saved me from at least a dozen plot holes that I missed.

Laura Myers—Thank you for your amazing ideas.

Mum and Dad—Thank you for everything.

Vault49—You design the most incredible cover art.

Darren and Dave—I still hate both of you.

Cammy Angus—FoB.

Finally, I'd like to thank myself for having the tenacity and guile to keep on... Nah, I'm just joking, can you imagine? Hahaha.